"Twenty-five million dollars!"

The two voices blended as one, a rare thing in Jeff and Julian Diamond. Both pairs of eyes were wide with astonishment at their grandfather's pronouncement.

Bartholomew Diamond leaned back in his chair and let the notion of the bet sink in. The Diamonds had always had everything they wanted—except this generation's continuation of the family line. Jeff and Julian were leery of love and marriage. Bart knew it was his duty to convince his grandsons to acquire wives and families. That he made it a competition only made it more enjoyable. And the brothers loved a challenge. He knew neither would—or could—pass.

"Your inheritance. Why wait? It's yours—or rather *only* one of yours—if you marry and are in the family way by the end of the year. Besides, I'll be damned before I give my money to the IRS." Bart held his breath, hoping they'd take the bait.

"So how about it, guys? Married and in the family way by the end of the year or no money for either of you." Bart knew the deal was too good to resist.

Dear Reader,

We're thrilled to bring you a special American Romance novel—*Diamond Daddies*. It's the first time you get *two full romances in one novel*. Author Linda Cajio proves she's a talented storyteller with a flair for the innovative.

Go ahead and meet twin brothers Jeff and Julian Diamond—two confirmed bachelors who are about to discover that a man's greatest fortune is his family. Just in time for Father's Day!

We know you'll enjoy this unique book. Please write and let us know how much you liked it.

Best regards,

Debra Matteucci
Senior Editor & Editorial Coordinator
Harlequin Books
300 East 42nd Street
New York, NY 10017

Diamond
Daddies

LINDA CAJIO

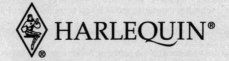

HARLEQUIN®

TORONTO • NEW YORK • LONDON
AMSTERDAM • PARIS • SYDNEY • HAMBURG
STOCKHOLM • ATHENS • TOKYO • MILAN • MADRID
PRAGUE • WARSAW • BUDAPEST • AUCKLAND

This book is for Jimmy the Dip. Just keep on doing what
you're doing and Susan will have plenty of stories—and
I'll have plenty of inspiration. Thanks, Jim!

ISBN 0-373-16779-2

DIAMOND DADDIES

Copyright © 1999 by Linda Cajio.

All rights reserved. Except for use in any review, the reproduction or
utilization of this work in whole or in part in any form by any electronic,
mechanical or other means, now known or hereafter invented, including
xerography, photocopying and recording, or in any information storage
or retrieval system, is forbidden without the written permission of the
publisher, Harlequin Enterprises Limited, 225 Duncan Mill Road,
Don Mills, Ontario, Canada M3B 3K9.

All characters in this book have no existence outside the imagination of
the author and have no relation whatsoever to anyone bearing the same
name or names. They are not even distantly inspired by any individual
known or unknown to the author, and all incidents are pure invention.

This edition published by arrangement with Harlequin Books S.A.

® and TM are trademarks of the publisher. Trademarks indicated with
® are registered in the United States Patent and Trademark Office, the
Canadian Trade Marks Office and in other countries.

Look us up on-line at: http://www.romance.net

Printed in U.S.A.

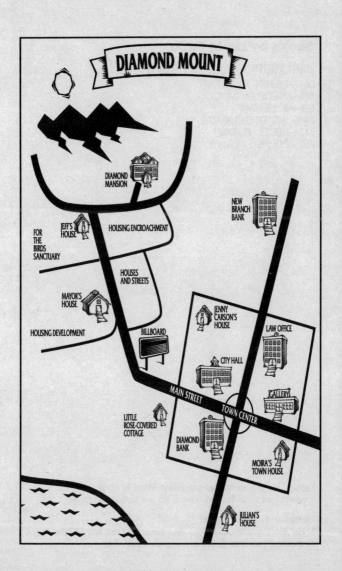

Books by Linda Cajio

HARLEQUIN AMERICAN ROMANCE

Don't miss any of our special offers. Write to us at the
following address for information on our newest releases.

Harlequin Reader Service
U.S.: 3010 Walden Ave., P.O. Box 1325, Buffalo, NY 14269
Canadian: P.O. Box 609, Fort Erie, Ont. L2A 5X3

The Bet

Prologue

Father's Day

"Twenty-five million dollars!"

The two voices blended as one, a rare thing in Jeff and Julian Diamond. In their thirties, the brothers, though twins, were fraternal, not identical. Jeff, the elder, was medium height, muscular, with reddish brown hair and green eyes. He was a veterinarian by trade, specializing in birds by desire—and a few bricks short of a load as far as certain family members were concerned. Julian stood a couple of inches taller and was more slender. His eyes were green, like Jeff's, but his hair was nearly black and finer. Banks were living breathing things to him. "Hey, somebody has to play with the money" was his philosophy.

Both pairs of eyes were wide with astonishment at their grandfather's pronouncement. The old man, eighty-two, with hair the color of iron to match his will, just chuckled. The dinner at the antique table commissioned by a coal baron ancestor was going as planned. Bartholemew Diamond had sat atop his mountain, in the family mansion outside the town of Diamond Mount, Pennsylvania, and made sure he had all the right carrots on their strings before he presented his wishes to his grandsons.

"Twenty-five million," he repeated. "Your inheritance. But why wait and why share? It's yours, or rather *only one* of yours if you marry and are in the family way by the end of the year. But only one. Whoever gets there first gets the money."

Dead silence reigned over the dinner, as if Bart Diamond's repetition of the challenge had actually made the words believable. He leaned back in his chair and let the notion of the bet sink in. The Diamonds of Diamond's Mount had always had everything they wanted—except this generation's continuation of the family line. He had raised these boys, his own son, Edmund, eschewing parenting for the jet set and the latest wife, a twenty-year-old. Bart loved his grandsons all the more because of that. But the two had been scared off love and marriage. Bart knew it was his duty to kick start his grandsons into acquiring wives and families. That he had kicked them for a loop only made it more enjoyable. He was an old man with little entertainment. He couldn't wait to see what the two would do.

"You're an old bastard," Jeff said finally.

Bart glared at his grandson. "I didn't get where I am by *not* being one, boy. Ask anyone when we sold off the banking chain ten years ago—"

"And left me to rebuild it," Julian said dryly. "All my life I'd thought I would come into the firm, only there wasn't one when I got out of college. Jeff's right. You are an old bastard."

"What's the matter with you two?" Bart demanded, pounding a fist on the table. The china, straight from England, trembled, their famous Royal Worcester pattern in danger of chipping. "You boys always loved a challenge. Didn't you cry, Jeff, when Julian's Little League team went to the state finals and yours didn't? Didn't you throw a temper tantrum, Julian, when Jeff got first prize for his science project while you got an honorable mention? It's always been that way between you two. You were always competing with each other. I'm just upping the ante as it were. Winner takes all, and you don't have to wait for me to die. Where's that Diamond spirit? Hell, if you're not going to take me up on my offer, then I might as well give the damn money away, to see it do some good some-where. I'll be damned before I give it to the IRS. You know what? I *will* give it away."

He held his breath, hoping they'd take the bait.

"Now don't be hasty," Julian said.

"If you're going to give it away, give it to my bird sanc-tuary," Jeff added, beginning to grin, not about to let his brother get ahead of him. "It'll do a great deal of good there."

"Or give to my bank expansion," Julian said, grinning even wider. "It'll do a lot of good there. And make us more money besides."

"Nope." Bart thrust out his jaw. "My mind's made up. Married and in the family way by the end of the year or no money for either of you."

The two looked at him in disgust, but the old man could see the wheels turning inside. He knew the deal was too good to resist. Oh, he'd have some decent compensation for the loser, but he wanted a winner. If left to their own devices, these two would never make a move toward commitment again. Both boys had married briefly, both marriages ending in divorce. Gun-shy was all they were now.

"I'm a stubborn old man," Bart added for good measure. "I've already put the money in a trust with the stipulation that you be married and in the family way before the end of the year or it goes to charity. My lawyer had a hissy fit, but he tied it up in ironclad knots. You know him. You can sue for-ever, but no judge will find fault with the legal arrangements."

"All right," Julian said finally, eyes narrowing with anger. "I'm against this, but I just want to go on record that you're leaving us no choice. Is he, Jeff?"

"No, he's not," Jeff answered, thrusting out his jaw. "You ever think you'll split us for good with this insane bet? It's not even a level playing field. Julian has prospects. I don't."

"It doesn't mean a thing," Bart said, truly believing it. "You're more ready to commit than he is. You two love each other too much to let it split you. And I love you both the same."

They said nothing more, but they didn't need to. Their grandfather knew they had accepted.

Bart Diamond grinned roguishly. "Flag's down, boys. You're off and running."

Jeff

~ Part One ~

Gentlemen, Place Your Wagers

Chapter One

"It's robbing Peter to pay Paul..."

Muttering in disgust, Jeff Diamond sat in his home office on a brilliant Sunday afternoon in June and stared at the pile of unpaid bills on the desk before him. It was stacked neatly and six inches thick—at least. Most he'd had for months and all of them were for sanctuary expenses. For the Birds cost the world to run. A few checks lay next to the bills, their total amount less than a quarter of what he owed. Same old, same old with his vet practice, he acknowledged. Not enough of one to pay the other.

"Damn, I can't even rob Harvey to pay Peter and Paul."

Birds perched by the window squawked, then ruffled their feathers as if in sympathy with their owner's plight. His shows, using the cockatoo and the parrots, helped to bring in the smaller income pile. The birds in the aviary outdoors, however, created the big expense pile. Popeye, the African vulture, waddled past the desk. The three-foot-tall bird was clearly curious about what disturbed his other exotic brethren and intended to apply his distinctive squint to it.

Jeff ran his hands through his hair in frustration, then began to weed through the mess. *Pay the mortgage, pay the feed, forget the lights and gas and everything else....*

Twenty-five million dollars.

The misery of bill paying brought his grandfather's wager

to the forefront. Despite his desperation, he must have been more insane than old Bart to even think about the damn thing, let alone agree. Well, he hadn't exactly agreed. He just hadn't said no to it.

He'd agreed and he knew it.

His brother, Julian, had snapped it up, but Julian had prospects of winning, namely Moira Carson, his girlfriend for over a year, while Jeff was a very confirmed bachelor. Even with prospects, Jeff knew he could never qualify under the terms of the bet, anyway. Never—not that the reasons mattered any longer. Jeff was well past it.

Julian would win hands-down even though Jeff admitted he needed the money more than his banking brother. He had to find funding *now*. He'd eaten through his own trust fund to support For the Birds, as well as using all profits from his small veterinary practice. He was a Diamond, but for all intents and purposes, a piece of coal. The family savvy had passed him by.

Twenty-five million.

The birds squawked again, louder this time, stress clear in their call. Frowning, Jeff rose and went over to the window to see what attracted their attention.

Two young boys, towheads of about seven and five, crept along the side of the house. They turned the corner, very sneakily. Jeff grinned. "We got company, gang."

He went out his office door, grateful to leave his bill paying, or lack thereof, behind. Popeye waddled along like a faithful puppy. Jeff moved swiftly and quietly. The two boys, intent on what was ahead of them, never realized they'd been caught even when Jeff came up to them from the rear.

Grinning widely, Jeff leaned forward and said, "Boo."

The boys screamed and spun around, then started to run. Jeff captured them by the arms, and one of them landed a good kick to his shins. "Hey, guys, it's okay. You're not in trouble unless you kick me again."

The two stilled. Jeff let them go, although pleased to have had a little fun at their expense. He always had kids from the housing developments down the road poking around the ten-acre sanctuary. Twin pairs of blue eyes stared at him, then caught sight of the vulture. The older one asked, "Is that your bird?"

"Yeah. Meet Popeye," Jeff said.

"Hi, Popeye," the boys said in unison, relaxing now that the threat was over. Even though they weren't twins, they reminded him of Julian and himself when they'd been boys. They had always been close-knit and comfortable with each other from a young age. Even their inevitable friendly rivalries hadn't marred that.

Popeye bobbed his head in greeting, helped by Jeff's signal. The bird was well trained and used to children from the shows Jeff did at local schools and such. The boys giggled while Jeff squatted on his haunches and fed Popeye one of the small biscuits that he always had on him.

"Does he bite?" the younger asked.

"He doesn't mean to, but sometimes it's hard for him to tell the difference between a biscuit and a hand that smells like the biscuit it's holding," Jeff said. "I get my fingers out of the way real fast. What's your name?"

"Bobby. This is my brother, Stevie."

"Pleased to meet you guys." Jeff shook hands. "New to the neighborhood?"

"Yeah." The boy's mouth turned down. With his fair hair, he looked like a glum angel. "We used to live in California."

"Nice place," Jeff said. California rang a bell but he couldn't place why.

"My mom got poor, and my dad didn't like it, so we left and hadda come live with Grandpa," little Stevie piped up.

Jeff's stomach lurched. He knew a mom who had two boys and lived in California. It couldn't be. She wasn't poor. *New York Times* bestselling authors weren't poor.

"Shut up, dork," Bobby said. "Mom said don't tell no-body."

Stevie looked solemn but said nothing.

"What's your last name?" Jeff asked.

"Miller. Can I pet him?"

Miller. Jeff felt ill. It truly couldn't be. The world had tons of Millers, even if a certain Miller's father lived next door and had a different last name. The boys looked nothing like her. Nothing. He found his voice. "Sure, just pet his back, though."

The boys stroked Popeye's back for a few moments until the bird waddled away to peck at the ground.

"He thinks he's a chicken," Jeff said. "Where's your grandpa live?"

"There." The boy pointed behind him.

"Next door?"

"Yeah."

Jeff's stomach churned. That was the Miller he knew, the one who had haunted him for years. "And what's your mom's name?"

"Mom," Stevie said, following Popeye.

"Idiot," Bobby scoffed. "He means Mom's name name." He turned to Jeff. "It's Paula."

The world tilted on its axis, rolling drunkenly in Jeff's vision for a long moment. Yet his heart swelled with an odd exhilaration. She couldn't be back. He would have known. He would have felt it. Wouldn't he?

"Hey, guys! Where do you belong? Not here."

Jeff froze at the voice that was so familiar, even after fifteen years. His heart pounded, although he managed to look up casually. She walked toward them, smiling like the world had given her pearls. It had. Jeff squinted against the blindingly bright sun. Paula Miranda Helpern-Miller moved as if the angels had placed little clouds under her feet. Her body, still lithe like a young girl's and exactly as he remembered it, swayed with grace. Her breasts were small and her hips subtly curved.

Her dark hair, with its sun-streaked highlights, cascaded in waves around her shoulders. Her features were small and symmetrical, with brandy-colored eyes, full lips and perfect skin. The California tan only emphasized good health and an earthy sensuality.

"Mom!" The boys ran to her, hugging her.

Mom. Jeff looked at the two boys and knew in his heart that they should have been his, because *she* should have been his.

Slowly he rose to his feet, tossing the treats in a pile for Popeye to devour. Paula moved toward him, composed and smiling like nothing had ever happened between them.

It shouldn't matter, he thought. It didn't matter. He was long past it.

"Does your father know you're here?" he asked her.

Paula's smile faltered. Okay, he thought, so he wasn't as "past it" as he'd thought he was.

"Don't worry. I'll sic Popeye on him," he said quickly to cover his vulnerability. Damn, in one question, he'd shown her just how much he still hurt. "How are you, Paula? Your boys were just telling me that you've moved back."

For one fleeting moment, she looked at a loss, but she recovered. Jeff wondered if he'd imagined it as she said, "It's good to see you again. How's your brother, Julian?"

"Fine," he managed to get out, knowing his brother was doing a helluva lot better than he was in many respects. Her voice, always low and sultry, washed over him as before, leaving him disoriented.

He stretched out his hand in a peace offering. She took it. He hadn't really thought about the simple courtesy other than that he meant to shake politely, he truly did, but somehow his fingers curved around her warm flesh and he held her hand instead. Moving it up and down would break the flood of emotions raging inside him. Paula stared at him, her brandy eyes as wide and as luminous as he remembered. He could gaze into those depths, mesmerized forever. Her perfume, unchanged in fifteen years, tormented his senses. Her body was so close, he could easily reach out and touch her breast, her waist, see if time and children had changed her. He didn't care if they had. This was Paula, and in a heartbeat of a second he wanted her all over again.

Then he remembered she had chosen her father over *him*.

The spell broke. Jeff dropped her hand, feeling burned. Paula had caved in to her father's pressure and dumped him fifteen years ago. She'd been just seventeen, with a sweet, placating nature. She'd left town shortly afterward for college and had never come back, which had helped some, Jeff admitted. Robert Helpern was mayor now of Diamond Mount, but he had always hated the Diamonds. He had hated Jeff most of all, especially when Paula and he had fallen in love. The feud had chilled after Helpern had broken them up, but not by much. Jeff had never forgiven him—or Paula.

Paula looked dubiously at Popeye, clearly not in the emotional state Jeff was. "I heard you bought the property next to Dad's a few years back. He rants that you've got a bunch of birds here, but he didn't say anything about *that*."

Jeff smiled, in spite of his feelings about her. Half his joy in finding the ten pristine, wooded acres was that it was a perfect sanctuary for his bird collection. The other half was that it annoyed the crap out of her father, who owned the property next door and had wanted Jeff's for his construction business's latest housing development. Jeff admitted he wasn't as mature as he should be, but he could happily live with that.

"I run a birds of prey sanctuary," Jeff said, "but that's still a bunch of birds. I like them, and they need a little help in coming back to this area…especially the predator hawks."

"You always were the nurturing sort," Paula said, smiling. Her smile could knock men over. It always did him. "I remember that nest of baby rabbits you found and insisted on nursing twenty-four hours a day."

Jeff smiled back. "I'm not a vet for nothing. How's the book business?"

"Fine."

She didn't quite look him in the eye. Paula wrote romances. Jeff had read every one—and in each thought he saw their relationship. The heat between them...the frenzied eagerness to be together at every waking moment...even the pain. She was the queen of love eternal and yet in real life had shredded the heart of a man who had offered her that kind of love. Jeff had gone on to marry elsewhere, but it hadn't worked. Now he lived like a monk—content until today.

"Mom, Mom. Look at Popeye! Isn't he silly?" Both kids started laughing.

Paula stepped back as the vulture loomed closer, his wings half spread as he half hopped, half waddled around her like a goofy-looking, bald-headed penguin. "What is that thing anyway?"

"A vulture," Jeff said. "Some idiot had wanted a vulture for a pet and had one smuggled into the country, then couldn't handle it. Popeye eventually wound up here at the sanctuary. I use him for show-and-tell at schools. He's pretty harmless."

"I'm not buying harmless. And I'm not buying pretty, either. Doesn't he scare the kids?"

"Your two boys were just fine with him," Jeff stated. "In fact, they've shown no fear at all, which is remarkable."

"He's funny," Stevie said, laughing at the bird.

Paula smiled. "Yes, he is funny, even if he looks like he wants to eat me for dinner. I bet those rabbits are glad they're long gone from here, now that you have Popeye."

"They've got more to worry about from the falcons than Popeye," Jeff said. On impulse, he added, "Want to see the place?"

"Thanks, but I just came to get the boys for Sunday dinner." Paula glanced back toward her father's house.

Jeff couldn't resist. "Take a few minutes, then, and come see my sanctuary."

He was tempted to add that sneaking around behind her father's back would be like old times. No sense reminding either of them about that.

Paula frowned for a moment while the boys jumped up and down and begged. "Okay, okay. You two are like yappy Chihuahuas."

The boys raced ahead as Jeff led them to the other side of the building. Popeye brought up the rear.

"The boys mentioned that you've moved back with your folks," Jeff said, to start a conversation and sate his curiosity. He had tons of it.

She shrugged. "Things change. It was time to come home."

"How does your…husband like it here?" He hated that he stumbled over the word *husband*.

"I'm divorced."

For one second hope glimmered inside Jeff. He squashed it immediately. *Just slam the door,* he thought. He was confronted with losing his beloved birds and his inheritance through an asinine wager he'd agreed to, and now here was Paula back, with children, to show him a life that would never be his. He didn't need to add that to the list of his current woes.

"Mommy, there's lots of birds here!" Stevie called out, his young voice impossibly high-pitched.

Jeff grinned. "He's found the falcon barn."

Paula's mouth turned down in dismay. "Will he get hurt?"

"It's fenced off. You'll see."

They did, when they reached the front of the building. The front doors of the old garage had been replaced with a wall of wire fencing. Inside, six beautiful small birds perched on tree stumps imbedded in the dirt floor. Eyes, sharp and watchful, gazed at them. Jeff gazed back, admiring the black-and-white feathering, always amazed at how precisely they seemed placed on the bodies. One flapped its wings for a moment, rising on the perch and giving a spectacular view of the hidden power the birds had. Their curved beaks dominated their faces.

"Wow," Paula said. "Do you hunt with them?"

"A bit," Jeff admitted. "They've got to learn to hunt for themselves if they're to go back to the wild."

Paula smiled at him. "I wrote a medieval, and had to study up on falconry. It hasn't changed much in ten centuries."

"Other than that I put 'em in my truck, rather than on a horse, and we head out for the open spaces, it's the same," Jeff said. "I've got one breeding pair, and one stud who mates with my special hat."

Paula raised her eyebrows. "Your *what?*"

Jeff shrugged. How could he explain the intricacies of getting birds to deliver the goods for artificial insemination? "It's complicated. I've found they don't mate well in captivity without a little help."

Neither did some humans, but that was another story, he thought wryly.

Paula looked dubious. "Okay."

"What's *mate?*" Stevie asked, while trying to poke a stick through the fencing to get the birds' attention.

"Making babies, like you guys once were," Jeff said matter-of-factly.

"Did you know us as babies?" Stevie asked.

Jeff smiled at the irony. "No. I wish I had."

"Do you got any kids?" Bobby asked.

"No. I never was that lucky." That question had once pained him whenever he'd been asked it. Today, it hurt all over again. He glanced at Paula. "I thought I would be a daddy someday."

Her lower lip trembled, and she thrust her jaw forward as if to stop it. She looked like she would cry at any moment.

"I knew it! I knew it!"

They turned to find Paula's father, Robert Helpern, stomping toward them. Big, brawny and boisterous, Robert glared, anger flushing the man's face.

"Home two days and you're already over here again. My God, Paula, when will you learn to stay away from this bastard?"

"Nice to see you, too," Jeff commented wryly. Dislike for the older man welled up inside him.

"Dad, that's enough," Paula said, her voice no-nonsense. "The boys snuck over here, and I'm bringing them home, okay?"

"See that you do. Your mother's had dinner ready for a half hour." Robert waved at his grandsons. "Let's go."

The boys protested, but clearly sensing the bitter undercurrents, they went with their grandfather. Paula smiled awkwardly, said a goodbye and followed behind the trio.

Not able to resist a parting shot, Jeff grinned and called out, "Come back again, guys."

The boys waved. Robert glared. Paula didn't respond. She was still doing whatever her father wanted, even though she'd stood up to him a little bit. Jeff knew it was for the best that they had broken up, especially with Robert's hostility toward him. Face it, no one could go home again.

Or could one?

A thread of logic told him that his grandfather only required he be married and "in the family way." Old Bart hadn't said how that family way was to be. Yet why, after fifteen years, at precisely the moment when Jeff needed her most, had Paula returned? Was it fate?

Jeff shook his head. He must be nuts to even consider such a loophole. His heart was wishing for something his brain knew perfectly well was impossible. He looked at Popeye. "I'm losing it."

Popeye nodded.

"NOW THIS IS OUR CAFETERIA and multipurpose room...."

Paula walked behind the school principal who proudly

showed off the amenities of the Diamond Mount Elementary School. Bobby looked bored, but Stevie was curious, all wide-eyed and full of questions. Paula smiled wryly at her sons. School was still new to up-and-coming kindergartners while jaded second-graders had no doubt seen it all. Emily Barton, the principal, clearly wanted to show off the place to the mayor's daughter, to impress her with reasons on why to send her sons here in the fall.

"Like I can afford a private school…" Paula murmured to herself. The book business wasn't what it used to be. Neither was her bank balance, since she'd been dropped by her former publisher for lowering sales figures. She wasn't the only author to be caught in the downsizing of publishing. A big-spender ex-husband had drained her savings, until she'd had to move back in with her parents—or starve. She added out loud, "I think I should have starved."

The principal turned. "I beg your pardon?"

"Just clearing my throat," Paula said to her.

Mrs. Barton said, "This is the last school the Diamond family built, you know. It's amazing how much money they put into our school system…and how much we miss them, frankly."

The statement was very true, and yet Paula was surprised that the woman would say it in front of the mayor's daughter. Her father disliked any criticism after he'd campaigned to break the Diamond family's hold on the town. Paula loved her father, but the man had never forgiven the Diamonds for not backing his company's development plans years ago. It wasn't until the Diamonds sold their bank chain that her father had made any progress in bringing suburbia to the mountains.

Paula wished he hadn't. She had liked the rural feel of Diamond Mount. Now the town resembled a bedroom community in Southern California, like the place she'd just left. Unfortunately, she had accepted her father's demands about a lot of things, to keep the family peace. And paid dearly for doing so.

She had paid with Jeff.

"I'm surprised the family still doesn't donate to the district," she said, knowing the Diamonds had been philanthropists in the past.

"There's a scholarship fund and such from the family, but they don't build the actual school buildings like they used to, which saved the town a great deal of money. Jeff still comes back and does lectures with his birds for the children. He's doing one in just a few minutes—"

"Mommy, Mommy!" Stevie shouted. "Can we go?"

"No." Her automatic response shamed Paula. She tried for more logic. "You guys aren't in school here yet, so it isn't fair—"

"Oh, that's no problem at all," Emily Barton said, smiling at Stevie. "You're more than welcome to attend."

Bobby and Stevie started chattering about their meeting with Popeye the crazy vulture. If the ground opened under her feet and swallowed her, Paula decided she wouldn't complain. Anything to avoid Jeff again.

She closed her eyes for a moment against the ache in her heart. Looking for the boys the other day had been an exercise in pain resurrection. It had hurt to see Jeff. Yet she had known, when she'd come back to town, that a meeting was bound to happen. She thought she handled herself well until he said he wished he'd seen her boys as babies. How many times had she wished that herself—and wished for more with him? How many times she had known he would have been a better father to her children than their biological parent? Dylan had been all charm and no substance. He'd ignored the boys and wouldn't take a regular job while waiting for his big acting break, preferring to live off Paula's earnings until they were in debt up to their eyebrows. She'd been looking for love in all the wrong places after she left Diamond Mount—and she'd found it.

That fact had been brought home to her the moment she'd been in range of Jeff again. His face was older, fuller, with sexy grooves running down either side of his mouth. His eyes were agate green, harder now than fifteen years ago. She had always been nearly eye-to-eye with him, for he'd never been overly tall like his brother, and his body was more muscular than most men's. Not heavy with muscles, but definitely defined. She'd had an overwhelming urge to run her fingers down his chest and only stopped herself through sheer willpower.

Definitely defined.

But his smile, that charming mix of boyish delight and knowing male, had cut right through her, just as it always had. How she'd ever hung on to her willpower was a miracle. How she had ever left him in the first place was her sin. She'd written twelve books and published ten and every damn one of her heroes had been Jeff in some form. Seeing him once more, she'd been mesmerized—until her father had shown up and made her feel like a child all over again. If only she had been older, when she'd first met Jeff. Or less scared of parental authority, more mature. She'd made poor choices in the past fifteen years. Her children had been hurt, and now she had to get on her feet again financially and out of her parents' house. She had to make her new life, without reacting to Jeff.

"All right, boys," Paula said finally, wanting to prove she was ready to do the latter. "We'll stay for Jeff's talk."

"Yeah!" Bobby and Stevie cheered.

The school's multipurpose room was already filled with kids and teachers when they arrived there. The noise level was deafening until Jeff appeared from behind a half-opened curtain on the little stage. The kids' voices snapped off as if with a switch.

He looks good, Paula thought, her gaze drawn to his tight jeans and dark green T-shirt. A fabulous white cockatoo sat on his shoulder.

"Kids, meet Elvis," Jeff said. His voice was miked. Kids

shouted the bird's name. The creature appeared unflustered by the noise. "Elvis, say hello to the kids."

"'You ain't nothing but a hound dog,'" Elvis sang on cue.

The bird did a number of tricks and sang more of Elvis's songs, as well. Paula sat in amazement at Jeff's patience and gentleness with the cockatoo and the children. He brought out Popeye, who only had to lope along like a drunken sailor to be a big hit. He also brought out a peregrine falcon and several parrots, the former majestic, the latter clever. Jeff talked all the time about the birds and what they do in the wild and why they needed open spaces. As he did, Paula found his voice hypnotizing her with his inflections and soothing words. It didn't matter what he said. It never had. She had been seventeen and he had been twenty when they'd first met. Even then he had been a giving man. Even then he had possessed a voice that reached into her soul. If only he hadn't been a Diamond. If only she had been braver.

She didn't think he knew she was in the audience until he suddenly looked directly at her and said, "I'd like the lovely young lady in the blue top to come up on stage and help me with the last birds I have here today."

Paula stared at him, then pointed to herself. "Me?"

"I'm not asking Sandra Bullock," he replied, grinning mischievously and beckoning to her.

"Oh, no," she said, shaking her head.

"Mom, you gotta do it," Bobby said.

Stevie took her arm and yanked at her. "Here, I'll help you, Mom."

Paula, with tons of second thoughts, let her youngest drag her up on the stage to where Jeff was smiling. Stevie returned to his seat, leaving her in a moment of panic as she felt hundreds of pairs of eyes on her. Thank God they were kids.

"What are you doing?" she whispered to Jeff.

Having fun, he mouthed. To her horror, he left her standing alone while he went behind the curtain for a few moments. She could see cages set up, most occupied by the various bird performers. He got several out of one cage and brought them into view.

Three small parrots sat on a stick, their body feathers a soft green while their faces had patches of peach down. They huddled against one another.

"This is Leo, Nardo and DiCaprio," Jeff announced to the audience. As he did, he coaxed each one from its perch onto his finger, then coaxed one onto each of Paula's shoulders. The last he sat directly on the top of her head. "These are lovebirds. Usually they stay in pairs and mate for life, but these three are brothers who like being together. I don't ask."

Paula didn't laugh along with the rest of the adults over the joke that the kids didn't get. She was too busy trying not to scream at the foursome Jeff had going with her. She could feel the birds' sharp claws clinging to her skin through her clothes and hair. It wasn't that they hurt her, but their nails tickled. The two on her shoulders immediately cuddled against her cheek, their feathers incredibly soft. She was afraid to move, afraid to startle them into taking flight, or worse, clawing her. She could see her boys giggling and knew whatever dignity she had with them was permanently shredded.

"Doesn't she look cute?" Jeff asked the audience. The kids applauded and cheered. The one on her head flapped his wings but didn't take off. The two on her shoulders trembled.

"You're a dead man, Jeff Diamond," she muttered.

He put his hand over his mike. "You usually said that when I got you all hot and bothered right before we had to sneak home."

Paula blushed furiously. He was flirting with her. No, she thought. He would never do that. Rather, he was having fun at her expense. Any humiliation on her part no doubt made him feel justified. She admitted she would endure it, knowing he *was* justified in having a little revenge.

"Pretty as Mrs. Miller looks," Jeff began, although it both-

ered Paula that he called her by her married name, "this is
what birds will have to do if we don't set aside land for them
to thrive, like I have at For the Birds sanctuary…"

Paula felt something warm slowly drip down the back of her
head and blurted out, "He peed on me."

The kids burst into laughter. Jeff raised his eyebrows.

"Have you been a bad boy, Leo?" he said to the bird. His
question was ruined by the huge grin on his face.

"Yes, he's been a bad boy," Paula snapped, wanting to
reach up and remove the creature and stop the awful sensation.
She had no clue how to get the damn thing off her without
scaring the other two. God only knew what they would do to
her.

"Leo, for shame," Jeff said. To the audience, he added,
"But you see what will happen if birds can't live anymore in
the wild. Just ask any New Yorker."

"Wonderful, I'm an environmental plug," Paula said in a
low voice to him.

Jeff led her behind the curtain as the kids applauded the
special finale she had provided. He was laughing, too, when
he coaxed that bad boy, Leo, onto his finger. Nardo and
DiCaprio took more coaxing because they liked her shoulders
too well.

Paula let out a huge breath of relief when she was free of
the birds. "You ever do that to me again, Jeff—"

"And you'll what?" he asked, grinning.

"I'll make sure your head will have bathroom duty. The
damn thing peed on me!"

Jeff chuckled. "Birds don't pee."

"What the hell do you mean birds don't pee?" she demanded, sending some of the parrots fluttering as they recognized her hostility.

"They only do one thing, and it's altogether, if you get my
drift."

"You mean he…oh, great," Paula said, disgusted with this further news.

"It's happened to me plenty of times, believe me, honey. Here, I'll fix it."

He stepped close to her, getting out a handkerchief as he did. Carefully he righted all birdy wrongs.

Paula tried to stand nonchalantly, but he was inches away from her. A wave of heat washed through her veins. Her lower body already throbbed with his proximity. It didn't matter what he was doing—even wiping bird poo off her. She wanted him.

Jeff paused, his mouth inches from hers as if he sensed her need. He lowered his head until their lips touched. The pressure was barely noticeable, but Paula felt as if a freight train had run her over. Her senses dimmed to everything but him. Her nerve endings shivered, like she'd been struck by lightning. Jeff was kissing her again and that was all that mattered.

In an instant the kiss was over. Even as he straightened and stepped back from her, giving them both a breathing space, Paula became aware of children filing past the curtain. Several glanced their way, grinned and waved.

"Why are you back, Paula?" he asked.

She swallowed, trying to moisten her throat enough to find her voice. "I'm broke and I'm divorced, with two boys to raise. It's as simple as that."

"But you were on the bestseller lists," Jeff said, frowning.

"And now I'm off." Better that he should think she came home for desperate financial reasons. Instead of only to get her life back in order.

"So you'll be here for a while?"

"Until I get a job."

"No more writing? That's a shame. I liked all your books."

Paula swallowed. She'd never thought he would read one, yet he implied he'd read them all. Had he recognized himself in them? She hoped not. "Thank you."

Jeff just smiled. "Thank you for helping today."

"I'm a terrific bathroom for your birds," she said, making a face.

"You're more than that. Much more."

She didn't want to think what he meant by that.

Chapter Two

Jeff circled his prey, scanning the area for any parental disruptions. She was alone.

He casually lengthened his strides, moving past the other mall strollers and closing the distance between him and Paula. He could have closed it completely, but his gaze was drawn to the sway of her hips in the short sundress. Strappy sandals enhanced her slim calves and ankles. He'd always loved her long, long legs—especially when they were wrapped around his waist while he was deep inside her.

The attraction was as strong as ever. Stronger. He knew what he had missed for fifteen years.

She paused in front of a store window, and Jeff almost passed her, his pace too quick. She swung around, clearly seeing his reflection in the glass. Her ponytail touched her shoulders. The sundress hinted at the curves of her breasts before skimming over her hips. He realized he was openly staring and covered his mistake with an innocent greeting.

"Hi. Window shopping still a favorite hobby?" He grinned at her, pleased with his nonchalant attitude.

"That's all it is," she said, then grimaced. "Hi, yourself. How're the Three Stooges?"

Jeff blinked, confused. Then understood. "Oh, the lovebirds? They're fine. Thanks for helping the other day at the school. You were great."

"I don't know about that," she replied, smiling a little. He decided he was forgiven when she added, "My kids loved it, though. I've enrolled them for next year."

Jeff's heart thumped wildly. She was planning to be around for more than a while. He felt as if fate *were* creating an opportunity for him, no matter what the past.

"Up here buying birdseed?" she asked.

"I couldn't afford it from here." He couldn't afford it from anywhere, but that was another story. "I have to return some jeans, so I thought I'd do it before my evening hours at the practice. How about you? You're really not window shopping, are you?"

She shrugged. "I like to get away and think."

"Starting a new book?"

She nodded, but didn't look enthusiastic. "I'm having trouble adjusting to my new work environment."

He hoped she needed help with research, then decided he ought to hit himself on the head with a two-by-four to get rid of what he was thinking. Instead of listening to his common sense, however, he said, "How about a cup of coffee at the Bean-Counter? They make a great latte."

"Do you think that's a wise idea?" she asked, not dancing around the things between them.

"No, but I think we need to just talk."

"A man wanting to just talk." Paula shook her head. "You never were stereotypical."

He smiled at her. "Nope, too dull. Come on, risk getting grounded and have a coffee on me."

Paula laughed. "There's a pun in there somewhere, but okay. A latte sounds good." She shivered as if on cue. "I'm still on California weather. Either that, or they've got the air-conditioning on too low."

Jeff took off his jacket and wrapped it around her shoulders. The garment had never looked better. Paula smiled gratefully at him.

He couldn't resist lowering his mouth to hers. The kiss was poignant and fierce all at the same time. He laved her tongue with his, feeling her melt against him as she always did. Her hands curled around his biceps, nails digging into his skin and muscles, as if she would fall were she to let go. She moaned in the back of her throat. Her breasts pressed into his chest. He could actually feel her nipples harden through the material. His blood heated in his veins. He had wanted this for so long...

Paula suddenly pulled away and stepped back. She stared at him, her eyes wide with desire and shock. "I'm sorry. That shouldn't have happened."

"That has been waiting to happen for a long time," he countered, his own breath coming heavily. They never would have done this publicly fifteen years ago.

"Maybe," she conceded. "But it won't happen again."

He raised his eyebrows in a cynical response.

"It was just a remnant of old dreams," she said.

"I doubt it, but never mind. You need coffee and so do I."

He took her arm and led her to the food court. It felt good to touch her...right, as if she were his again. He thought of the irony. When they'd been together, they never would have acknowledged each other publicly for fear of her getting in trouble with her father. Now, as adults, he could touch her all he wanted and he wanted to—a lot.

They got their drinks and sat across from each other at one of the many cozy tables under the skylight. A water fountain bubbled merrily next to them, while leafy plants in large tubs gave some intimacy from other patrons in the food court. Intimacy would have been easy, anyway, for the mall traffic was light at three in the afternoon. It didn't hurt that her father probably didn't have a crony here who would report this meeting to him.

He hoped. That kiss was pretty public—and that had been exciting in itself.

Paula sipped her latte, then smiled over at him. "This is nice."

Jeff knew she didn't want to discuss what had just happened. Maybe it would be better not to, since he wasn't sure he was emotionally equipped to deal with it, either.

He smiled back. "Yes, it is. Now tell me about your book. Can I be in it?"

She blushed and looked away. Jeff realized she truly had been writing about him. He grinned. "I'm already in them, aren't I? Hot damn!"

She turned more red. "I hate to burst your bubble, but no, you're not in my books."

Liar, he thought. "You're missing a good thing, then." He was referring to the books but knew it could mean more. "It'd be a great book if you had a bunch of people sneaking around to have sex."

"They call that mainstream." She shook her head ruefully. "I do love stories between *two* people sneaking about to have sex."

"That was us in real life."

His statement lay out there, like an unexploded bomb.

Paula rubbed the top of the metal table with her forefinger, as if to remove the baked white enamel. Finally she looked up. "Yes, it was us. I'm sorry."

"You regret your choice?" he asked, needing to know she hadn't wanted to do what her father had forced on them both.

"I regret…hurting you."

It wasn't the answer he was looking for. "Why? Did you want to break it off with me in some other way?"

"No." Her mouth turned down. "No. I was too young, barely seventeen. You were young, still in college."

"You were scared of your father."

"Who wouldn't be at that age?" She straightened and drank fully from the cup.

"Why did you really come home?" he asked.

"I told you. Because I'm broke and divorced and I need to get my life back in order." Her voice was strong, determined, as if she were making some emphatic point. "That's the only reason I'm here, okay? Thanks for the latte. I need to get going."

Slipping off his jacket, she rose from the table and walked away before he could protest.

"Hey, what about your book?" he called after her. "Don't you want my help with it?"

She waved a goodbye to him for an answer.

"Well, damn," Jeff muttered, watching his quarry get away.

All the way home, he wondered what the heck he was doing with Paula. Maybe it was the bet. Twenty-five million was a lot of money, and Paula just dropped in his lap the ready-made solution. But he knew he'd have wanted her even if it hadn't been for the twenty-five million. Caution had flown out the window the moment he'd seen her again. None of the past had mattered.

Several birds on a fence caught his eye as he neared his home. Jeff stopped the car and got out. He slowly walked over to the group. The small starlings flew up, but the big red macaw just sat. Its wings were clipped and the bird was capable only of short flights.

"Talulah? What are you doing out here?" he asked, stretching his arm out.

Talulah hopped onto the human perch, then walked up to settle on Jeff's shoulder. The bird's heavy claws clung gently to his shirt.

"Hello," Talulah said.

"Hello, yourself." Jeff frowned, trying to figure out how the bird got loose from the house.

He heard a distinctive call just beyond some bushes, one usually imitated around Thanksgiving time. "Orville? Is that you?"

He caught sight of a flash of brown among the greenery.

Then it was gone. How had Orville the turkey gotten loose from his cage? Jeff made a face as he vaguely remembered opening the kitchen window. He hadn't gotten new screening for the storm window and he bet Talulah had escaped that way. Probably the rest of the parrot crew was out. Orville's pen, however, was outside.

A car's engine drew near. Jeff saw it was Paula at the wheel. He waved her over. She slowed the car when she reached him. Bobby sat next to her while Stevie was in the back. She must have picked them up from somewhere on her way home from the mall.

"Anything wrong?" she asked.

"I've got birds loose," he said. "I just wanted to ask you to be careful because they're probably walking. Their flight wings are clipped."

"Oh."

"Can we help find them, Mr. Diamond?" Bobby asked eagerly. Stevie chimed in. "Please, please, please?"

Jeff chuckled. "Sure."

Paula didn't look thrilled, but she pulled her car onto the grass verge. The boys scrambled out.

"All the house birds are probably missing," Jeff said. "I've got Talulah here. But the lovebirds might be out, and Elvis. And Orville, my turkey. I heard him in the bushes over there."

Immediately the boys ran off toward the bushes, shouting Orville's name.

"If I see Orville again, I'll be lucky," Jeff muttered, knowing the boys would, in their innocence, drive the turkey farther into the bush.

"What can I do?" Paula asked.

Jeff said, "Start looking for the crew. I'm praying the falcons aren't loose. They'll be hell to get back."

"I thought you wanted them free."

"When they're ready. They're not ready."

"Oh." They started hunting together for his lost birds. Jeff had coaxed Talulah off his shoulder and settled her on the back of his seat in the car, leaving the windows cracked a few inches for ventilation. Paula found the lovebirds fairly quickly, the three keeping together as they always did. Her boys, having given up on Orville, took the trio, their small fingers gentle. Jeff was impressed with the care they used. He was relieved to find Elvis the cockatoo, but eventually gave up on Orville.

"He's been lovesick," Jeff said, sighing. He and Paula walked back to the cars behind the boys. "The mating season just passed and he's had no luck, mainly because I don't have a female for him."

Paula gaped. "Lovesick? How do turkeys get lovesick?"

"Just like everything else when they ain't getting any," he replied, wondering if he'd been lovesick for her all these years. Sometimes he'd felt like that. He had a lot in common with Orville.

Paula said nothing.

As they trooped back to the car, Bobby asked, "Can we ride with you?"

"Sure," Jeff replied. Paula gave him a look that had "no" written all over it. He just grinned at her, unrepentant.

In his car Jeff drove slowly, so as not to upset the birds, which weren't in cages. Elvis and Talulah squawked a little, but that was all. They were used to being in a moving vehicle. Paula followed behind in her car. Jeff noticed the boys instinctively stroked the birds to soothe them whenever they flapped their wings.

"You guys are good at that," he commented.

Both grinned. "Thanks." Then the questions began. "How long do they live?" "How'd you get them?" "Can I feed 'em sometime?" "What do you feed them? Mice?" "Ugh! How about cake? I bet they like cake. I do."

Jeff laughed and answered their questions and more. He realized they were starved for male attention. An idea popped into his head. Since his conversation with Paula had not gone exactly as he'd wanted, this new notion might ease them together.

"I need helpers," he said. "How would you guys like a job? A few hours every day and then one hour every afternoon, after school starts. I'll pay you fifty cents for each hour you work."

"Yeah! Yeah!"

Jeff grinned. Okay, so they were working for slave-labor wages, but they didn't know that. Besides, mostly they'd just fill water and food bowls for him. Maybe clean out a cage or two, nothing worth more than a half a dollar an hour, anyway.

At the house Jeff found his concerns for more escapees was alleviated when he saw the falcons and Popeye sitting happily on log stumps in their respective outdoor pens. Orville's cage was closed, leaving Jeff at a loss to explain the turkey's great escape. Turkeys were a lot smarter than people thought. He cursed at the house window he must have left open. "I've got to get that screen fixed."

"Nice that you know the word, but my kids didn't," Paula said, reminding him of his audience.

"Aw, we already knew it, Mom," Bobby said, looking disappointed.

"From where?" Paula demanded, her hands on her hips.

"From you," Stevie said blithely. "When that car ran that red light and almost hit us. You said it then. Real loud."

Paula looked heavenward. Jeff chuckled. Paula glared at him, but helped him with returning the birds to the house. She, like the boys, seemed to have an affinity for aviary things. She herded the boys out the door, but Jeff stopped her for a moment. Her arm felt warm under his fingers, as if already picking up his body heat.

"Thanks." He kissed her cheek, although he wanted to do more.

Her smile was vulnerable. "You're welcome."

"I'm not apologizing for the earlier kiss," he added. "I never will."

She slipped away, the thought going with her.

"WE GOT JOBS."

Paula set down her fork at Bobby's predinner pronouncement. Her parents were at a Rotary Club banquet, so she and the boys had the house and the dinner table to themselves. Unfortunately, her mother had insisted on cooking their dinner before she left. The roast pork didn't look appetizing. Neither did the vegetables. Paula had a feeling her repulsion was due to more than a heavy meal on a warm summery day.

"What did you say?" she asked, unsure she heard right.

"We got jobs. With Mr. Diamond," Stevie said this time, digging into his mashed potatoes. "Do I hafta eat the Brussels sprouts? They taste like stinky sour-crap."

Paula had no time to judge the Brussels sprout issue or her son's choice of words. Her brain whirled with "job" implications.

"What are you talking about?" she asked carefully, staring at her sons.

"Mr. Diamond said we could come over every day and help with the birds." Bobby smiled.

"Feeding them and all," Stevie added for good measure. "He'll pay us a whole fifty cents an hour!"

"I think we shoulda asked for a dollar," Bobby said, pursing his lips. "Fifty cents isn't enough for the ice cream man."

"You're not asking anyone anything," Paul said, feeling her blood pressure shoot up into the danger zone. "Mr. Diamond never should have offered you jobs."

"But we need the money, Mom," Bobby protested, his expression dismayed. "You said so yourself. That's why we're living at Grandpa's and not back home."

"We don't need anyone's charity," Paula said.

"We're taking Grandpa's," Bobby replied quickly. "Grandma even said so."

"I'll eat my Brussels sprouts if we can keep our jobs," Stevie offered, making a face.

"No job," Paula said.

Stevie burst into tears. "I want my job! I want my job!"

He shoved away the bowl of Brussels sprouts, then jumped up and ran from the table.

"Steven Miller, you come back here!" Paula shouted uselessly after him.

"He just wants a job, Mom," Bobby commented, taking a big bite out of his meat.

Man, Paula thought. If anyone else had offered the job to her boys, would she feel resistant? Her heart told her it was more than pride versus charity that put her against the idea of the boys working for Jeff. Jeff, of all people. And what would her father say if she let the boys work for Jeff? She shivered. He'd go ballistic. Her boys in close proximity to Jeff…the thought pained her, as if all her regrets were about to erupt.

A person could not go through life carrying regrets, she told herself for the nth time. She needed to stop doing that now.

"Eat your sour-crap," Paula said to Bobby, taking a forkful of her sprouts. She shivered as she ate the overcooked greens. Way overcooked. Her boys were making more of a sacrifice than she'd realized.

The next morning she went straight to Jeff's house, determined to nip this job thing in the bud. Only Jeff wasn't at the house. He was in the peregrine barn.

He stood in the enclosure, arms folded across his chest, looking stoic. He wore a hat, fedora shaped, on his head. A falcon fluttered just above the headgear, wings outstretched. The other birds were nowhere to be seen.

"Hi," Jeff said, not moving. "It'll be just a minute more until Oscar here finishes mating with my hat."

Paula gaped at him from beyond the wire barrier. "He's what?"

"Shh." His voice was low and gentle, as if he didn't want to disturb the bird's doings. "Quiet. It's a helluva thing to get this guy going, believe me."

The bird fluttered some more, his tail feathers moving rhythmically for a few moments. Oscar suddenly stopped and seemed to collapse onto the hat. Paula opened her mouth. Jeff put a forefinger up to stop her. Very slowly he stepped to a perch, then helped the falcon onto it. The bird blinked once, although its eyes looked dull. Jeff left the barn and came outside.

He grinned as he took off the hat, holding it level. "Hi."

"Hi, yourself." Paula peered at the object of Oscar's affection. "He really didn't mate with it...did he?"

Jeff tilted it slightly until she caught sight of a kind of soft plastic well in the back of the hat. Inside was a milky substance.

"One happy Oscar then," Jeff commented. "One whipped Oscar now. Come on in the house. I've got to get this extracted and refrigerated right away, until I can repackage and ship it off to a center that impregnates females and raises the hatchlings. We're trying to see if we can get male birds to copulate out of season, in order to build up a gene pool. They usually mate in early spring. So far so good."

"How did you get him to do that?" she asked, dutifully following him.

"Pheromones and hours of training," he replied, glancing at her. "The technique was perfected by the Colorado Peregrine Resource Center. Peregrines are breeding in captivity now, but there aren't enough out there in the wild yet, so we help out with artificial insemination."

Her heart swelled with pride, as if she had a right to feel a part of his accomplishments. "You always were clever and kinky. But a hat!"

"Love at first sight always worked for me."

He led her to his lab, where he placed the bird's semen in test tubes and put them in the refrigerator. He looked so damn good in tight jeans and a polo shirt, she thought, loving the way his brow furrowed with concentration. Leave it to him to be resourceful. He always had been, when it came to their personal mating habits. Did they ever mate! She felt the tingles of awareness deep inside and knew she still wanted to mate with him.

He turned to her. "I know you didn't come over for the Jeff and Oscar porn show. What's up?"

Her brain clicked back into place. "Jobs."

"You want one, too?" he asked, grinning at her.

"No." She cleared her throat and was self-conscious about the obvious state of her emotions. "It was lovely of you to offer my sons a job, but they can't accept charity."

"It's not charity," he said. "I could use some help around here, and they're big enough to lug water bowls and such. They're nice boys, Paula. Very responsible and good with the birds. They'll have a terrific opportunity here to learn about something they'll never get in school. That's not a bad thing, even if it is attached to me."

He sounded so logical that she had trouble finding a reasonable objection in return. Finally she settled on the universal answer to such dilemmas. "We'll see."

"Send them over this afternoon," he said, taking the answer for the reluctant yes that it was.

Paula sighed, feeling like she had walked in the door with her eyes wide-open and still tripped all over her feet.

"We're done here," he said. "Let's go into my living room and I'll go over with you what I mean for the boys to do. That way you'll be reassured that it is work but not too much for them."

Paula knew every moment spent in his presence brought her

closer and closer to resurrecting the past, one she couldn't afford to face. But she couldn't resist, either. "Okay."

Seated in wing chairs in his very masculine oak and leather living room, Jeff went through his routine with the birds until she pretty much understood her sons would only be getting food ready, making sure the water bins were filled and other small details children could handle. It was all nice and polite, clinical almost, with no sensual undercurrents. Well, a little one, she thought ruefully, but not anything she couldn't ignore for the moment. When she got up to leave, he stood with her, within arm's reach.

"I..." He paused, then added, "I like your boys, Paula. They're good kids and enthusiastic, like young birds on their first flight. I know I'll enjoy having them around, to be brutally honest. I won't ever have a chance for my own."

She gaped at him, not sure she heard right.

He looked at her steadily. "I got married after you left and that's when we found out I was sterile. Rebecca wanted kids, so she moved on. What a joke, all those times you and I were so careful to use protection and complained when we did. We never needed it."

"Jeff," Paula said, something inside her easing away at his loss. Tears clogged her throat. Clearly he needed to reach out to her kids, who were hurting in their own way. She wanted to hold him, to wipe away everything that had happened to them over the years.

"Being sterile mattered a lot to my pride, then," he added. "I never told anyone before, not even Julian. But it doesn't matter anymore. It hasn't for a long time. I guess that's why I'm telling you. I always told you things I never told anyone else, but I want you to understand that I'm making the offer for more than a need of cheap labor. I'd like to spend time with your kids."

He had told her special things, she thought. She knew about the time he'd gone duck hunting as a young teenager and how he'd cried in his room after shooting one. She knew he had secretly swapped his brother's better bike tires for his own one time, something else Julian probably still didn't know. She knew he had been devastated when his mother passed away from cancer shortly after winning custody of the twins in an acrimonious divorce. She knew he'd always felt his father had loved Julian more, because the man found Jeff "too strange" as a child to comprehend. Now this.

His sterility would never have mattered to her if things had worked out differently between them. She would have loved him for himself alone, not for any children they couldn't have conceived. She would never have "moved on," like his wife had.

"You can borrow my boys anytime," she said, smiling.

"Thank you." He leaned forward and kissed her.

She'd expected he would, and she met him halfway. The kiss held gratitude, compassion and latent fire. But they had already come together twice in this way before, and the fire won out this time. Jeff pulled her fully against him. Paula wound her arms around his shoulders and met his tongue boldly. Her body melded perfectly with his. Breast to chest, hip to hip, thigh to thigh, they had always been a perfect physical fit. It had been other things that had not fit well—like her father.

Paula shoved those objections aside. She was an adult now, and she could kiss whoever she wanted. She wanted to kiss Jeff.

She clung to him, kissing as if he was the last man on earth. Her tongue mated with his, faster and faster, until the kiss was a frenzied jumble of emotions and needs. His hands stroked her back, then cupped her derriere, his fingers digging in as he pressed his arousal against her. She had loved that, just had loved to feel how much he wanted her, right from the first touch of their lips. She teased him a little bit, lifting away and pressing back even harder to meet him. His hand slid up her side and cupped one breast, kneading her flesh while his thumb circled her nipple.

Paula moaned in the back of her throat, knowing that it felt as good as it ever had with him. Nothing in her life since she left him had even come close to matching the desire Jeff always aroused in her. The kiss went on so long, she wasn't sure she was even breathing anymore. She wasn't sure she needed to, as the world lovingly dimmed. Jeff's mouth eased from hers, and he kissed her hard on the cheek.

"I have missed you," he whispered, kissing her chin, her throat, her jawline with those wonderful little biting kisses she remembered so well.

"I want you," she murmured, running her hands down his back and feeling the strong muscles there. He was heavier, mature, with the promise of virility over eagerness this time.

"You don't mean it," he said.

"Oh, yes," she murmured, knowing she never meant anything more in her life. She might be turned upside down in a lot of ways, but on wanting Jeff she was sure. And she did not regret it. How could she, when she had dreamed of it night after night, after she'd left?

She reached up and kissed him again, taking his mouth as fiercely as one of his falcons would take a sparrow from the sky. She let her fingers drop below his trim waist, reacquainting herself with the hard curves of his buttocks. She explored his flesh through his jeans, the feel of male muscles under the heavy denim creating delightful little shocks along her palms' nerve endings. Wickedly she moved her hand around his hipbone and cupped him in her fingers.

Jeff groaned and buried his face in her neck. His breath was hot on her skin, sending her blood spinning through her veins. He pressed his lips to her ear. "Nothing changes. *Nothing.*"

"Nothing," she echoed, knowing nothing *had* changed in her heart.

Somehow she found herself on his sofa, Jeff on top of her.

He pushed her blouse over her head before stripping her bra away. His cheekbones were flushed with desire, his expression intense. He lowered his mouth and suckled her nipples until they puckered into nubs. Paula bucked against him, feeling as if she would explode. She wanted more and pulled his shirt open, running her palms along the mat of hair on his chest.

"You have more," she whispered, while he rose up and worked at her jeans.

He grinned. "I am a hairy beast."

"What does that make me?"

"A beauty." He removed the rest of her clothes until she lay naked before him, unashamed. She didn't think of the curve of her belly or the silvery lines on it, marks of childbirth. This was Jeff, and it wouldn't matter. He kissed her at the junction of her thighs. "The most beautiful of all."

He shed his jeans and boxers, his arousal rock hard as he knelt between her thighs. She wrapped her legs around him without hesitation, the young lovers' knowledge of each other blending with the overlying maturity.

He invaded her body slowly, with great care and delight, his fullness pressing her open even as she sheathed him tightly. Her heart had already become one with his, and when they moved together Paula knew it was more than a mating. It was a renewal. She knew it as she met each thrust with her own. She knew it when they moved instinctively quicker, faster, to capture the elusive fulfillment. She knew it when the heat burst inside her like a million tiny droplets throbbing through every fiber of her being. She knew it when Jeff thrust one last time, catching her up and holding her, pouring himself into her, as if he would never let her go again. Jeff was inside her and nothing else mattered.

When they surfaced in the aftermath, Paula smiled. She caressed his back, his skin cool and yet damp with perspiration. "I've missed you, Jeff."

He kissed her cheek. "I've missed you."

They spoke of nothing more, neither willing to ruin the contentment as they lay in each other's arms.

When Paula eventually went home, she felt as if she were walking on air. The cliché seemed all too real. Jeff had sent her home this way many times in the past. In the kitchen she discovered her parents sitting over coffee.

"Where were you?" her father asked, eyeing her closely and frowning.

Paula smiled dreamily. "I went for a walk."

"Not over to that bastard's house."

In an instant Paula's dreamy state vanished faster than the dodo bird. Time warped back fifteen years, and she felt intimidated again, humiliated that she felt that way, and angry over her whereabouts being questioned—and over her father's favorite nasty term for Jeff. She forced herself to be calm, however. "What does it matter, Dad? I'm not seventeen. For Pete's sake, I've been on my own for years."

"It matters, and you damn well know it. Just like his grandfather blocked my business before he sold that bank of his, that bastard and his birds are keeping me from finishing off the development up here. Vindictive, that's what those Diamonds are. They don't like anyone making money they don't have a hunk of. But that'll change." Her father smiled grimly. "I'm just warning you that I'm not putting up with him sniffing around your skirts again, just to get at me."

Too late, Paula thought. Jeff had already done more than sniff.

Chapter Three

"Howdy, stranger."

Jeff grinned as he got in line at the post office behind Paula. She smiled at him, although her eyes turned smoky as she glanced at his chest, then back up to his face. One touch, he thought, and the clock had turned back to their first time together.

"Hi." She still smiled, even as she looked more cautiously at the other patrons in the small place.

Jeff wished he hadn't seen the reaction. For all her talk of starting a new life, she still worried about what might be said to her father. She hadn't boldly called him since their lovemaking a few days ago. Then again, neither had he called her, just made sure he ran into her like this. Now who was the chicken? How could he be, after sharing about his sterility with her, after sharing his body intimately *in* hers?

To distract himself, he focused on the big mailing envelope under her arm. He decided to keep the meeting light.

"New book done? Were you inspired by something? Mmm? Mmm?"

She chuckled, her shoulders relaxing. "New proposal. Oh yeah, I was inspired…by Oscar and his hat. Have you caught Orville yet?"

Jeff sighed. "No, although a couple of kids reported seeing him in the Farmer's Glen development."

"I think I heard him singing 'Somewhere Out There.'"

"I think I was singing that," Jeff muttered. He leaned forward and whispered in her ear. "How about coffee? My place?"

Paula shivered a delicious little shudder that had him desperate to plant love bites along her throat.

"Next!" the clerk called out.

"Hi, Sam," Jeff said to the postal clerk, waving as Paula stepped to the window. "You remember Paula Helpern, don't you? The mayor's daughter? Her name's Miller now. Paula, Sam's dad ran the hardware store before you left."

"Oh, sure," Paula said, shaking hands with Sam. "Nice to see you."

"Nice to see you, too," Sam said. He motioned between her and Jeff "Hey! You two—?"

"No, no," Paula said quickly. "Just old friends."

The term hurt—and left him doubting his status with her after their lovemaking.

"Right." Jeff just winked, determined not to let his thoughts show, then pointed to the package. "Take care of that, Sam. It's her book. She's a famous author."

"Hardly," Paula scoffed.

"She *is*," Jeff said, rubbing her back. "The best."

He realized his unconscious gesture of support and dropped his hand away—but not without one last pat. The hell with it, he decided. *He* wasn't a kid anymore.

Sam took care of Paula's package, then sold Jeff the stamps he needed. Jeff walked out of the post office with Paula. The day was beautiful, cool and sunny. Diamond Mount loomed above them, the mountain verdant with fir trees.

Jeff drew in a deep breath of air, then touched Paula's elbow. "Come on. Coffee on me again."

Paula sighed. "It's too pretty a day to argue. But just coffee and just in town."

"You're no fun."

She smiled like a little satisfied cat. "Wanna bet?"

Jeff laughed. He kept his hand on her elbow as they walked together, just liking to touch her. Her skin was smooth, like silk, and he could feel the warmth of her heating his fingers.

They strolled along Main Street, with its quaint little specialty shops that somehow survived the local mall. People smiled at them and said hello. Some recognized Paula. The whole feeling was so right that he wished he had had it for the past fifteen years.

They settled at one of the little tables outside the Yum-Yum Ice Cream parlor on the corner of Union and Main. The world that was Diamond Mount passed by on a regular basis.

After their coffees arrived, Jeff said, "I've missed you. Why haven't you called?"

"I've been working," she said, looking pleased with herself.

"I *did* inspire you."

She flushed. "Well…maybe unblocked me."

Jeff sent her a raspberry. "I sound like a plumber's helper. That's great for the libido."

"Yours never needed any help."

"Not where you were concerned." He grew serious. "Paula, where are we going with this?"

"I don't know," she admitted. She ran her fingers across her forehead. "It's complicated between us. Too much baggage in the past and in the present."

"Then let's take it a day at a time," Jeff said. "So what time do you want to go out tonight?"

Paula burst into laughter. "That's a day at a time?"

"Works for me. Eight o'clock?"

"I'm not ready yet for that."

"Paula! My God. I heard you were back."

Jeff groaned under his breath at his brother's voice. Julian stood by their table with his longtime girlfriend, Moira Carson. Both looked tall, poised and elegant in near-matching business suits. His brother was definitely anal-retentive. At Julian's open arms, Paula rose and hugged him, very pleased to see him. Julian had always liked Paula, but he shot Jeff a look that asked if he were nuts for being with her again. Jeff just grinned smugly back at his brother. The one looking less pleased was Moira, who stood patiently next to Julian. She had a dozen pink roses resting along one arm.

Jeff rose and gave her a hello hug. Why not, he thought. His brother was having fun. "Why you put up with that idiot is a mystery to me, Moira. You're too good for him."

"I was beginning to wonder the same thing myself, but he gave me flowers." Moira actually sounded touched.

Moira had three Pomeranians she doted on. It occurred to Jeff the doting was a manifestation of her maternal needs. Those "damned, spoiled, puffballs of hers," as Julian called them, ensured she'd leap at any offer Julian made for marriage and kids. Jeff liked the poms. He didn't know what the holdup was with Moira, but Julian was an ass for not yet proposing. Jeff could take advantage of it.

"I'm surprised to see you two together," Julian said. "Last time I think your dad was chasing Jeff with a shotgun."

"It was a wooden spoon," Jeff said, remembering how her father had come after him, after catching him in Paula's bedroom in the wee morning hours. Paula had broken up with him the next day.

Paula flushed, clearly remembering, too. "We're just friends."

Julian looked straight at Jeff—and smiled broadly.

Jeff took Paula's hand and lifted it to his mouth, giving her fingers a kiss. "*Old* friends. Some things never change."

Julian's eyebrows shot up and he blurted out, "Are you…" He paused. "We'd love to chat but we have to go, don't we, honey?"

"'Bye," Jeff said, waving as Julian hustled Moira away.

"What was that all about?" Paula asked, after they sat down again.

Jeff shrugged. "Who knows with Julian. He's like that friend of Ferris Bueller's, in the movie. Stick a piece of coal up his butt and it would come out a diamond."

"You are bad," Paula said and laughed.

Jeff grinned. "I'm fun."

The thought stuck in Jeff's head after they parted. He didn't press for a date, the conversation with his brother giving him an idea. Maybe seeing Julian and Moira together had added to his plan.

That evening he found himself on the edge of the Helpern property, grateful that Robert Helpern didn't like dogs and therefore didn't own one. The lights in the house eventually went out one by one as he watched. How many times had he parked his car off the road and waited like this for the household to go to bed? Too many and not nearly enough. He only had to walk over the property line now. He knew, after seeing the slender form against the shade, that Paula's room hadn't been changed. He had also seen that the boys were in the back bedroom, both of them having poked their heads out and warbled for Orville, the still-missing turkey.

Orville's eventual return warble in the distance seem to be a rallying cry for Jeff. When he was sure the house was asleep, he moved silently across the lawn and climbed the porch balustrade to the roof. He crept across it until he came to Paula's open window.

"Paula," he said in a low voice. "Open the screen."

"Jeff?" Her voice was alert, not sleepy. He heard a rustle and a movement inside the darkened room. Her face appeared at the window. She opened it wider and whispered, "Are you nuts!"

"It would see n so. Open that screen and let me in. Please."

"No, I—"

"Please." He shivered against the night air. He should have worn more than a T-shirt.

She hesitated a moment, then pushed the screen up from its inside latches. He squeezed through the opening. Barely.

"It wasn't that tight before," he commented, frowning.

"You aren't the boy you were before," she said. "Now what's this about?"

He smiled and reached for her. "Fun."

She evaded him. "Jeff. You said we would take this one day at a time."

"But I said nothing about the nights." This time he caught her in his arms. He nuzzled her throat. "Paula, we won't know where we're going unless we explore what's there."

She resisted another moment, then relaxed against him. "You *are* crazy."

"Only with you."

He kissed her thoroughly. Her response was everything he could hope for, passionate and emotional. She pressed her body fully to his, as her arm wound around his neck. Their tongues swirled together.

"I must be nuts," she whispered when the kiss finally ended. "Why can't I stay away from you?"

"We never could stay away from each other, and we never will," he murmured. "Romeo and Juliet. Remember how we thought that?"

He eased her onto her bed. Neither spoke above a breath. They didn't need to. Their mouths and hands and bodies communicated on the most intimate of levels. As they shed their clothes, darkness enshrouded them in its cocoon. Jeff felt as if he could hear nothing, see nothing, feel nothing except Paula. He knew they could be interrupted at any moment, with disastrous results, but it had always been this way between them, every part of him infinitely attuned to her. The past didn't matter, the complicated present didn't matter, twenty-five million dollars didn't matter. All he knew or cared about was that she was back in his life and he could have her again.

Desperate to be joined with her, he eased himself into her

almost at once. Her moist folds held him in their already hot, wet grip. Her taut nipples burned his chest, and her legs wound tightly around his hips. He rolled them to their sides and took her nipple in his mouth, laving it with his tongue and nipping slightly with his teeth. Paula smothered a moan, but he heard it and knew it was just for his ears. They rocked together slowly, Paula's nails digging into his back. She would leave marks. She always did. The bed hardly moved.

"I want you so much," she whispered. "I don't care. I don't care."

She did care. He knew she did and knew she meant what this would cost her emotionally and with her family. Not the boys—her parents. But she was risking it again. For him.

The frenzy between them rose. Jeff could feel it in himself, in her, yet they both kept their movements slow, controlled. That only added to the intensity. Paula's hips bucked and she moaned again. Jeff captured the sound with a searing kiss, taking in the expression of her climax even as he completely buried himself in her one last time. His soul poured into her, wiser and yet more hungry than it had ever been before. The darkness totally enwrapped them both for long, long minutes.

When they surfaced, she stroked his face from temple to jaw with her forefinger. "What am I going to do with you? What am I going to do with me?"

He kissed her bare shoulder, his lips feeling the fragile bone under the warm flesh. "We'll find a way."

He could have her forever, he thought. And he could save the sanctuary. She *had* come back into his life at the right time.

"HE'LL COME BACK if you let him off the jess?"

Paula frowned as she asked the question, concerned that the beautiful peregrine falcon wouldn't return. The bird perched on Jeff's wrist. A heavy gauntlet protected him from Oscar's tearing claws. Jeff might be getting him ready eventually for release into the wild, but that didn't mean Oscar wouldn't do an Orville and disappear to go looking for a ladylove.

"He'll come back," Jeff said, with incredible surety. "Oscar likes to test himself sometimes, that's why I have a little transmitter on him in case he goes after something. But he's not ready for release yet, and he knows it."

He took the hood off the falcon's head, then loosened the tether on his leg. Oscar looked around, blinking only once. Jeff flung his heavily padded arm up. Oscar spread his wings, beating them fiercely to save himself from falling. The air caught under the bird and lifted him into the currents, the tiny bells on the trailing thongs of leather attached to his legs jingling merrily with the breezes.

Jeff came and stood next to her, putting his arm around her as they watched the bird rise higher into the blue sky. "Just like you came back."

Paula turned and smiled at him. She hadn't felt this happy in years. She and Jeff had so much to sort out still, a lot of the past to wash away. Then there was her father. Clearly, his feelings for the Diamond family hadn't changed. She didn't want to alienate him any more than she had fifteen years ago. He was a good man; he just had a blind spot when it came to Jeff's family. Only she was an adult now, and that made a difference.

One day at a time, she thought, because she wanted Jeff and her to work out.

Jeff leaned over and nuzzled her ear. His breath fanned her flesh, sending spirals of delicious shivers along her nerve endings. "You smell terrific."

"You are a sex fiend."

He lifted his head and grinned. "And this is a complaint?"

She chuckled. "Not hardly. But this isn't the place."

In the few days since he had come to her bedroom the first time, they had found little niches during the daytime for talking and cuddling—and a bit more—while he'd spent the nights in her bedroom, both of them smothering cries of pleasure. Jeff was like a drug she had to have to live. His yard, however, with her boys going in and out of buildings to fill bird feeders, wasn't the right place to feed her addiction.

"Jeff! Jeff! Look who's following me!"

Stevie could hardly contain his excitement as Orville the turkey waddled intently behind the boy. Stevie didn't run, just walked fast, but seeing the turkey's wings half spread and his neck extended sent Paula's shivers in another direction. "Be careful, honey!"

"I'll get him," Jeff said, heading toward boy and turkey. He intercepted Orville and herded him into his pen, securely latching the gate this time.

"Did ya see? Did ya see?" Stevie demanded, dancing around the two adults.

Jeff laughed and patted the boy on the back. "We saw. Great job, Stevie. Where did you spot him?"

"Behind the house. I just called to him and he came. I tried to catch him but then he scooted away from me."

"He's hungry," Paula said.

"Turkeys are smarter than people give them credit for," Jeff said. "I think he likes Stevie, though."

"I think he had a look at the world and said forget it," Paula commented, kissing her son on the cheek. "You did really well, sweetie."

Stevie grinned. "I gotta fill some more dishes or Bobby'll yell at me."

The child raced off. Jeff smiled indulgently as he watched. Paula smiled at him. She liked seeing his delight in her children and was glad she had allowed the boys their jobs with him. All three were getting a lot out of it. Four, if she counted her own visits while they worked. Her mother, always easily fooled, thought she and the boys went for a long walk every day. Her father still knew nothing about jobs and visits with Jeff.

Paula made a face of disgust. She had to stop hiding this. She *wasn't* a kid anymore, even if she had had to move home for financial support.

A light, happy sound caught her ears and she realized it was the falcon flying back their way. Jeff stepped to the most open spot in the yard and lifted his arm. He waited. The falcon came in like a bullet, before stopping at the last second to cling to the suede gauntlet. Jeff's arm jerked with the sudden weight and force, but he didn't drop the bird. Oscar flapped his wings once or twice, then folded them against his body. He looked around nonchalantly as if he hadn't been about to take Jeff's arm out of its socket.

"That's it?" Jeff asked the bird. "Just a look-see and home again?"

Oscar only stared in answer.

"Two home," Jeff said, grinning as he put Oscar in his pen.

Three, Paula thought. Hadn't she come home, too?

That evening, after dinner, Paula decided she would do the sneaking into bedrooms tonight. Another exploration, she thought. Until she overheard her father talking to her mother.

"He'll get the letter in a few days," her father said as he sat over evening coffee while her mother crocheted another of her endless afghans. "I got the zoning board to have an emergency meeting. It's a health violation in a residential zone. I've said that all along. Now they've hit him where it hurts—"

"Hit who were it hurts?" Paula asked, although her heart had made a good guess.

Her father jerked a thumb eastward, toward Jeff's house. "That bastard. He and his birds won't be thumbing their noses at the rest of us anymore. The zoning board's revoked his variance. Took them long enough. Diamond's gone as soon as the citation arrives."

"You can't do that, Dad!" Paula exclaimed.

"Now, dear—" her mother began.

"I can do it and I did do it." Her father was smug.

"You never bothered before. It's me, isn't it? It's all about me and Jeff again."

"Health violations."

"That a load of BS and you know it!" Paula snapped. "You maneuvered the zoning board into this, just to get at Jeff because I'm back. Because you think something's going on between us."

Her father didn't answer, just thrust his jaw out.

"I love you, Dad, but you're a bully sometimes."

"Don't talk to your father that way," her mother bleated.

"It's time someone did." Paula whirled on her heels and out the front door.

"Hey! Where are you going!" her father shouted after her.

She turned her head as she strode forward. "To Jeff's, to help him fight you. If you want to kick me out, then kick me out, Dad, but I won't let you get away with this."

She was at Jeff's in record time. He was just escorting out his last patient, a large German shepherd with a nasty row of stitches on its foreleg.

"Keep out of the trash can, Rudolph," Jeff admonished the dog, then said the same to the owner in the small area that doubled as waiting and examination room. When the two left, he turned to Paula and smiled broadly. "You timed that right."

He reached for her to kiss her, but she evaded him, knowing the first touch would turn her into mush and she'd never tell him what her father did. "Jeff, the zoning board has revoked your variance here."

"What?" He gaped at her. "What the heck are you talking about?"

"My father. My wonderful father got the zoning board to have some kind of meeting and revoke your variance here. You're getting a letter that says you and the birds have to go."

"He can't do that!" Jeff exclaimed.

"That's what I said. But he did it." Paula went to him and

put her arms around him. "I'm so sorry, Jeff. He's doing this because of me and you."

"He knows?"

"He does now. I told him I'd help you fight this." She raised her head. "What do you need me to do?"

"Just what you're doing." He caught her to him. "You stood up to your father about me. I can't believe it."

"I should have done it fifteen years ago." Paula smiled and put her arms around his neck. "Maybe this is why I came home."

Jeff kissed her, his mouth like a tender fire. She kissed him back with all her heart and soul.

"I love you," she whispered when his mouth eased from hers. "I never stopped. I wish I hadn't been a scared girl. I wish I could take back those fifteen years and give them to you, the way I should have done in the first place. I'm so sorry I hurt you then."

"We have to do this right," he said, taking her hand. "First we settle us, then we settle the rest."

She felt exactly the same as he did. She had taken flight finally, and brought herself truly home. Jeff led her to his bedroom, a place she had never been. On his nightstand was her senior class picture in a silver frame. Paula stared at it. "How did you get that? I never gave you one, not that size."

"I loved the small one you did give me, so I had it enlarged." He smiled at her and took her in his arms. "The Diamonds can get a thing or two done when they need to. It's been there since you've been back."

Tears welled in her eyes. "Jeff."

Their lovemaking was a storm of passion, regret and love. Paula strained against him longer and harder as they whispered all the things they'd wanted to say and had never been given a chance to do so before. They lay replete in the aftermath, entwined in each other's arms. Paula never wanted to let go, although she knew she would have to return and face her father.

"You can live here with me," Jeff whispered as if reading her thoughts. "You and the boys. Unless you have ties with your ex."

Paula shook her head. "No. He's off somewhere acting his heart out, my mistake, but my only regret is for my boys."

"We'll get married, Paula," Jeff said.

Paula's heart soared. She had wanted to hear those words fifteen years ago, but he had never offered them. Now he was asking. She had tons of reasons to say no, but life was giving her a second chance at love. Could she pass it up?

She was about to speak, when he laughed and added, "That'll frost everyone. Your father, my brother, Diamond Mount itself. The variance won't matter a damn then."

Paula frowned, having no clue why *everyone* would be "frosted." "What are you talking about?"

"Let's get married. As soon as we can." He got excited as he pulled her to him, physically and emotionally. "Before my brother, that's for sure. We get married, and I'll be in the family way with the kids, and we'll save the sanctuary. Hell, honey, we can move it anywhere in the world we please with twenty-five million dollars from my grandfather. They can revoke all they want, and it won't matter."

Paula pushed him off her and sat up in his bed, holding a sheet against her naked breasts. She had no clue what he was rambling on about, but every one of her senses knew—*knew*— it wasn't good. "What twenty-five million? What is all this?"

Jeff sat up. He put his arm around her. "A while ago, my grandfather told Julian and me that he would give twenty-five million dollars to the first one who got married and was in the family way before the year was out. The sanctuary's broke, I've run through my trust fund to keep it going this long. I figured I was doomed to lose because of my sterility, but then you came back and everything's the same. Better. You've got children. That's a family if I ever saw one." He chuckled. "Julian won't like the loophole but that's life. He's had two years with Moira and did nothing. Paula, marry me. Your boys are terrific and I think they'll accept me as a father. We'll be together at last, and we'll save the sanctuary, too. We'll never want for money in our lives…''

As he went on and on and Paula listened, she turned numb. Her teeth chattered with shock as the implications of what he was saying sank in. His attention was all because of a bet—not love. He didn't love her. He couldn't. How could he even suggest he loved her, while telling her they'd make a ton of money when they married. Another truth hit Paula. Her sons were the key. Even from his own mouth, Jeff admitted—admitted—that they were his loophole to win the bet. She had opened her heart to him and he had crushed it.

Paula felt her whole body roil with pain and anger. Twenty-five million dollars. Twenty-five! The thought of being used for so much money made her sick. And her sons, as well. God help her, she had been about to put them into a situation where they would be used, too. No matter what she had done in the past, she didn't deserve this. Neither did Bobby or Stevie.

She flung herself from the bed and grabbed her clothes. "No! This is revenge, pure and simple, isn't it? Use me, the woman who hurt you so badly before, to get back at my father and win a bet at the same time. A stinking bet! How ironic, what a nice twist on the past. Did you rub your hands together with glee when you hatched this plot?''

He looked dumbfounded. Nice trick, she thought cynically.

"Paula, it's not like that—''

"What else could it be? A sudden rush of love after fifteen years?'' She yanked on her clothes as she asked her questions. She answered them first. "Only I would be that stupid. No, you saw opportunity and you saw revenge in a nice little package. You're as bad as my father. I won't be winnings for any man, so take your bet and your variance and shove them where the sun doesn't shine, Jeff Diamond.''

She raced out of the room and out of the house. Tears

streamed down her face as she walked home. She couldn't believe he would play on her emotions just to win a bet. She and her sons would be used like commodities. It figured. She should have known this was false, an illusion. No relationship moved this fast or this smoothly. Jeff must have been laughing up his sleeve the whole time.

"Congratulations," she muttered, swiping at the flow of tears than didn't stop. She had come home to change her life and she had made a mess of it all over again.

Julian

~ Part Two ~

Little Brother Takes His Turn at the Wheel

Chapter Four

"Shut up!"

Julian Diamond practically growled the words at the three yapping furballs barring his way. The Pomeranians ignored his command as always, their barking growing more frantic as they lunged at him, then leaped away. They looked like miniature hairy foxes, but not nearly as bright as those feral creatures. They did have the ability to keep him trapped in the foyer. Stairs wound up along the opposite wall. Too bad he couldn't reach them, he thought. They'd provided an escape hatch before from the three dogs. Every Tuesday and Friday nights for the past year, he had come to Moira Carson's straight from work for dinner and a sleepover. One would think the dinky half-wit creatures would let him in the door just once without the display of ferocity.

"Puppies! Quiet, please."

The dogs suddenly went silent. They raced to their mistress.

Moira stood on the threshold of her home's front room. No attorney's tailored suit in sight this time, she was dressed in a pair of navy khakis and a button-down pink-and-white-striped shirt with its tails hanging out. Julian noted the odd fact that she hadn't tucked in the shirt as she normally would have. It should have marred her usual perfection, yet he found himself intrigued by the change. She looked earthy...unconsciously sexy. He liked it.

She bent and stroked each one of her pets, their entire hind ends wagging in delight at her attention. "What good babies. You'd give a rottweiler a run for its money. Anastasia. Sergei. Doodles." Each dog stilled as its name was called. "Go get your treats in your bowls."

The three raced off to the kitchen at a speed a greyhound would envy. Julian walked over to Moira and said, "Dammit, why the hell are they still barking at me after a year?"

Moira smiled. "They're just protecting me."

"But I'm a banker, not a robber! You spoil them, honey." He kissed her cheek, then kissed her full on the mouth. It wasn't his customary greeting to her, but he felt affectionate. He'd better, he thought, knowing what was facing him down the barrel of the metaphorical gun his grandfather held to his head. He'd already started his campaign with flowers and candy.

To his surprise she stiffened at his words, her bottom lip trembling as if she would cry. "I do *not* spoil them!"

Tears spilled over suddenly, trickling down her cheeks. Shocked, Julian stepped back. He had *never* seen Moira cry in their entire time together. "Moira, honey, I didn't mean anything by it."

She swiped at her eyes, but the waterworks didn't stop. If anything, they got worse. "You *never* mean anything by it. You don't care to make friends with my dogs. You never did! I've never asked anything of you but that. Why can't you do something for me once?"

Julian stared at her, dumbfounded by her unusual outburst. The dogs materialized in the doorway, their beady eyes assessing the situation. Anastasia recognized the problem first. Before Moira could stop her, the little dog launched herself at Julian, faster than a speeding bullet. Sergei and Doodles followed their leader in an all-out attack.

Julian grabbed the stair banister and leaped over it. The dogs, confused for a crucial moment, spun in circles where he'd just stood, trying to find their "vanished" quarry. They spotted him on the stairs and the race began again. Or would have.

"*Stop!*" Julian roared.

The dogs skidded to a halt at the foot of the stairs, tumbling over each other in confusion, Julian's tone and decibel level taking them by surprise.

Moira clapped her hands and called each by name again. "Bad puppies. Bed!" Three pairs of ears went back as if on cue. Anastasia and Sergei walked dejectedly toward the kitchen and their daybeds. Doodles looked at Moira, his snout opening in a smile and his tail wagging hopefully. Moira pointed to the kitchen. "Bed!"

Doodles slumped into the kitchen.

"I'm so sorry," Moira said, rushing to him as he came down the steps. She wrapped him in a clingy embrace, something else she *never* did when the dogs acted up around him. She kissed his face all over. "Poor Julian. It's all my fault. I'll stop spoiling them so much, I promise."

Julian was about to ask what was wrong with her, then clamped his lips shut. A part of him was kind of liking this affection. Another part of him noted it was all to the good for what he had to do. Yet another part of him didn't like it at all. He wrapped his arms around her and kissed her passionately.

She hesitated, just as she always did, that wonderful split second of indecision about whether to match what he offered. Anyone else would see it as a rejection, but he was undeterred. She always weighed her options before responding, and he liked that the most about her. When her tongue mated with his, all cool fire, he ran his hands down her back to cup her derriere. He loved the way her curves fit his grasp. She looked like Rene Russo, had Michelle Pfeiffer's poise and Marilyn Monroe's underlying earthiness. Best of all, Moira was an attorney. She understood business, and understood his personal needs.

The only problem was that their relationship never truly progressed from the occasional business lunch, discreet dinners and sex several nights a week. They rarely called each other in between times. They never got closer emotionally. That was something Julian needed to change—and in a hurry. Jeff was about to make an ass out of himself again with Paula Helpern-Miller.

As he eased his lips from hers, he whispered, "Let's forget dinner and go right to bed. I'm more hungry for you."

Moira chuckled and pushed him away. "Don't be silly. You *always* have to eat first. I've got takeout from the Szechuan Palace. It'll be cold if we don't eat it now."

She went into the kitchen. Julian had no choice but to follow her. The dogs eyed him from their individual beds along the back wall. Julian glared back at them, curling his lips slightly in response to their growls. Unfortunately, the sound was not at all threatening.

"You need to give them each a biscuit," Moira said, opening a large jar on the counter and digging out three treats. "If you make friends with them, they'll stop acting like you're a burglar."

"They act worse than that," he muttered, but took the hard cookies from her. "Last time we did this, Anastasia nearly took off my hand."

"Keep your fingers out of the way."

"Keep my fingers out of the way," Julian mimicked wryly as he approached the puff pack. He offered a treat to the two males, but they turned away, snubbing him. He set a biscuit in front of each bed. Anastasia, however, snatched up the treat so quickly, he nearly did lose a finger. The other two, seeing her heading toward their biscuits, were fast to reach for them.

"That's better," Moira said proudly as she opened cartons and served up their dinner.

"Hey! While they're eating, let's go upstairs—"

Moira laughed, dismissing his suggestion. "We'd have Mu-shu Pork all over the bed. No thanks."

As they sat and ate, Julian found himself watching Moira.

She had swept her mass of brown curls up away from her face. Escaping tendrils trickled down her nape. Her skin was creamy and her features soft, delicate. Yet her jaw held a stubborn bent. Her lips were thoroughly kissable. He remembered that was the first thing that had attracted him to her. That and she never asked personal questions. Neither did he. It had suited him at first, and yet as time went along, he had been afraid to break her self-containment even though he sometimes wanted to.

But things were different now, and he had to push a little. If his new bank branch expansion went the way he hoped, he would need to win the bet. "Moira, you've never talked about your ex-husband. I mean I know you had one, but you've never said exactly what happened in your marriage."

She stilled. "Why would you want to know that?"

He shrugged. "I don't know. Curiosity."

It sounded incredibly lame to his ears after all these months of mutually agreed-upon privacy, but she bought it because she pursed her lips, then said, "It's the usual story. He cheated on me. He said I was…umm…emotionally distant and unsatisfying."

"Really?" The first he could understand, although tonight she'd been all emotions, one right after the other. The second…Julian grinned. "I've never found you unsatisfying."

"Oh." She looked ready to cry again.

Julian wondered what the heck he might have said wrong. He realized this was the moment when he should reveal something of his former marriage. He had told her from the beginning that he was relationship-shy—and he *had* been then—but he'd never told her what happened in his marriage. "My wife said I was a workaholic. She sued me for half of everything and nearly got it all. I knew then that she only wanted my money. I should have had you for a lawyer. You would have ensured she received nothing, or next to nothing. After all, you worked corporate New York before you came back here." Julian smiled, proud that he knew *something* about her past.

"I wouldn't have represented you. I don't do divorce work, as you know."

He nodded, not surprised. She was scrupulous about ethics. "Farmers Bank chain is considering my bid to buy their three branches. It will officially start my expansion for Diamond Bank," he said, going to safe ground: business.

She smiled with pleasure, obviously feeling the same way. "Julian, that's wonderful, but it takes a lot of cash to fund a venture like that."

"I've got sources." He was sitting across from his biggest one, yet the notion rubbed him the wrong way.

He tried for sex again. Maybe that would be better. "Sure you don't want to go upstairs…?"

Moira waved chopsticks at him. "Finish your dinner. I've got some new books from the library for us."

Julian knew that despite his efforts, the evening was rapidly falling back into its normal pattern. Library books meant soft music and reading came next. He was right.

A little later, Moira sat in her chair with the latest literary bestseller. Julian sat in his "designated" chair with another. Debussy played in the background. The dogs lay sprawled in her lap, occasionally jostling for the best position. The words on the page swam before his gaze. He wanted to take the book from her and give her a rip-roaring, steamy novel while he had the latest, equally hot, men's thriller. He wanted them side by side on the couch, touching and stripping away clothes as they read the best parts out loud to each other. He wanted the Rolling Stones or the Kinks blaring hard-edged rock music from the stereo. And he wanted the dogs in Pomerania. *Now.*

He tried his favorite ploy to move the evening along to better things. "I've got an early meeting tomorrow."

Moira folded her book closed and lowered her reading glasses. "I suppose it is getting late."

Not the rockets-and-fireworks answer he'd been looking for. Julian sighed as he rose, then took her hand and pulled her up from the chair. The dogs protested as they were forced from their human sofa. Julian nodded to the three. "Moira, can we do something about them tonight? I'm not in the mood for an audience."

She looked surprised. "I suppose. Puppies, bed."

The dogs looked as surprised as she, but went to their dog beds with reluctance. Each one gave Julian a dirty look before it did, just to let him knew it knew he was the cause of their banishment. Julian just grinned back at the canine rug rats.

He and Moira climbed the stairs to her bedroom. He put his arm around her and was puzzled when she started at the gesture. She turned and looked at him, then smiled like a shy girl. The vulnerable expression pleased Julian. She wasn't quite as self-contained as usual.

Their normal procedure was to both undress separately, then meet in the bed. This time, Julian felt he should hold her first, maybe kiss her. As he did and she melted against him, he realized Moira meant a good deal to him. In his heart he knew she would make a fine wife, bet or no bet. Maybe he was ready for marriage again.

Moira eased her lips from his. "Julian, you feel so good."

"So do you." He took her mouth fiercely, all sorts of emotions suddenly surfacing at her words. Somehow, he had to make her his. He had to have the world know she was his.

Her tongue mated hungrily, dueling and darting, teasing and enticing. He cupped her breasts, kneading the flesh while circling her nipples with his thumbs. Moira pushed herself against him, as if she would absorb him into her body, make them one. Her fingers dug into his buttocks, urging him to take her. Instant heat wasn't Moira's habit, but Julian liked the change in her. He had no clue why she was so eager for him, but he'd be damned if he'd complain about it. Sometimes he felt a distance in her and he always held back then. Not tonight. After her earlier reticence, he wasn't about to let this go.

He began unbuttoning her blouse, his mouth following the

opening down her cleavage. Moira's hands went up under his shirt and raked his back. He pushed the blouse away and got her bra unfastened. When her breasts were free, he teased one with his tongue and rubbed the edges of his teeth over the sensitive point. Moira went electric.

She dragged him down on the bed, pulling at his clothes in a vain attempt to get him naked. She ripped the buttons open on his sinfully expensive shirt. Julian chuckled and sat up, pushing it off and yanking off his T-shirt, while she worked on his trousers. She kissed his bare chest as she did, running her tongue around his flat nipple. He sucked in his breath at the hard pull of sensations jolting through him. If this was what she felt when he did the same, no wonder she was going nuts on him. Why hadn't she before tonight?

He forgot the question when she whispered, "I l-l-l—I want you, Julian. How I want you tonight."

She freed him from his clothes, stroking him beyond wanting until he felt he had to take her immediately. They never worried about protection, Moira being on the pill. He slid the rest of her clothes from her and slipped inside her, astonished at the way her moist heat enclosed him so tightly. Never had Moira been such a tigress before. She wrapped her legs around him and kissed him with a frenzied passion that left him breathless. They moved together, their aggressiveness blending into mutual need. She whispered things to him. He didn't know the words but understood their meaning and thrust faster and harder. She met him at every turn until she froze and cried out, clinging to him in her ecstasy. Julian met her even then, his climax the strongest he'd ever experienced in his life. He drained himself into her, feeling her pulse and absorbing it all to make them one.

He collapsed on top of her, exhausted. Perspiration trickled from his temples, and his limbs felt like gelatin. He couldn't decide whether it was from the intensity of their union or whether he was that out of shape.

"Wow," he murmured. "We should have come to bed earlier."

She nodded in answer. He thought she was too exhausted to speak, then realized he was feeling more wetness on his face than from sweat. He turned his head toward her and touched her face. Tears were pouring down her cheeks. "Moira, you're crying. Did I hurt you?"

"No, oh, no." She gulped and cried more. "I don't know why I'm crying. I'm just crying, okay?"

"Okay." He didn't know what to say. Jeff would be witty at a moment like this. Julian tried to lighten the mood. "Don't worry. It'll last longer next time. I promise."

"Oh, Julian." She wrapped her arms around his neck and burst into tears.

Thoroughly bewildered, Julian held her as she wept copiously. A piece of himself seemed to leave him and move over to her. He couldn't describe the feeling, but knew that it had happened. When she finally hiccuped and quieted, he said, "You want to tell me what that was all about?"

She gave a watery laugh, sounding ruefully amused. "I know you won't believe me, but it was nothing, Julian. Honest, just some aftermath of a good lovemaking...a good session."

"Honest?"

"Honest."

Her voice sounded sure and firm—and lighthearted. He didn't think she could fake it. "Okay." The way she changed moods made him brave. "Moira, have you ever thought about us. Our relationship?"

Her tone turned unmistakably wary. "What do you mean?"

"I don't know." He wondered how to broach the bet and sensed he needed to do it obliquely. "Well...are you wanting more from it?"

She didn't hesitate. "No."

Julian couldn't imagine a more flat-out answer for anything. His heart dropped with a terrible thud. Now what would he do?

"IT'S NOT NEGOTIABLE, Harvey. I'm sorry, but my client's adamant. He wants full restitution for six trees accidentally dug out and removed by your landscape company. *Igottago.*"

Moira sped through the last words, banged down the phone by her bedside and raced for the bathroom. Her stomach roiled over, in spite of deliberately not eating breakfast this morning. When she returned to her bedroom, she collapsed on the bed, exhausted and ill. The dogs gathered around her body, their little warm forms like ovens against her. She knew they were snuggling in for an extra morning snooze. Her still-upset stomach told her they might not get one.

"It *must* be a virus," she muttered. Only it was the oddest virus she'd ever experienced. For the past few weeks it had hit in the mornings, was normally nonexistent in the evenings, left her exhausted when she woke but restless when she went to bed, had her alternately laughing and crying, joyous and angry, and oddest of all, she hadn't had her period yet. She didn't want to think what it could actually mean.

Julian would kill her.

Her telephone rang again. She had always had her office calls forwarded to her home for convenience, but it was damned inconvenient now. Especially as it was bound to be Harvey Wintzer, who would no doubt ream her out for hanging up on him. She sighed, knowing she'd have to take her medicine.

"Hello, Harvey," she said, skipping the identifying courtesies when she answered. "I'm sorry I hung up on you. I had a problem here suddenly crop up."

It was about to crop up again, she thought, when her stomach lurched ominously.

"It's Julian. Who the hell is Harvey?"

Moira yelped and dropped the receiver. Her stomach flipped

completely over and she raced for the bathroom, not caring that she left a hanging telephone behind with someone on it. The dogs started barking at the sound of Julian calling her name. Whether it was another attack of morning sickness or an attack of fear, it was a false alarm. She staggered back to the telephone.

"Sorry, Julian," she said in her coolest of voices, while she signaled for doggy silence. "Doodles knocked over the phone and I had to get it. And Harvey is a contractor, one of my clients is suing him. That's all I can say."

"Oh. I thought the house was burning down."

She wondered if he would have come over and rescued her. The question was unanswerable, since she didn't know how Julian really felt. When they'd first dated, Julian had laid ground rules for their involvement. Oh, not in dictatorial terms, but when a man said he'd been in a bad relationship that had scarred him for life, that he would be forever cautious, he was making it clear he wasn't in the market for anything more emotional than dinner and sex. Unfortunately she had fallen in love with him right from the beginning. By the time he'd indicated he wasn't looking for more, she was already so far in she couldn't get out. She had spent months, now, hoping he would eventually come around to her way of thinking.

Every time they made love she almost said "I love you," but knew he would vanish if she did. Last night, she had nearly blown it with all the clinging and weeping. He must have sensed her true feelings, because he'd asked about deepening the relationship. She had denied it immediately, knowing any other answer would have him running. No wonder she was weepy.

For a year now, she had deliberately kept a part of herself aloof from him, hoping he would come around. Oh, he'd come around all right—for dinner and sex on Tuesdays and Fridays like clockwork. Weekends might or might not entail another date. It depended on Julian's mood. Waiting for Julian to deepen the relationship was like waiting for Darla to make up her mind between Alfalfa and Spanky.

It must be her, she thought. Hadn't Bill, her ex, complained about her not fulfilling his "emotional needs" in the divorce? She'd thought she might ease herself into a relationship as much as she'd thought to ease Julian in, as well. Instead, like a million other women, she'd given the man the cow, so why would he now buy the milk?

Had she ever given the milk last night. Never had she been so open and aggressive with him. He seemed to like it, too. Maybe there was hope.

Even as he chatted with her about the possibility of getting away to the Maryland shore for the weekend, depression set in for Moira, and she listened absently. When she hung up, feeling like it was another weekend of Moira being the vessel for Julian's cup-bearing ways, the hope in her died. She decided she would have to face what was physically wrong with her. It had better not be what she suspected.

Her doctor managed to fit her in right away. When she finally walked out of his office, she wished he hadn't. Her worst fears had been confirmed. She was pregnant. She didn't believe it. She was on the pill...well except that time several months back when she'd messed up taking a few. She could have sworn she was safe, anyway, but her condition had been verified by a simple test that turned a stick blue. Who knew science could make it so easy to change people's lives?

Moira groaned and squeezed her eyes shut against the tears that threatened. She was having the baby, no question. She could well support it, and God knew, she wanted it badly. Only how would she ever tell Julian about this? His probable reaction made her sick all over again.

"Hi, Moira."

She looked up and saw several of her mother's mah-jongg friends waving to her from across the street. She smiled and waved back, although her stomach did a flip that had nothing to do with morning sickness.

"Oh, God," Moira moaned, knowing telling her mother would be as bad as telling Julian. It didn't matter that she was thirty-two and a successful attorney. Her mother would rant and rave—especially about Julian being the father. Jenny Carson didn't care for Julian. Maybe Mom and the dogs knew something she didn't.

Moira finally dragged herself into her office, knowing she had to work, but another shock awaited her there. A huge basket of flowers sat on her receptionist's desk. Julian sat in her office.

"Hi, honey," he said, getting up and kissing her on the cheek. "Where were you? Did you see the flowers? I thought they'd be better than candy. You didn't seem to like that last time."

His aftershave, usually a subtle blend of musk and male, overpowered her senses. Her stomach protested. Moira moved away before she did something to show, rather than tell, him her condition. She waved him back into the client wing chair while she went behind her desk and sat.

She looked at him, truly looked at him, assessing him for the news she'd have to impart. His suit was impeccable Armani and fit his lean form to perfection. He had no gray in his nearly black hair that was brushed away from his face. She knew he didn't blow-dry it into place; it just fell naturally. His features were strong and handsome, with high cheekbones and a lightly tanned complexion. His mobile mouth promised delights, but his eyes were a beautiful jewel-green. Would the baby have those wonderful eyes? She hoped so. They gave him a hint of vulnerability, only Julian was about as vulnerable as a water buffalo. But would he be a good father? The answer scared her with how much she didn't know about him.

"The flowers are beautiful, Julian," she said finally. "What's the occasion?"

He grinned, then winked. "Last night. Now that was an occasion."

Moira blinked. Julian was flirting with her. Julian who laid out business rules for relationships was actually flirting with her.

Moira frowned. "I don't understand you. You never gave me flowers before."

"I...I just wanted to say I appreciate you."

A sudden rush of emotions nearly had Moira on another crying jag. She suppressed the threatening tears. "I...thank you, Julian. You're very sweet."

She chuckled at his frustrated expression, knowing he probably hated to be called sweet. *He has a right to know about the baby.* She forced the internal command aside, nowhere near ready to tell him about his impending fatherhood.

"I wanted to go over plans for the weekend," he said. "I thought we'd go to a bed-and-breakfast on the Chesapeake somewhere. Maybe by Annapolis. We could go out in a little fishing boat on the bay. We just sit in the boat, throw a line out and just let it rock us into relaxing—"

Key words formed in Moira's mind, even as she remembered his earlier mention about the Maryland shore. Words that hadn't hit her until now. *Boat. Rocking. Sick. Really* sick.

"Julian, I can't go." The words came out before she could stop them. She realized she had to give some explanation. "I have work, for one thing. And I can't just up and leave the dogs."

"You never said anything about this when we talked on the phone."

"Well, I didn't know you were already planning fishing or I would have."

"Can't you kennel the dogs?" he asked. "Or leave them with your mother?"

"She says they howl constantly when I'm not there, and I can't arrange a kennel in a day. They're booked way in advance." She waved a hand. "Never mind that. I need to talk with you about something."

He sat up. "Okay."

She opened her mouth, truly opened her mouth to tell him about the baby. "My mother's mah-jongg group is coming to the house tonight for a special tournament, since I have the space she doesn't."

Chicken, she called herself. She *had* to tell him, but he looked too cool and urbane to be anyone's daddy, so she just couldn't say the words to him, no matter how much she willed herself to. Who could, when Julian was so adamant with boundaries for relationships?

He smiled. "No problem. It's not our night for dinner, anyway."

Moira clenched her jaw shut at the barrier just thrown up in her face. Finally she pried her mouth open. "You're right. There is *no* problem."

"You look stressed. Why don't you come over tonight and get away from the crowd? You could even bring the dogs. As long as they stay in the kitchen. As a matter of fact, we could sit out on the back veranda. I'm thinking I ought to get new furniture for it. I'd like your opinion."

"Mine?" Moira gaped at the notion. "But you always go to Mark Decorators for everything."

"I know. I just want to see what you think first."

"Okay," she said, feeling like she was having an out-of-body experience. Julian had *never* offered his house as a refuge before from her mother's meetings, let alone offer one to her dogs. He was being nice. He was being caring, more attentive. And the flowers were wonderful. Last night he'd seemed eager for intimacy, very different from his usual regimen. Maybe he truly had wanted sex first and dinner after. Did he suspect something different in her and needed to acknowledge it? Could he be ready to take the next step in a relationship? Of course, after he took the step, he'd have to take the great leap into fatherhood.

Maybe tonight was a better time to tell him. The office was awkward at best. She liked the idea of it being in his home, on a more personal level for such an announcement.

"Okay," she said louder. "I'll come over tonight with the puppies."

His upper lip curled for a second at the mention of the dogs. She couldn't expect instant miracles, but more exposure to her pets would be good for all concerned.

Tonight she would give him her big news. It would be a humdinger of an evening.

Chapter Five

"...and I've ordered Grand Marnier cake for dessert."

Julian sat back with pride as he rattled off the dinner he'd preordered at the Mountain View Restaurant, one of Diamond Mount's better places. Now that he was courting Moira, he had wanted to treat her to a very special dinner and had spared no attention to detail. Half the town was sitting around them on this Friday night. Julian liked them seeing him with the brightest and most beautiful woman he'd ever known.

"Steak and lobster?" she echoed. "Potatoes Anna, green beans in a buttery white sauce and a cake loaded with liqueur?"

Somehow it didn't sound so good when she said it. "I can order you something else."

"Oh, no. No. It's wonderful, really."

He accepted her smile. She was probably just annoyed that he had ordered for her. Moira liked to be in control, but his aim was to make her give it up, surprise her with little things that would bring her closer to him. Like having her assess his house for new furniture. That was an important event in a relationship. He found he actually liked having her opinion. The flowers helped, too, in easing them forward, but it was time to take their relationship to the next level. Several next levels.

"How are you doing with the acquisition of Farmers Bank chain?" she asked, gazing at him with interest.

Moira loved business. He wished his heart was in it tonight. "On course. I've got my bid in with the holding payment. I've had to put up my bank as collateral on that."

"You're risking everything."

"It's worth everything." The words sounded hollow. As he looked across the table at her beautiful face, he knew that nothing would be worth losing her.

"Have you ever considered children, Moira?" he asked, figuring a discussion of kids would be next-level material. Besides, he was tired of bank stuff.

She jumped, bumping her glass of water with her hand. She grabbed it before it tipped over. Julian helped her right it, but when he would have taken her hand, she snatched her fingers away.

"Children?" She sounded like one of Jeff's parrots on a learning curve, repeating everything it heard. "Why do you want to know about children?"

He suddenly felt a pit yawning in front of him. Moira was skittish about marriage and family for reasons of her own, and he'd forgotten that. He decided he'd better backtrack. "Well, I was just curious. We've never discussed our opinions about children. Usually we're talking about interest rates and stock prices."

"What do *you* think about children?" she asked, clearly reluctant to go first.

Julian swallowed, feeling as insecure as a fourteen-year-old boy on his first date. The wrong answer would ensure he was dead in the water with Moira and the bet. He chose honesty, deciding he had to know how she felt. He did like kids, and he did want one, that was part of the appeal of his grandfather's bet. If she was adamantly against children, he would have to move on to another woman. The notion, however, caused a great slice of pain in his chest. He wondered if he were having a heart attack, then dismissed the idea.

"Kids are okay, I suppose," he said, hedging his bets a little.

Her expression turned strange, unreadable. Julian frowned, feeling like he'd fallen into that pit. He couldn't stand it. "Do you like kids?"

Her lower jaw thrust forward, but she nodded in agreement. "Kids are fine."

Her voice sounded trembly, like she wanted to cry. She'd been this way for the past few days, either very happy or very upset. Must be PMS, he thought. Yet Moira had never suffered with it before.

"Here's dinner!" she said cheerfully, as the waiter, a huge platter on his shoulder, stopped at their table.

The man hefted the platter down and set the edge beside Moira's seat. Aromas of rare roast beef and sweet seafood combined with rich, clinging cream and tart vegetable scents, wafting up from the plates. Julian inhaled deeply, then sighed with pleasure as his brain and stomach signaled "Ready to Eat."

"Oh," Moira said, staring at the plate the waiter put in front of her. The steak glistened with juices. The lobster puffed from its shell. White sauce spread across cooked green beans and over a molded tower of potato slices laden with paprika.

"Looks spectacular, doesn't it?" Julian commented, as his plated was set in front of him. "And smells sensational. Look at how the sauce is turning pink from the steak juices."

Moira leaped from the table and dashed away, her hand over her mouth. She banged into several restaurant patrons, nearly knocking them over. She made a mad dash for the hallway where the rest rooms were and vanished. Everyone stared after her, the restaurant silent.

Julian gaped, stunned at her actions. Finally he found his voice and said to the waiter, "I guess she didn't like the steak."

"Shall I take it back?" the man asked.

Julian nodded. "Package it up, please, and bring me the check."

He was waiting for Moira outside the ladies' room when she emerged. She looked pale and shaken. "Are you ill?"

"God, yes." She straightened. "I'm sorry, Julian."

"It's okay. I've taken care of the bill so we can go anytime you're ready." He put an arm around her to help her to the car. He had a doggie bag in his free hand. "Is it a virus? You don't feel warm."

"Something I swallowed, that's for sure," she said, then shook herself. As they walked out of the restaurant together, she was fairly steady, to his surprise. She said, "Julian, I have something—"

"I'll say." He chuckled wryly. "You've got one helluva flu bug. It hit fast, didn't it?"

"Well…mmm…yes. Julian, I—"

"Don't worry about it," he interjected, knowing she would. "It's okay, honey. I'll take you home and tuck you in bed and stay with you tonight."

"You will?"

She looked so astonished that he frowned. "Yes, of course, I will."

She melted into a huge smile. "Oh, Julian. You're wonderful."

Despite the ruined dinner, it was worth it, he thought. He was making progress anyway.

He felt as if he was making even more progress on Sunday when he took her to the local lake for boating and a picnic. He'd once punted on the Thames in England, near Oxford University where the river was little more than a stream. English women loved being rowed. It wouldn't hurt to trot out the American version, he admitted, having rented a rowboat ahead of time. Moira's flu bug turned out to be a short-lived virus, dying almost as quickly as it started. But he had thoroughly enjoyed coddling her through it. He felt she was now ready for the intimate picnic he'd planned. When presented with the fait accompli, Moira's reaction wasn't quite what he'd hoped.

She stared at the vessel tied to the dock. "It's got water in the bottom. We'll sink before we get five feet out!"

"It's sound, honey." He bent down and tapped the boat's sides. "See? The guy would get sued if he didn't keep them in shape. Here, hop in."

He got into the boat, then held out his hand to help her do the same. She wore a white, floaty knit dress, a blue sweater draped over her shoulders with the sleeves tied in front of her, and gold jewelry. She took his fingers with a death grip and gingerly stepped in. The boat rocked precariously close to flipping.

"It's going under!" she yelped, grabbing on to him.

He laughed as the boat stopped rocking. "It's okay. Just sit down. Here."

He untied her sweater and put it on the seat so her dress wouldn't get dirty. She sat on it. Unfortunately the hem of her dress sank right into the little puddle of water in the bottom of the boat.

Moira lifted her wet hem, eyed Julian sourly, then wrung out the dirty water from the edge of her dress. She hiked it up above her knees.

"Ready?" Julian asked, slipping the oars into their oarlocks.

"As I'll ever be," she replied grimly while he pushed off from the dock.

They bounced right back in, Julian having left the anchor rope still tied to a piling. He slipped it off and got them out onto the water this time.

"Isn't this romantic?" he asked, maneuvering the oars in and out of the water. He maneuvered the boat right in a circle.

Moira groaned and hung over the edge of the boat. "Julian, if this got any more romantic I'd have an ulcer. Do you know what you're doing?"

"I used to." He straightened out the boat and began to row. The boat moved forward in proper manner. "Here we go!"

Crisis over, Moira lifted her head. "That's the sixty-four-thousand-dollar question."

"Twenty-five million," he muttered.

"Twenty-five million what?"

"Nothing. Isn't this nice?"

"I think so."

Within five minutes Julian knew it *wasn't* nice. Although he worked out regularly, he wasn't prepared for the effort needed to row two people and a heavy craft around a large lake. As he struggled with the oars, he felt like they were in quicksand. The sun beat down on them mercilessly; sweat poured from his temples, belying the low humidity in the air. His shirt stuck to his back. The best place for his feet, in order to have proper purchase to pull on the oars, was smack-dab in the middle of the puddle. His Italian loafers looked like they'd swum over from Rome.

He rowed back to the dock. "That was nice."

Moira smiled knowingly. "Oh, absolutely. When do we sky-dive?"

"Not in my lifetime." He tied up the boat and helped her out. "Let's relax and have our picnic."

"We'll probably get attacked by ants," Moira predicted.

The attack, when it came, wasn't from ants. Julian had set-tled their blanket in a nice shady spot under a tree. Cool breezes caressed their limbs. They had a beautiful view of the lake. Its serenity was soothing, and one would never know the water was a cesspit of trouble for a rowboat. Julian was even willing to forget the torture he'd just been through. He opened the basket, packed by Mike's Deli and Specialty Shop at the mall. They had cold fried chicken and potato salad, sweet pickles and black olives.

Moira took one bite and became ill.

"It's gone bad," Julian said, as he held her head. He nearly got sick with her.

"No!" Moira gasped, finally lying on her back. She looked even more pale than she had the other night. "I think it was the boat ride that did me in. All that rocking."

"No. It's the food. Even I don't feel so good." He paused.

"Unless you've still got that virus thing. Maybe you ought to see a doctor."

"No, I'm fine, really. I'm just not much of a sailor."

"I guess not," he said dubiously. He didn't like the idea that she might be ill and hiding it. He didn't like the idea of her being ill, period. He had an urge to protect her from such things.

"I'm sorry, Julian." She started to chuckle. "Somehow I don't think we're outdoor people. Give us a French menu in a setting even Bill Gates couldn't afford and we're gangbusters."

He laughed ruefully while swatting at a horsefly. "Raw sushi we can handle, but the lake they came from is too much."

Moira groaned. "I don't think I can handle sushi just now."

"Sorry about that."

"Give me a few minutes and then let's go home," she suggested. "You and the puppies can eat the picnic stuff. I'll just lie on the sofa and not watch."

He was reduced to dating the dogs now. The notion must have shown on his face because she reached over and squeezed his hand.

"You're so sweet to give me a little romance, Julian," she said. "I wish I could live up to my end of it."

He bent down and kissed her forehead. "You live up to it, believe me, honey."

Now this was progress, he thought happily.

SHE COULDN'T TELL HIM.

Moira sighed as she watched Julian, who sat in a den chair and coaxed Anastasia to take a piece of chicken meat scraped off the bone. The dog sniffed it delicately, then grabbed the morsel as if she hadn't eaten in two days. Sergei and Doodles crowded in on Julian, now wanting to get what their sister had.

"Moochers," she murmured affectionately. Louder, she said, "It's good to see you getting along with them."

"Yeah...ouch!" Julian yanked back his hand and stared at his forefinger. "The little bastard nipped me!"

Doodles and Sergei, sensing his change of mood, immediately began barking at him.

Moira sighed. So much for getting along. "Puppies, hush!"

The two stopped, although their gazes glittered with animosity at Julian. Julian's gaze glittered back.

Maybe it was his lack of affection for dogs that made her hang back from telling him he would be a father. If he couldn't reach out to one type of innocent creature, how would he ever reach out to another? She'd tried to do the right thing, several times. The night she was at his house, she'd tried to tell him. The night at the restaurant, too. How many times had she opened her mouth to say the words or put her hand on the telephone receiver to call and tell him? She chickened out each time. Somehow she couldn't bring herself to utter the words that would totally change their relationship. Having Julian in some capacity was better than having no Julian at all.

Only she couldn't keep faking a virus or the flu, either. He was already asking about doctors and such. It had been that damn boat. And the icky-looking white sauce at the restaurant. Both had set her off. Yet Julian had been so sweet about her "bouts." She'd had hope for him. And then there was today with the dogs.

He would hate her when she told him. And she would have to soon.

"Your eyes look glazed over," he said, getting her attention. "Are you sure you're feeling better?"

"I'm sure."

He came over to her and sat on the edge of the sofa. He pushed back her hair in the most gentle of gestures. "I don't like you being sick. I'm calling your doctor."

Julian talking to her doctor was like Brutus chatting up Caesar on the Ides of March, Moira thought, trying not to panic. "Julian, I'm fine. Truly I am." She put her hand to his cheek, feeling the beginnings of a beard. She loved his five-o'clock shadow. To her, it was an earthy break in his immaculate armor. "You're wonderful for worrying about me."

He grinned. "I am?"

"Yes." Love welled up inside her before she could suppress it. "You are a wonderful man under that financier's exterior."

"You think so?"

He sounded unsure, a phenomenon for a man like Julian, who controlled millions of dollars in his bank. Moira smiled and caressed his jaw. "Yes, I definitely think so."

He bent down and kissed her, a tender kiss that held more than affection. She wound her arms around his shoulders, her fingers stroking the muscles of his back. He felt incredibly strong, a counterpoint to her feminine softness that always excited her. His tongue met hers in a gentle duel that mimicked something far more intimate. Desperate to touch him, to imprint herself on his senses, she caressed his hair, his cheeks, his arms, his back, even his thigh as he sat next to her.

"My God, woman," he whispered, his breath hot on her ear. "You're not sick."

She giggled. "Only a little and only for you."

He kissed her fiercely this time, as if he would absorb her into himself. Moira's head spun. She had only revealed a small part of her feelings for him, and he had responded in a way she had never hoped for. Maybe…maybe if she seduced him into loving her, he would love the baby, too. At least be receptive to the idea. Sex for love was the oldest exchange on the planet.

And the most unpalatable.

Moira eased out of the kiss and out of his embrace. She sat up. The room swam a little but righted itself. "I'm okay now." Her head pounded with the onslaught of a sudden headache. She rubbed her temples. "Maybe."

"I'm making an appointment at the doctor's for you tomorrow,'' he said, frowning with concern while trying to ease her back onto the sofa.

She resisted, instead rising to her feet. "No. I'll make the appointment, Julian, just to reassure you, all right?''

"All right." He stood, then gave her a relieved smile. "I'll go with you. Just call and tell me the time.''

God help her, Moira thought, feeling a panic attack in full force. She gazed at him, at those beautiful and puzzled jewel-green eyes, and knew she could no longer keep her secret. She *had* to tell him.

"I've got ice cream for dessert," she said, cursing the words that came from her mouth.

"Ice cream!" He gaped at her. "You want ice cream? You? You never eat ice cream. You always said it tastes like frozen butter. And you're sick. You got sick today. Again. Ice cream will only make you sicker.''

She shrugged. "Well, I found a brand I like. And it was just the boat ride, Julian. I'm no sailor. How many times do I have to tell you that?''

She walked toward the kitchen. He followed her, saying, "I would have said you're no ice cream eater, either.''

Normally she wasn't, but her taste buds had gone quirky on her in recent days, and she found herself craving ice cream. Superhot foods and supercold ones seemed to settle her stomach better than tepid things like salads and such. And she needed calcium. Ice cream had sounded really good one day, so she'd gotten some and discovered she had been missing out on a great thing.

"Jungle mint chocolate or pistachio harbor?" she asked, opening her freezer door. The dogs gathered at her feet, yipping for a treat of ice cream.

"Neither." Julian stared at her. "I don't understand you. First, you can't eat a thing, then you're eating outlandish ice cream. I feel like I don't know you anymore. It's confusing. And exciting.''

Moira grinned at him. "Alluring through pistachio harbor. I think I like being unique."

He nuzzled her nape. "You are unique."

His new affection brought her up short. Did he know something about the baby already? Was that why he was so eager to get her to the doctor, so she would be forced to reveal her pregnancy? Maybe he wanted her only because he really wanted the baby. She rounded on him. "You've been different lately, too, Julian. What's that all about?"

He raised his eyebrows in astonishment. "What?"

"All this affection, this wining and dining and boating and flowers and everything else you've been doing which, it just occurred to me, you've never done before. Why all of a sudden? Why are you treating me differently now?"

"I don't know," he blurted out. His expression changed to one of control, the Julian she usually saw. "I didn't know I was being any different to you."

"Well, you are. Why?"

He gazed at her, then opened his mouth, closed it, then opened it again. "I know you said no the other night to this, but I would like to try for the next level in our relationship."

"Oh, God," she murmured, her heart nearly bursting with joy.

"I'm hoping to persuade you to my way of thinking."

He looked vulnerable, scared almost, as if her turning him down would ruin him forever. Her common sense surfaced, and she realized that even though he was making an overture, it still wasn't anywhere near love. She could scare him off with a too-eager answer.

Taking a deep breath, she smiled. "I know I was negative before, but I've been rethinking things, too. I'd like us to try a deeper relationship."

He smiled happily, like a little kid. "This is great."

"Yes, it is." She chuckled and offered up her two half gallons. "Let's celebrate."

"Give me that jungle mint thing," he said, then kissed her cheek. "I'm glad."

So was she. In fact, she was still floating when Julian stormed into her office three days later, waving a letter in her face.

"This was just delivered by courier," he said, slapping the paper down her desk. He was furious, his hair disheveled, and a coffee stain marred his normally pristine white shirt.

Moira read the letter slowly, taking in the devastating news. Parsons Banking Conglomerate had made a preemptive strike against Diamond Bank for the Farmers Bank branches, offering money beyond Julian's capacity to raise. Worse, they announced their intent to gain a majority stock in Julian's company. Not only was the expansion in dire jeopardy, so was Julian's livelihood. And his dream of rebuilding Diamond Bank to what it once was.

"Oh, God," she murmured, shocked. "Julian, it's a hostile takeover."

"I know. I hold a higher percentage of stock than any of my stockholders, but I don't have fifty-one percent. I knew I would be vulnerable, but I needed the cash for the expansion so I sold off that safe percentage."

Her heart broke for him, knowing he had a nice arrangement with Farmers that would have benefitted both banks—and would have started him on his dream of rebuilding Diamond Bank to a chain again.

"Who is Parsons?" she asked.

"An eastern Pennsylvania bank chain," he said. "They've never shown an interest in this end of the state before. Now suddenly they are. Someone must have got them to bid."

Moira folded her arms on her desk and looked at him. "I assume we will fight this."

"We?" He smiled slowly. "Hell, yes. I came to you before I even went to the bank's attorneys. I trust you the most."

Moira grinned at words she'd never thought she would hear

from Julian Diamond. The pleasure she felt combined with her already rushing adrenaline over the coming fight with Parsons. When she first got out of law school she worked for a firm in New York that handled corporate matters. The everyday, frenetic pressure got to her, and she came home to Diamond Mount, but once in a while like this was stimulating.

"All right then. I know a law firm in Pittsburgh that handles corporate raiders. We'll get them working on this now, so you have every legal advantage. In the meantime, can you get cash together to buy up a majority of the public stock? The quicker you are to lay down your funds, the better to lock Parsons out."

He was quiet for a minute. "I may have something soon."

"Good. If not, we may have to find you a white knight to put up the rest of the money to block the takeover, yet who won't reach a majority of the stock themselves."

He walked around the desk and pulled her to her feet, kissing her thoroughly. When they surfaced at last, Moira blinked, her brain still in a dreamy fog.

"You are so exciting when you're talking business," he said, taking little love bites on her throat. "I'm watching you, so poised, so calm, so cutthroat. Nothing gets to you, does it?"

She laughed, half with humor and half with irony. "You do."

"Good."

He unbuttoned her red power blouse and pushed it aside. When he would have undone her bra, Moira stopped him, afraid he would see the heavy fullness and darkening nipples in her changing breasts.

He pressed the button on the phone. Moira's secretary came on the line. He said, "No interruptions, please. We're having a conference."

"Moira?" Nancy's voice was hesitant.

"It's okay, Nancy."

Julian let go of the intercom button. He smiled devilishly. "Where was I? Oh, yes."

She knew she should resist him, not make love, not when she was withholding vital information from him. Everything would change when it did. Yet she wanted him so badly. They'd never done anything wicked in her office. Never once had Julian deviated from his normal routine. Next level, she thought, the words holding a wonderfully delicious promise.

When he unhooked her bra, though, all her trepidation returned. He couldn't miss the changes in her body. But he did miss. He kissed her breasts, took them in his hands, brought her burgeoning nipples to sensitive peaks. Never once did he comment on them looking different.

But she knew they were different. Every touch, every caress, every press of lips and tongue on her breasts drove her insane with sensation overload. She clawed at Julian's clothes and her own, needing to be free of encumbrances. She needed to mate wildly with him.

Straddling him in her office chair, she took him inside herself so quickly, *he* gasped with the shock of it. She thrust harder and faster, barely waiting for him to respond in kind, so hungry was she for him. Sweet darkness pressed down on her senses until she thought she would faint from the pleasure-pain inside, then the darkness burst into a thousand brilliant showers of incredible satisfaction. Somehow she bit back the words of love, suppressed the need once more. And a little of her bliss dissipated.

Julian clutched her to him when his own pleasure came. Spent, he collapsed back in the chair, taking her with him. "Woman, you are a tigress. I love it."

So close, she thought, feeling unshed tears pushing at her eyes. But he never quite said the words she needed. Keeping it light, she said, "See? You don't know everything about me."

"Hell, no." He kissed her breast. "I've got to get over here more with bank mergers. Who knew they were so sexy?"

She chuckled, feeling the sadness pass. "I knew."

He kissed her breast again. "So beautiful. I've always thought so."

Numbwit. He couldn't see any difference. No wonder she felt as if she were in a losing battle. She bolstered herself with the idea of them being on the "next level." He was like the tortoise, slow and steady.

Eventually she'd win the race.

Chapter Six

"Hello, puppies."

Julian grinned when the three rug rats actually wagged their tails at his greeting. They looked almost pleased to see him. He was almost pleased to see them. Heck, if this was the "next level" in the relationship, he should have gotten onboard long ago.

Moira smiled at him. She looked sexy and sweet, vulnerable and gorgeous, all things woman. He *definitely* should have been onboard long ago.

Unable to resist, he put his arm around her waist and pulled her to him, kissing her deeply. Her arms wound around his neck, her fingers stroking his hair. He admitted he couldn't think of a thing finer in this world than kissing her.

"Umm," he murmured. "You taste good."

"Thank you." She eased from him. "I've got seafood tonight."

"From Barney's?" he asked eagerly. Barney's was a little shop by the mall that sold very fresh seafood at very reasonable prices. Julian had no clue how the guy made money, especially being at least eight hours from the Delaware and Chesapeake bays. Everything had to be shipped in.

She grinned. "Yes. We have that art gallery opening to go to tonight, remember? My mother's expecting us. She got Spencer to locate his gallery here. She's been after him for years to take it out of Pittsburgh where he's had it. We are on command to go tonight."

Julian groaned in disgust. Moira's mother was a real estate agent, for whom social appearances were important.

Moira held out a lure. "I got raw clams for you. I don't know how you can eat that stuff."

"It's a gift." He headed for the kitchen and the refrigerator, where a plain brown bag sat. "Aw, you didn't shuck them."

"I'm not insane." She wrinkled her nose. "You take care of that, and I'll take care of my nice flounder."

Besides the clams, she had bought lobster tails and some hush puppies, another of Barney's specialties. Julian took pleasure in prying open the clam shells. After loosening the clam with a small knife, he loaded it with hot sauce and slurped it down, the sting of the peppers blending perfectly with the moist meat.

Moira held her hand to her mouth and groaned as she watched him.

"What?" he asked, puzzled.

She swallowed. "Nothing. Isn't that unsanitary? Don't they have some kind of dreaded disease now?"

Julian loaded another with hot sauce. "I'll risk it."

"I'll go into the den. Let me know when you're done."

She actually left him alone in the kitchen. Julian looked at the three doggie amigos, who looked back at him with similar bafflement. He shrugged. "Who understands women?"

"Not idiotic men," a voice replied from the den.

Since he was already risking his life with seafood, he gave each of the dogs a biscuit from the container. *Miraculous,* he thought. They'd accepted their treats graciously, and he'd come away with four fingers and a thumb still intact. Maybe it was the raw clam smell that kept the animals cautious. It had certainly made Moira cautious—all the way to the den.

"I talked with the bank attorneys, honey," he called out. "They're getting right on the little problem."

"Good," she called back. "I talked with the Pittsburgh firm today. They've contacted Parsons's attorneys and let them know you would be fighting the takeover." Her voice turned lighter. "I let the mayor know this afternoon when I saw him on Commerce Street."

Julian walked to the den doorway. He grinned at her. "What'd he say?"

She made a face. "He was very surprised you were fighting it, *not* that a takeover was in progress. He already knows. Can you not hold that clam while you're talking to me? *Please.*"

"You're getting funny about things," he commented, feeling like he was insensitive to her. "Do you think Helpern went to them and encouraged the takeover?"

"Anyone would be funny about raw clams, and yes I thought that about the mayor's reaction. He's got a construction firm, doesn't he? And it doesn't do business at Diamond Bank. Even I know the man's spine would snap before he put his money with your family."

"Good point, and the dogs seem to like the clams even if you don't. They're hanging by me, not you."

"They're ding-dongs," she replied. "Now go back to the kitchen."

"I feel like I'm banished. Got any beer to go with my dinner?" he asked.

"In the fridge."

He felt fortified when they walked into Diamond Mount's latest community venture, Spencer Fine Arts. Diamond Bank held the mortgage on the place. Julian smiled in pleasure at the thought. Through Jenny Carson's efforts, he'd brought a little culture to the town and made a little money while he was at it. Spencer Fine Arts was packed with Diamond Mount citizens who were more nosy than anything about the gallery's opening.

Fortification was helped with a glass of white wine. While Julian sipped his, he noticed Moira had none. "Where's your wine? I'll get it."

"No." Moira shook her head. "I don't want any."

"No wine?" Julian murmured more to himself than to her. Moira liked white wine, but he realized he hadn't noticed her drinking any lately.

Mark Spencer, a retired New Yorker, bussed Moira on both cheeks. She was his attorney as well as a patron. "You look smashing, my dear. Those extra few pounds suit you. What are you doing? Bulking up?"

Moira blushed. "No, no. Just eating a little more ice cream than I should."

"Well, it's marvelous on you." He grabbed someone, who turned out to be a council member. "Mary Jean, doesn't Moira look terrific?"

The councilor started, then grinned a little. "You do look different. Your color looks...I don't know. Heightened. But, yes, Mark's right. You look terrific. Did you cut your hair? No, but your face looks a little fuller. Not puffy, but rounded, softened. Oh, dear. I'm trying to compliment you, and I'm making a mess of it."

Moira protested good-naturedly. Julian just stared at her, his curiosity surfacing. She *did* look different. Her face did look fuller. Her breasts, too. They'd been more full the other night, or so it seemed to him. And her color was more pink. He'd noticed some paleness before, but that was when she was sick. Oddly, despite a stomach virus, she had gained some weight, enough to round the edges. Moira was tall and could pass for a model. Now she looked more like a young Ann-Margaret.

Moira gave Julian a look as she took Mary Jean's arm and led her off so naturally that a moment passed before Julian realized his private attorney was about to pump the councilor for information regarding Parsons and the local government's part in their bid to kill his expansion and take over his bank.

"Don't you think she looks fabulous?" Mark asked him, referring to Moira.

"The most beautiful shark in the world," Julian murmured happily.

Mark only chuckled, although Julian doubted the man understood the joke. Mark showed him around the cluster of paintings from an up-and-coming artist Mark knew. Probably an old boyfriend of Mark's, Julian thought, shrugging away Mark's sexual preference. The old guy was nice, a friend of Moira's mother, and the rest didn't matter. Moira's mother appeared, as if the thought conjured her.

"Julian," Jenny Carson said by way of greeting.

Like daughter, like mother. Julian smiled, despite her cool tones. "Hi, Jenny. How's the mah-jongg crowd?"

"Doing well. I'm surprised you're here. Normally you don't come out with Moira."

Julian set his jaw. "Yes, I do."

"I don't think so." She turned to Mark. "When was the last time Julian went anywhere with Moira…let alone to an art show?"

Mark thought for a long moment, not an encouraging sign. "Well, I see them at lunchtime upon occasion."

"See?" Julian said, feeling vindicated.

"And did you see them more than 'upon occasion'?" Jenny asked triumphantly.

Mark shrugged.

"We've been busy," Julian said lamely.

Jenny laughed. "Right. Still…" The older version of Moira looked thoughtful. "Moira has been different lately. Happier sometimes and sometimes very stressed."

"I've noticed that," Julian said, eager to discuss Moira's new quirks with someone who knew her extremely well. "So she isn't like that all the time?"

"No, but it's interesting that you've been seeing my daughter for a year and you don't even know what she's like all the time. So what are you doing to her to cause her stress?"

"Me! Why would you think I caused Moira any grief?"

Jenny snorted in disgust. "Because she was content before she met you, and now she's not."

"What the hell does that mean?" Julian demanded.

Mark said, "Much as I love family dirt, this is too much for me. Ta."

Mark left, but Jenny stayed put, her chin thrust out. Julian had always sensed the woman's hostility to him, but couldn't figure out how he'd offended her. Knowing Moira would be upset to find the two of them fighting, he tried placating the woman. "Jenny, I didn't do anything to Moira to upset her. She's been funny lately, that's true, and if you know why, please explain it to me. Maybe it's the dogs. I know they drive me crazy."

"Mom!" Moira came up and kissed her mother's cheek, effectively rescuing Julian from further interrogation. "I'm having a great time, aren't you?"

"That's debatable," her mother replied, arching an eyebrow at Julian.

"You'd debate the sun on whether it's got ultraviolet rays," Moira said. She linked her arm through Julian's while still keeping the other around her mother's waist. "My two favorite people. You're so special—"

Moira's voice suddenly choked. She looked as if she had tears in her eyes. Before Julian could tell if she did, she waved her hand and raced off for the powder room.

"See? I didn't do that," Julian said to Jenny, although Moira's abrupt departure troubled him.

"Neither did I," Jenny said, frowning worriedly. "You wait here. I'll go see what this is all about."

Mother followed daughter. Julian considered ignoring her order and following both, but the sight of Mayor Robert Helpern caught his eye. He detoured around a display of watercolors until he stood next to the mayor.

"Bob," Julian said, knowing the mayor hated being called by the nickname.

"Bob" turned, started, then smiled like a great white shark in an oceanful of swimmers. "Diamond. I hear tell you've got money problems at your bank."

"No problems," Julian replied with complete confidence.

"No…" The mayor frowned. "But there's a takeover threat to your bank. With Parsons."

"Why would you think that?" Julian asked, taking a sip from his wineglass.

"Because I told them—" Robert stopped himself. "Play cagey like the rest of your family if you want. I *know* you've got troubles, and I'll give you a bit more. Parsons Bank just applied to the council to expand their newly expected acquisition, the former Farmers Bank, into a regional office. They move quick. They're kicking you out, boy, and you know it. I'll be laughing when they do."

"Whatever happened that you hate the Diamond family so much?" Julian asked, keeping his voice low so the other gallery patrons wouldn't hear him. "Did my father date your wife when you were all in high school? Did one of our dogs crap on your lawn or something? Did my brother get Paula pregnant and abandon her? Or was there some other equally horrible thing one of my family perpetrated on one of yours? The answer is no to all of them, and you damn well know it, so what *is* your problem with me, Helpern?"

"I don't like the way the Diamonds have ruled everything in this town," the mayor sneered. "And yes, they blocked my development business years ago, costing me a fortune, so I do 'damn well know it.'" He thrust a finger at Julian. "And you shut your mouth about my daughter while you're at it."

"Okay." Julian grinned, despite the anger boiling inside him. "I was only making a point. I like Paula—"

The finger nearly jammed his nose, as it suddenly swung in front of him again. "You stay away from her, too!"

Helpern stomped away. Julian glanced around. People were

staring at him, clearly having heard the last bit of the mayor's tirade. *Hell,* he thought.

Putting on a social face, he sought out Moira and her mother. Jenny stood outside the powder room, her arm around her daughter.

"What was that all about?" she asked, nodding toward Mayor Helpern.

"Bank mergers." He looked at Moira. "Are you all right, honey?"

Moira sighed. "Yes, except for making an ass of myself, which I've been doing lately. Never mind me. What did the mayor say?"

Julian grinned. "He asked me about the merger, and I told him I had no clue what he was talking about."

Moira laughed, while her mother frowned. "I wish I'd been there for that. I'd have loved to have seen the windbag's face. Why do we keep electing him?"

"Because he's built up the half of the town the Diamonds didn't," Jenny said. "If a Diamond doesn't run for office, people want a Helpern on the job."

"Maybe I ought to run for mayor," Julian mused.

"Jeff would be better," Jenny said. "Everyone likes him."

Except the mayor, Julian admitted, although that wasn't an ace in the hole where the bet was concerned. His competition opening a regional office in Diamond Mount was not good news. In fact it was disastrous. It meant that if he could stave them off on taking over his own bank, they would heavily pursue his customers. If they got his bank, they would be entrenched in this area. It would be difficult to pry them out, should he be able to restart yet another bank.

"Dammit," Julian muttered, knowing he'd worked too hard to let that happen without a battle. A war.

"What now?" Jenny said, firming her lips into a disapproving line.

"Julian?" Moira asked.

He let out a breath of exasperation and told her about the regional office. Jenny looked shocked. Moira looked thoughtful.

"That's what Mary Ellen told me." She grinned. "I think there's a bit of collusion going on here…especially if Helpern has accounts already with Parsons, which we surmise. His construction business might be attractive enough to give him entrée in influencing a bank's expansion."

Julian immediately caught her intent. "I think you are the most marvelous woman in the world."

"Ooo," Moira cooed. "I think a certain mayor is in for a rude awakening. I'm feeling *much* better now."

He leaned over and kissed her. "I love it when you talk attorney."

"You two are scary," Jenny said, shivering. "It's like you have business telepathy."

Feeling expansive, Julian kissed Jenny on the cheek. "Thanks."

He wasn't feeling expansive a few nights later when his brother called him at home. They talked about their respective run-ins with the mayor of Diamond Mount before Jeff broached another subject.

"You've got clear sailing, you lucky bastard," Jeff said, clearly frustrated. "I told Paula about the bet, and that was the last I saw of her."

"What?" Julian's stomach churned ominously, although he couldn't figure out why.

"She dumped me. Again." Jeff let loose a string of curses. "I thought she would understand what winning meant to the sanctuary. I thought she would be amused at the irony of getting all that money, now that we're finally back together. It was like a reward for the years we were forced apart. She thinks I was trying to use her. Now that's irony."

Julian had a vision of Moira's recent emotional mood

swings. Suddenly the mystery of his ominous stomach churning was explained. In detail. "Oh. God, I'm sorry, Jeff."

He meant it. He *was* sorry his brother had been hurt yet again by the woman he loved and could never let go. While he had warned Jeff time and again to get a life, he ultimately wanted his brother's happiness. Paula made him happy.

"Thanks." It was a measure of the bond between them that Jeff knew Julian's feelings were sincere. "Well, little brother, go get 'em. Just slip me a million or two, to keep me going here."

"Wait a minute," Julian said. "Did you try talking to her? The whole town knows you've been in love with her for years, I think. Doesn't that count for something with her?"

Jeff laughed. "You'd better stop trying to help me, or you'll lose the sure thing. When did you get so generous?"

"I just like a little competition," Julian said, chuckling. He sobered. "Seriously, Jeff. Did you talk to her?"

"I wasn't given the chance."

When Julian hung up, his stomach had more acid than an antacid commercial. The thought of asking Moira to marry him and having the proposal blow up in his face went beyond the bet. He and she were incredibly compatible. Even her mother, who disliked him, said so. He could no longer put off telling Moira about the money. But he had to tell her in a way that allowed her to see the benefits. Moira was different from Paula. More logical, more sensible. Her needs were less emotion oriented than the regular person.

Julian straightened in his favorite wing chair. Of course, Moira's needs were less emotion oriented. She was an attorney, a businesswoman, first and foremost. Look at the way she threw herself into his hostile takeover problems. She loved a good fight.

Citing Jenny Carson yet again, he reminded himself that he and Moira had a "telepathy" about many things. He only had to be honest with her about his grandfather's bet, approach the proposal from a business standpoint and she would see it all clearly. Then she would be his. Forever.

The notion of wife and children filling his quiet house pleased him greatly. Not any wife and not any children. Moira and *their* children. And a banking chain that would set the standard for service and wealth.

All he had to do was avoid his brother's mistakes. A piece of cake.

"YOU'RE PREGNANT."

Moira gaped at her mother as the two cleaned up after the Historical Society meeting that had been held at her mother's house. Next meeting was her turn.

"Oh, don't look so shocked," her mother said. "You're puffy around the jawline, you're eating like a horse, yet avoiding tepid foods like the nuts and candies today. You look worn-out and you took a five-minute snooze during Alma Carter's discussion about rug beaters in the nineteenth century."

"God, I didn't snore, did I?" Moira asked anxiously.

"A snort maybe here or there. No one noticed because you were in the back with me." Her mother arched her brow. "I see you're not denying it. Thank you."

"You didn't give me a chance," Moira muttered in disgust.

"Julian doesn't know, does he?"

Moira set the paper plates down on the counter and sighed. "No. Not yet. I'm trying to figure out how to tell him."

"Opening your mouth and letting the words out works really well, dear." Her mother paused. "Yes, I know he'll take off like Superman on a mission. Shame on him, but you *must* tell."

"I know." Moira groaned at the thought. "I've tried, Mom. Honestly. But even though he says he wants a deeper relationship with me, I don't want to scare him off first thing. I'm looking for a really good time to tell him."

"In the delivery room does not work. A little before that. How far along are you?"

"About three months the doctor figures. And don't give me any lectures on taking birth control or not having sex. I screwed up the first and I'm kicking myself over the second. I'm also a grown woman who accepts her responsibilities."

"They sent your great-aunt Fredda away to stay with a cousin for a year when she got pregnant, a deep, dark family secret," her mother commented.

"Sad Aunt Fredda?"

"Now you know why. She had to give up the baby, for one thing. And she loved the man and never got over him, so my mother always told me. I don't want you sad, and I would hate the thought of never seeing my grandchild. But you do have to tell Julian. How he reacts is up to him."

"You're right."

Moira knew her mother was right even as she waited for Julian to pick her up for a "special" dinner a week later.

When Julian came in the front door, he immediately sent the three dogs into spasms of delight by tossing them real sugar cookies.

"That's not good for them," Moira said sternly as the dogs gobbled up their treats.

"I've got to make friends with them somehow." He pulled her to him and kissed her like a man too long starved for a woman. His mouth lashed fire and his hands were everywhere at once. Moira gasped for breath when he finally released her.

"I think I know what I want for dinner," he said, bringing her to him again.

"Julian!" Moira felt as if her body were burning even as she protested. "This isn't like you."

He chuckled and actually leered at her. "I know."

She relaxed against him. "I think I like it."

"I hope so, because I do." He nuzzled her neck. "Do you think we could be late for our reservation at the Viennese Café?"

"Not on a Friday night," she said, stretching back. Her pelvis rubbed intimately against his. He grinned at her as she added, "You got us reservations there? Wow, I thought it was a month's wait."

"Not when you hold the mortgage. Mike's very accommodating with special customers. We've got the best table. I think the mayor won't be happy. He was supposed to have it for tonight, so Mike tells me."

Moira laughed. "Then we can't be late."

"But when we get home..." Julian kissed her breasts through her soft linen dress. "These are different, more full. More round." He straightened her up. "You look different, too. Have I told you that?"

"Must be the company," she murmured, yet knew time had run out on her secret.

Her mother's words came back to haunt her. She had to tell him. Tonight over dinner. Julian would never make a scene in public. Neither would she. After all, they made their respective livings from their images. That meant he and she should be able to discuss the situation without histrionics or walkouts. Maybe his wanting to make friends with the dogs was yet another good sign for her. Moira's stomach churned, anyway.

Julian frowned. "What's wrong? You're not sick again, are you?"

"No, and I went to the doctor, too." She wasn't lying. "I'm in perfect health."

"Great." He kissed her again. "How late do you think we could get away with on that reservation?"

"Not as late as we'd like."

By the time they got to the car, Moira felt as if she were in a sex-crazed movie. Julian was acting all loving and sensual, the latter nearly doing them both in several times before they finally admitted on reservations over bed—for the moment. The anticipation of when they came home was already intense. She could feel it in him as well as in herself.

How to tell him about the baby...

It looked as if the entire town had turned out for the news at the Viennese Café. The restaurant was mobbed. They greeted people, many of whom invited them for a social drink. A large group of townspeople invited them to a birthday party being held in the side room. Julian declined, and she was glad. She wanted to be alone with him. She felt as special as the evening promised. Somehow, despite all her worries, she knew she would tell him tonight about the baby. And he would take it well. It went beyond his currently expansive mood. He was happy. Surely, in his mid-thirties, he would·want a baby. Hadn't they even talked about family a little?

Now, she thought, as the waiter held out the chair for her at the best table by the fireplace. She would tell him during this dinner.

After the waiter left, Julian smiled at her, then set a small box on her plate. A ring-size box.

Moira's hands shook as she lifted it and snapped the lid open. A large, very, very expensive, pear-shaped diamond winked at her, its facets reflecting rainbows from the candle-light.

"I know we only just talked about deepening our relationship, Moira," Julian said. "But I think I can give you some excellent business reasons for moving up on the timetable."

Moira glanced away from the ring and at Julian. His smile faltered slightly, showing his vulnerability. The word *business* rang hollowly through her. He plunged ahead with whatever he was saying.

"We care about each other, deeply I think. That's good. I know we are eventually heading toward a step like this, provided all things come together properly in our relationship. It was just a matter of time, another year or so, I'm sure is all it would have taken..."

Another year or so. Moira could feel her hands tremble, and the reason had nothing to do with the expensive rock she held.

"...I know you will see, from a purely business standpoint,

why our marrying sooner is beneficial. *Very* beneficial from a logical standpoint.'' He paused. ''My grandfather has challenged my brother and me to marry and be in the family way before the end of the year. Whichever of us does it first will receive twenty-five million dollars from him.''

''Twenty-five million dollars!'' Moira gasped, drawing the attention of neighboring diners.

Julian nodded. ''That money would cut the merger threat to nothing. Moira, if you marry me I pledge to you that you will get half the profits from my bank expansion for the rest of your life, no strings attached. You can draw up the contract, honey, and make it as ironclad as you want—''

''Wait a minute!'' she exclaimed, his words sinking in. ''You mean this ring…all of this…is because of a bet?''

Julian faltered. ''No, no. It's a marriage proposal—''

''For a bet.''

''Well, yes and no. Technically.''

''*Technically,* to have a child, so you can satisfy some half-senile old man and get a hunk of dough.''

''No. No!'' Julian's easily read expression was one of panic. ''Honey, Moira, no. He's not senile, maybe just a little crazy. But…it's a business proposition *and* a marriage proposal. I thought you would like that—''

She snapped the ring box shut and slammed it on the table. ''I'm nothing but a business proposition to you!''

''No. Moira, sit down.'' She had half risen in her chair. People stared at them. Julian added, ''I've done this badly.''

''No.'' Moira sat and calmed herself, but a cold chill wrapped around her heart. She now knew exactly what she meant to him. ''You've done this very well, Julian. You've presented an excellent case for a marriage between us—''

''I knew you would appreciate it on business terms,'' he broke in, brightening.

''Oh, I do. The terms are so businesslike that you've given me an incentive that would choke Godzilla.'' She half rose again. "I have wasted more time on you than Guinevere wasted on Launcelot. Now I'm a bet, a lousy bet. You are nothing more than a whore for money, Julian Diamond. But I won't be one with you."

At that moment a waiter passed their table, a lovely chocolate cake on his tray as he headed for the birthday room. Moira stood and snatched it into her hands. She dumped the cake, plate and all, over Julian's head. The entire restaurant gasped as one, while the maître d', Mike Robinson, hurried over to their table. But Mike was too late. The plate tilted for a moment, then hit the floor, shattering into pieces. Hunks of cake sat on Julian's hair like a hat. He never looked better as far as Moira was concerned.

Moira watched the spongy devil's food drip down the sides of Julian's cheeks. Icing clung to his eyes. He blinked woodenly.

"There," she said. "Have your cake and eat it, too, Julian Diamond. But put that bet where the sun doesn't shine."

She stormed out of the restaurant, in front of the town, damn glad to have found out what Julian Diamond was really like.

A bet. She and her baby were a bet?

Not on her life.

Mid-Logue

Time for Grandfather to Make the First Call

Chapter Seven

Bart Diamond surveyed his grandsons. He wondered how they liked his little wager so far and assured himself they no doubt hated it, yet were racing neck and neck. What Jeff had said last time was true: Julian, with his ongoing relationship with Moira Carson, had a huge advantage. But then Paula Helpern-Miller had come home and right into Jeff's lap.

Bart remembered that episode in his grandson's life. If he had known about that idiot Helpern's interference, he would have paid the man off handsomely to let his daughter see the boy. More than handsomely. Of course, he would have continued to block the mayor's proposed development of what was now the sanctuary. The place was the prettiest part of the mountain and should be preserved. But Jeff needed to earn it, to know how precious it was. Paula was back, both she and Jeff older and wiser. The advantage was now nil.

Julian, too, needed to ''earn'' his bank. The family shouldn't have sold it out from under the boy, but at the time, the veteran members were either old and tired, like himself, or uninterested, like his son. Julian had been caught in the lull of family talent. Now the boy faced a takeover. Adversity would make Julian stronger, as well.

''So, boys, how's your quest for love?'' he asked, as the table was cleared and brandies were poured. Bart believed in a formal and fortifying evening meal. It came from marrying a good Englishwoman, he acknowledged. Aloud, he added, "Or did you both give up and call me a bastard again?"

The two chuckled. As much as they didn't look alike, they sounded alike, both having deep baritones. They used to sing as kids. Bart wondered if he could get them to do "Embraceable You." Matter of fact, he had had to pay them to sing that, if he remembered rightly. Little twerps.

"No, we haven't called you a bastard lately," Julian admitted.

"Speak for yourself," Jeff countered.

"So things are going well?" Bart asked.

"Oh, yeah," Jeff answered.

"Like clockwork," Julian replied.

"I think you're going to pay out double the bet," Jeff added.

Bart smiled, thoroughly amused. He'd heard Paula had dumped Jeff while Moira had dumped cake all over Julian. Both were besieged in their sacred places, the sanctuary and the bank. And both were probably as miserable as two men could get.

A few complications never hurt anyone, he decided. "You two think you're doing that well, eh?"

"Very well," Julian added. He cleared his throat. "Grandfather, I have a business matter to discuss with you—"

"If it's about the hostile takeover and Parsons's new bank offices, I've heard." He stared grimly at Julian. "Work your way through it, boy. It'll be good for you."

"I think I'll skip a plea for sanctuary funds," Jeff said.

"Smart thinking." Bart leaned back in his chair. "What doesn't kill us makes us stronger."

"This from a guy born with a silver spoon in his mouth," Jeff said.

"If mine was silver, yours was gold. Just bring me a bride and a grandchild, and his or hers will be platinum." Bart laughed. "That's not a bad thing."

AFTER THE DINNER with the elderly ogre, Jeff and Julian stood outside their grandfather's home and contemplated a beautiful June night.

"We lied our butts off in there," Julian commented, taking the common denominator approach to the dinner with their grandfather.

"Well, Julian, brides and children are obviously not for me," Jeff said. "This time it was me who drove Paula away. How could I have been so stupid to tell her about the bet?"

"You weren't alone," Julian muttered, in disgust.

Jeff looked at him. "What do you mean?"

Julian turned down his mouth, miserable. "I thought Moira would appreciate a business proposal so I made one. After all we're both professionals."

"Christ! You didn't offer her part of the money to marry you, did you?"

"It seemed like a good idea at the time."

"You're a worse idiot than I am," Jeff said, shaking his head. "I'm sorry about Moira. She's a terrific person, and she deserves better than you."

"That's what I'm thinking. I'm sorry about Paula. You have always loved her. I'm not sure she deserves you, but there were extenuating circumstances. Her dad is a pain in the ass. At best."

"Paula's worth it. Now that we've assessed our dismal love life..." Jeff made a face. "This marriage and family thing is harder than I thought."

"It sure is. Especially when you want the best," Julian said. "Moira and Paula were the best, weren't they?"

Jeff grinned wryly. "We're back to square one."

Jeff

~ Part Three ~

Hey! The Bet's Not Won Yet

Chapter Eight

"Popeye, my boy, you're actually more cheerful than me."

The vulture was sitting on the roof of the hawk's barn and hunkered down even lower when he heard his name. The poor thing's head drooped pathetically on his shoulders. Popeye looked sick.

Jeff felt sick.

He held the letter from the zoning board that officially threatened to revoke his variance for the sanctuary, the letter that Paula had warned him about. He had to appear in court before the week was out for a hearing. That seemed like nothing, compared to what had happened with Paula. He had refused to admit defeat with his grandfather, since the old man was so intent on needling him and his brother about the bet—that damnable bet that had set a chain of emotional mishaps into play. If that bet had never existed and Paula had come home...

"What's wrong with Popeye?"

Jeff glanced up, startled to find Bobby and Stevie next to him. He hadn't even heard the boys approach.

"What are you guys doing here?" he asked.

Stevie giggled. "We're 'aposed to work for you, remember?"

"But I thought..." Jeff paused, as the obvious occurred to him. "Does your mom know you're here?"

"Sure." Bobby nodded. He didn't look Jeff quite in the eye.

Jeff opened his mouth to send the boys home when it occurred to him that sleeping dogs were better left alone. Better he shouldn't ask, then he wouldn't know for sure.

He desperately wanted to ask them about Paula, however, but resisted. That would put the kids in the middle, which wasn't fair to them. He'd be damned before he would ask what their grandfather was doing, something nearly as tempting, under the circumstances, as knowing about Paula. But he wouldn't turn the boys into spies, either.

"You're right, Stevie. You guys have jobs. The first thing we have to do is get Popeye down from the roof," Jeff said. "He flew up there, but he hates landings so he won't come down."

"I know!"

Stevie ran to the shed where Jeff kept his lures. The young boy came back with a length of heavy twine which had an object attached to its end. Popeye's head lifted when he saw Stevie.

"Look, he likes it!" Stevie began whirling the twine, the stuffed animal on the end flopping heavily up and down with the boy's efforts.

A vulture is a vulture is a vulture, Jeff thought, panic shooting through him as he ran for Stevie to stop him. Popeye, in birdie innocence, might decide a small boy was more intriguing than a doll to capture. He wouldn't mean to hurt Stevie, but Popeye was still a wild animal. The bird might even view the boy's quick movements as a threat and attack. "Stevie, wait!"

The vulture suddenly swooped between Jeff and Stevie. He snagged the stuffed animal, then thudded to earth. Popeye flipped over in a complete somersault. He straightened upright, toy still in his beak, flapped his wings once and looked at Jeff.

"Good bird," Jeff said automatically while his gaze searched for any broken bones.

"Yippee!" Stevie yelled, jumping up and down. Bobby fell on the ground laughing.

Jeff took the twine from the boy. "Steve, never, ever do that again. Popeye looks like a happy goofball, but he's a bird. If he ever touched you, I would have to destroy him—"

"But it wouldn't be his fault!" Stevie wailed, starting to cry.

Jeff hardened his heart against the tears. He had to make the point first. "I know. But that doesn't change anything." He put his arm around Stevie. "You did great, but let's let me get him down from the roof next time."

Stevie nodded, clearly seeing the point. He wiped at his face, while Jeff patted his back affectionately. A shaft of pleasure and pride coursed through his body. The emotions wrapped around him, telling him what he wanted and what he might never have. Screw the bet, he thought, although he knew he would need the money more than ever, if he had to move the sanctuary. He wanted kids for himself...and he wished it could be these two boys. They had attached themselves to his heart almost from the moment he'd seen them sneaking around his house.

He patted Bobby's back, just for good measure, then sent the boys to their chores. After he got Popeye into the house, he worked with the parrots for a little while, their bawdiness and their showmanship making him chuckle. They were really "on" today, he admitted.

The boys came in to take care of the indoor birds' cages. They sat, instead, and laughed at the birds. Elvis rode his tiny trike across the long table Jeff had set up for practice. The bird sang "Hound Dog" as he did. Even Jeff chuckled when one of the parrots walked to the middle of the tightrope, then suddenly spun over and under in a complete circle.

"'The Lord helps those who help themselves,'" the bird intoned.

The solution to his problems smacked Jeff right in the forehead. "The birds!"

"Pretty neat," Stevie replied.

"No, the variance—" He realized who he was talking to. "I just had a thought about something, guys. Don't mind me."

Bobby glanced at the ceiling, then back, sort of at Jeff. "I...we know about that thing Grandpa sent you. Mom had a big fight with him about it."

"Yeah!" Stevie said, grinning. "She yelled at him louder than she yelled at me when I broke her computer."

"That must have been pretty loud," Jeff commented, hope on more than one front surging through his veins.

"It was."

"Since you know, then you know the sanctuary's in a little trouble. I'll understand if you guys can't work here anymore."

"We're working," Bobby said, reaching out to stroke Elvis's headcomb of white feathers. Stevie nodded in agreement.

Jeff smiled at their loyalty, vowing to savor whatever little time he had with them. But the birds had given him an idea about how he could save the sanctuary. He would charm it out of the judge.

Several days later, when he saw the grim face of Judge Herbert T. Morrison, Jeff wondered if he was asking too much of Popeye, Oscar, et al., to charm the man into a stay of execution. Judge Morrison looked like he ate fowl for breakfast, lunch and dinner. Fortunately the judge had held his job for so long that he was considered to be impartial and not at all worried about who he offended with his verdicts. That meant he wouldn't be biased against him. As an advantage, Judge Morrison had a poodle he doted on. Jeff had saved Suzie's life when she had had to have a C-section for her litter of puppies. That had to count for something. A little bias in his direction wasn't a bad thing.

The courtroom was packed with people, all clearly interested in the proceedings. Robert Helpern sat in the front row, not far from Jeff. Jeff ignored him. Instead, he looked around for his attorney, who hadn't shown up. The man, someone Jeff had used for estate planning, had said he would be here.

As the gavel banged down, Jeff turned back to face the judge, forcing down panic.

A muffled thud drew him around again, just in time to see Paula and the boys slipping into the courtroom, the heavy door shutting behind them.

"Hi, Jeff!" Stevie called out, waving enthusiastically.

Jeff grinned at him and Bobby, who waved in a more "cool" fashion while they stood in the back of the room. Stevie and Bobby might not be his attorney, but he felt he had friends in the room. Last, he glanced at Paula—and found his gaze frozen. It was the first time he'd seen her since their fight.

She looked terrific in a white top and long, flowered skirt— the kind of outfit popular when they had been kids together and now was fashionable again. It gave Jeff a sense of being back in time. Yet her face showed experience, wisdom. And pain. She hurt. No doubt she came to gloat. He couldn't blame her.

Jeff turned back to the judge. He had to wait for several other cases to be heard before his, municipal court being full. The undercurrent of Diamond Mount fascinated him. Move over soap operas, he thought, as a restraining order was issued between the local antiques shop owner and her estranged husband; a property line dispute was mediated between neighbors; and a jail sentence was pronounced against Old Man Simmons who refused to clean up his backyard, which had the appearance of a junkyard.

Judge Morrison was no-nonsense, but seemed to be fair. Jeff knew Popeye could be a real charmer. The parrots would be entertaining, certainly another plus, and Oscar was regal and virile. He had chosen each of them for their ability to make great first impressions. Once the judge viewed them in a favorable light, he was bound to view the variance in their favor. But he was still missing one team player.

"Diamond Mount versus Diamond," Dottie Marshall, the bailiff finally announced.

Jeff stood. Having been given a front-row seat with his cages, he didn't have to come forward.

"Where's your attorney?" Judge Morrison asked.

"He should be here," Jeff began, but was cut off by Bill Gruden, the town solicitor.

"Your Honor, I wish we could wait for Mr. Diamond's attorney, but we can't. The council's decision takes effect in less than thirty days. This will just delay the inevitable at great expense to the taxpayers—"

"I'll decide what's inevitable," the judge said. "Your point is valid, however. Mr. Diamond, where is your attorney?"

"I don't know," Jeff admitted. This was bad. He had to fix this faux pas and not turn off the judge. "But I'm prepared to go on without him."

Judge Morrison eyed him. "Are you sure?"

Hell no, Jeff thought, but said, "Yes, sir."

"So be it." The judge banged his gavel. "I will hear the case now."

Jeff forced himself to calm down. The judge didn't seem to like Bill Gruden, surprising, since the older man was nice. He had lots of things in his favor, so he felt good about pulling this off.

The city solicitor made the zoning board's case, then objected to the presence of the birds.

"I allowed these creatures in here," the judge said, eyeing Jeff, "because you said you had a point to make with them. Just do it quickly."

"Right, your honor." After opening the cage, Jeff led Pop eye out. The bird waddled over to the table. Everyone watched intently. "I've had a variance for ten years for my property, to run it as a sanctuary. Ten years, and suddenly it's revoked as a health hazard. Why, after ten years, does it present a hazard?"

Popeye stretched his wings, raised his back end and deposited a health hazard right in the center of the floor.

Dottie, the bailiff, yelped in surprise and outrage, several people shrieked and the judge banged his gavel to restore order. The parrots started shrieking, and worse, cursing at the top of their lungs, while Oscar the falcon, startled and feeling trapped with all the strange surroundings and noises, began banging against his cage and shrieking such a high-pitched "skree" that people covered their ears and shrieked even louder.

"I've seen enough," the judge bellowed over the noise, as he still pounded on his gavel. "The variance is revoked. You have thirty days to find these…these wild animals another home!"

"But your honor, where's due process?" Jeff asked, while he herded Popeye back into his carry cage.

"Right there in the middle of my floor!" the judge shouted back, pointing to Popeye's mess. "And are those two doing what I think they're doing?"

Jeff turned and looked at the parrots. He groaned. "How can you two mate at a time like this!"

"Out!" the judge ordered. "Court is in recess for ten minutes while you get your birds out of here, Mr. Diamond."

The spectators laughed amid the commotion. Jeff could feel his face heating as he picked up a cage and took it out the back door of the courtroom. A short corridor led to the parking lot where he had his van. Judge Morrison watched him with eagle eyes. He got the rest of the cages loaded up, while cursing his birds. Oscar might not have been rude, lewd or lascivious like his brethren, but neither had he been majestic.

So much for charming, Jeff acknowledged in complete disgust with his grand scheme.

"Next time get yourself a lawyer," Mayor Helpern said smugly as he walked by the van.

"Blow it out your butt," Jeff retorted, not having the energy nor the confidence for anything other than a childish dig.

"Why, you—"

"Dad, you won. Now go home."

Paula's voice was all business. Her father glared at her, looked like he was about to say something, then decided against it. He made his way toward his car.

"Does this mean you have to kill Popeye?" Stevie asked, tears streaking down his face.

"No." Jeff lifted the boy up and hugged him, glad to have the support of someone in the family…although Paula's reaction was encouraging. "It just means Popeye and I have to move."

"No." Stevie hugged him tightly.

"I'm so sorry, Jeff," Paula said.

Jeff stared at her over her son's shoulder. She looked as devastated by the judgment as he felt. His heart lifted, despite the threat to his well-being. Bobby had his arm around her waist, as if needing comfort, too. Paula rubbed Bobby's shoulder. Eventually Jeff set Stevie down, conscious of Paula waiting by his car.

He said, "Thanks for coming."

"I…the boys wanted to."

He wished she had wanted to, as well. Maybe she did, otherwise why would she have driven them to the hearing? And was that why she was sympathetic to him over the ruling? "I thought the birds would help, but I didn't get a chance to present anything."

Paula grinned reluctantly. "I would say that Popeye did too much presenting."

Jeff chuckled. "True."

"What will you do?" she asked.

"Do what your father suggests. Get a new lawyer, since mine didn't show up tonight."

"You're fighting the judgment?"

"Absolutely. And I'm leaving the birds at home when I do."

She smiled. "Good for you."

He smiled back, then sobered. "About the other night—"

Her expression changed. "No."

"I'm sorry—"

"Me, too. For a lot of things. I can see now that you did whatever you had to do to save your home. But that doesn't change anything between us." She turned her sons toward the parking lot. "Let's go, boys."

Jeff wanted to stop her, explain himself further. Only he was afraid he would fail as dismally as he had in the courtroom.

Robert Helpern's expression was on full-tilt gloat as Paula walked up to him. Whatever she said made his smirk vanish.

One person in the audience was on his side, Jeff thought. Maybe the most important one of all.

A little man bustled up to him. It was his missing attorney. "Oh, good! You're just going in. I was afraid I was too late."

"You were," Jeff replied. "And so was I."

Or was he?

"ARE YOU SURE you'll be okay?"

Paula smiled at her mother's worried expression. "Mom. I've been on my own for years and never burned my house down once. I promise I won't burn yours to the ground, okay? Now you and Dad go on your cruise and have fun."

"You're sure?" her mother asked nervously.

"I'm sure. Sure you don't want me to drive you to the airport to catch your flight?"

"No, no," her father said, coming onto the porch. "It's part of our trip every year, and I like driving us." He turned to her mother. "Come on, Darlene, the suitcases are already in my car. Nothing's better than the sea on a summer's day."

Paula chuckled. "Good thing Stevie's not going with you. He gets seasick in a rowboat."

Her father smiled expansively. "Even that wouldn't ruin the cruise for me this year. Two weeks in the Maritimes and when I come home *that*—" he pointed a thumb over his shoulder toward Jeff's property "—will be gone. Or as damn close to it as I could ask."

"Dad, don't start," Paula said. She hated that her father gloated. She hated that he had a right to, after Jeff lost his case. Her father should be gracious, but he'd probably rather fall off the Empire State Building than show the least sign of that.

"I'll start if I want, young lady," her father replied, glaring. "I've waited years for this. It's time the Diamonds found out they can't have everything they want." He softened a little. "Now, honey, you know he'd just hurt you all over again."

"No," she said, letting out her tension in a long breath. "I hurt him the first time and now it was payback. But I know that's all it was."

Her father put his arm around her in a hug. "See? Your old dad was right all along. Wasn't I, Darlene?"

"Oh, yes," her mother said, smiling at her husband.

Paula kissed them both goodbye and wondered how her dad could be blind to his own actions and her mother blind to him. Maybe that was why their marriage worked. She shivered at the thought and happily sent her parents off to their annual two-week cruise of the eastern Canadian provinces. That her father took a victory lap over Jeff bothered her.

"Hey, guys, where are you going?" she asked, when the boys began racing off after the driveway was clear of grandparents.

"Ahhh…fishing!" Bobby called back. He and Stevie raced faster.

"Without poles?" Paula frowned but not in puzzlement. She had a good hunch where her sons were headed. And if they were fishing, then she was flying with Popeye today.

To her own surprise, she didn't stop them. She should. The less contact with Jeff the better. While she might understand on some level about Jeff's need for a payback, she would never forgive him for planning to use her and her sons to win a bet.

And yet here she was, allowing the boys to go to their

"jobs" with his birds. Oddly, she didn't doubt his sincerity with her sons. He couldn't fake his behavior with them. He liked her sons, and for them, working with the birds had a positive effect on their lives. Her guilt surfaced at what her father had done to Jeff with the variance. She wanted to go to him and apologize, maybe hug him, just as she had wanted to the other night at the courthouse. He'd looked so hurt and vulnerable, especially when he'd held Stevie.

Paula shook the image away before it seeped into her heart even deeper. She and Jeff were over. Besides, what she planned to do while her parents were on their cruise would take care of any further developments on the Jeff front.

Two minutes with her checkbook and another five on the telephone with her agent told her the sad truth. Another rejection of an older manuscript making the rounds meant no relief to the empty wallet.

She had to get a paying job *now*. Living with her parents was no solution, even if the old vendetta hadn't risen like Lazarus from his grave. She needed to get away from them, just as she had before. She needed to get away from Jeff even more.

Paula set her checkbook down and drew in a steadying breath. She sucked in a little too much and started coughing from the sudden drying of her throat.

"Okay," she gasped, grabbing a cup of water and drinking it. When her throat calmed again, she added, "I came here to start my life over, and I'm gonna start it right from scratch."

She still felt that way when the boys came in for dinner—and cheered.

"Fun food!" Bobby said, happily eying the hot dogs, baked beans and salad.

"Mom, tell grandma not to cook no more," Stevie said, digging in.

"Not and live," Paula said, grinning. "So how's Popeye?"

"He's great," Stevie blithely replied. "He actually caught

the toy mouse today and he wouldn't give it…owww! Watcha hit me for, Bobby?"

Bobby's elbow had landed with precision in Stevie's mid-section, but was far too late to stop his younger brother's chattering.

"Oh," Stevie said suddenly, realizing he had given the game away. He brightened. "Mom, you never said we couldn't go over and do our jobs with Jeff."

"You're right, I didn't. However, what did you tell me earlier when I asked where you were going?" she questioned, raising her eyebrows. "Fishing, I believe was the answer. Not an honest answer."

Stevie set his hot dog down on his plate and stared at it. "No."

"Don't lie to me, all right?" she said. "No television tonight just to remind you of that."

Both boys groaned and whined, but Paula didn't budge. They gave it up when they saw she wasn't malleable to a kid's greatest persuader, nonstop begging.

"Well, can we still work there?" Bobby asked. "I feel real bad about what Grandpa did to Jeff and the sanctuary. That wasn't fair."

Stevie nodded around a mouthful of baked beans.

"No, it wasn't fair," Paula said.

"Why'd he do it?"

She wondered how to explain all that went into the situation and decided at last to give it the simplest of all. "Grandpa firmly believes the birds will hurt people or cause a health problem of some kind. That's why he thinks it's important that they be moved."

"I thought he just didn't like Jeff," Stevie said, childish innocence hitting the nail right on the head.

"It's not right, Mom," Bobby said.

"No, it isn't," Paula agreed. "I feel real bad that Grandpa's doing this, too."

"You oughta tell Jeff that, Mom," Stevie said. "He felt better when we told him we were sorry. He hugged me."

"He shook my hand." Bobby sounded prideful at being treated like a man.

Paula stared at her boys, tears clogging her throat. "You apologized to him?"

Stevie nodded. He was so solemn he stopped eating his hot dog for a second. "Yeah, Mom. I just had to."

"So you oughta, Mom," Bobby added for good measure. "Especially since you feel bad, too."

"I think you're right," Paula admitted. "Gosh, when did you guys get so smart?"

Stevie giggled. "When ya weren't lookin'."

But the boys being right was a whole lot easier to accept than actually doing the right thing. Paula's steps were leaden as she walked the last few feet to Jeff's back door. Several cars were in the small parking area, indicating his vet hours weren't yet finished.

"We better go back," Paula said, halting. "He's got patients."

"It's okay, Mom," Bobby replied, while Stevie tugged her hand. "We'll just wait and be after everybody else."

"I could pretend to be a dog," Stevie volunteered, laughing while Paula reluctantly moved forward.

If she was going to make a clean break with her old life and career, she had to apologize to Jeff for her father. Paula vowed to follow her own advice and do it fast. Unfortunately the office was a madhouse the moment they went inside. Two small poodles barked furiously at them while their owner yelled haplessly to get them to stop. A German shepherd cowered in a corner, trying to scramble under its owner's seat. A woman held a carrier up over her head, clearly afraid the dogs would go after the contents, a Siamese that yowled at siren decibels. On top of the deafening noise, the telephone rang and rang, with Elvis and his cohorts endlessly imitating the device and the dogs from the other room. From his examining room, Jeff yelled that he would be with whoever it was out there in a minute.

"Get the birds, boys, and I'll get the phone," Paula said briskly. "And watch those killer poodles over there while you're at it."

The boys raced past the poodles, temporarily sending them into apoplectic fits. Paula glared at the poodles, then picked up the receiver and said loudly, "Dr. Diamond's office."

The person wanted an appointment and thought Paula was the one to do it. She was about to tell the client otherwise, when she spied a book with names, dates and times off to the side. Smiling, she slid it to her and fit in Bill Barterman and Bitsy at six-thirty, next Tuesday between a Clark and a Mc-Claren. Grinning, she hung up the receiver and glanced around at the now-quiet waiting room.

Jeff stood on the threshold of the waiting room, smiling broadly.

"Bitsy Barterman needs her shots before she can go to the kennel," she said efficiently. "She'll be in next Tuesday at six-thirty."

"That was my dinner break but you're hired, anyway," Jeff replied.

Everyone laughed.

"Oh, Lord," Paula said, chuckling sheepishly. "I'll call the man back and change it."

"Nah. Bitsy's good about getting vaccinated. She'll take about five minutes." He pointed to the German shepherd. "Unlike Gunther here, the big baby. He kills on command, but bring him to the vet for a shot and he's a scaredy-cat. Can you hold the fort while I finish up? The phone's been ringing off the hook tonight."

"Sure."

He grinned. "I think everyone wants to get their visit in before I'm evicted."

Paula cleared her throat, giving herself a moment to gather her courage. "That's what I want to talk with you about—"

"Later," he said, but he smiled.

He hadn't asked why she was there, didn't act cold or angry or anything other than easygoing. Paula's stomach churned, knowing how that easiness would lure her into his spell again. It always had. She shouldn't have come.

But the telephone rang again, distracting her. Before she knew it, a half hour had passed. The boys came in at some point from the other room, after quieting the birds. Finally the office cleared of patients and their owners.

"Wow," Jeff said, slinging his stethoscope around his neck. He looked terrific in camp shorts and a plaid shirt, the casual opposite of his button-down twin. "What a night. How did you do out here?"

"You've got four more appointments this week and three for next week," Paula replied, from memory. "I didn't book anything on your dinner break."

He looked at his appointment book. "This is great. You really handled the phones."

"It's not rocket science," she said. "Just common sense and keeping your head screwed on straight. I did a lot of office temp work out in California this past year." Not a great moment in a writer's career, she acknowledge ruefully. But she came here for a purpose. She straightened. "Jeff, I want to apologize for my father's vendetta—"

"Why? It's not yours."

His comment threw her off her speech. "No. I know. But I'm not a party to it and I don't like it—"

"Tell him that, not me."

"I have." He wasn't making it easy for her. She looked at her sons who looked back, frowning. Although they didn't grasp the nuances, they did recognize that her apology wasn't going as well as theirs had. She told herself it didn't matter.

"I just wanted you to know I am sorry he's done this to you. It's time to go, boys—"

"Hang on," Jeff said. "I haven't had dinner yet, and I'd like some company. Elvis and the boys have to practice the act tonight. We're the entertainment at the local Boy Scout meeting on Saturday. We could use an audience."

"Well…"

"Please! Please, Mom!"

The boys begged shamelessly. This time Paula knew she would give in. What a mother she was, she thought, yet her insides warmed with anticipation. "Okay. As long as I'm not part of the act with the three lovebirds."

"I was hoping…" Jeff grinned at her.

"Forget it."

"To change the subject, because I'd probably better," he said, grinning, "I did call Moira, and she's going to work on the variance. She yelled at me for going without an attorney. She says I should have gotten an extension, instead of going ahead myself."

"You should know better, being a Diamond," Paula said.

"Hey, I thought it would be so logical to keep the variance that I wouldn't need an attorney's help," he said. "Being a Diamond doesn't keep one from stupidity."

She had a feeling he was talking about more than attorneys. An idea came to her and, seeing the potential subject diversion, she tapped the appointment book. "I think you've got some untapped help here for the sanctuary. You should start a petition about the variance and get all your clients to sign it. In fact, everywhere you go, you ought to have it with you for people to sign."

"What's a 'tition?" Stevie asked.

"It's a paper that people sign saying they all agree to something," Paula said. "Like in this case, people would sign saying they want the variance reinstated for the sanctuary. If a bunch of people sign it and it's presented to the people who took it away, they may change their minds again.''

"Oh." Stevie still looked bewildered.

Jeff didn't. He had a broad grin on his face. "That's perfect! I should have thought of it. I'll get Julian to put it in his bank.''

Paula chuckled. "There ya go. But start with dinner first.''

Paula kept her internal guard up against his charm. Clean break, new life, she thought. Not being just a means to win a bet. As long as she remembered the latter, she ought to be safe from pain. Very safe. She had come simply to apologize, and she had done that. She had even given him a fighting chance against her father, something that made her feel very good about herself again.

If a little politeness came out of her doing so, then she was fine with it. But it wouldn't be more.

She kept her distance from Jeff all evening, letting the boys and the parrots be her buffer against him. It worked fairly well, too. Except for the occasional urge to throw herself at him. But her boys were right about one thing. She did feel better for apologizing.

Chapter Nine

The world had *not* crashed down on him. In fact, things were looking up.

Jeff grinned as he looked over the list of clients who had signed his petition. In two days, it was almost a Who's Who of Diamond Mount. He had taken Paula's suggestion to heart and to extremes and had distributed petitions all over town. The post office had one, the drugstore had one, and of course his brother's bank had one. His biggest fear was that people would sign more than one time, inflating the lists. Still, the idea was to show community support rather than make legal points—and he was getting the former. Thanks to Paula.

Now that, he thought, was the best news of all. Nothing had been sweeter than hearing her on his telephone taking appointments as if she had done it all her life. He thought he'd been dreaming when he'd come out to find her at the desk. He hadn't been able to leave the resentment aside when she'd tried to talk about her father, to apologize. He couldn't help feeling that if she stopped worrying about her father's actions, she would be more willing to stand up to the man. Through the boys, Jeff had heard that the parents were away on their vacation. Two weeks.

The parrots began to squawk, indicating visitors. Jeff grinned and went outside. The boys were right on time for their jobs, as usual. This time their mother was with them. His grin broadened.

"Hi, guys."

Paula smiled at him, a genuine smile. He had an opening with her again, a crack so minuscule it couldn't be seen by the naked eye, but it was something to help him win her heart. If he wanted her.

Bets aside, he wanted her. After fifteen years, she was living and breathing in the same town as he. On the same street. He had never truly let her go before. And he knew, the moment she had walked out of his bedroom, that if he did let her go a second time, he would never survive.

The boys went off to do their work, but Paula didn't get back in her car right away.

"I hate to ask this," she began, looking wary, "but could the boys stay a little bit with you after their chores are done? I have a job interview, and no one will be home. It might run longer than I think."

"Sure," Jeff said, but her words started a chain reaction of thoughts within him. "Why are you going on a job interview? I thought you had a job. Writing."

Paula laughed wryly. "Oh, yes. The one that pays so regularly. I got another rejection, and I have to face financial facts. Mainly, I have no finances. Besides, I can't live with my folks forever. In fact, I can't live with them much longer."

Jeff's heart rose with eagerness. "Where do you plan to…ah…live?"

She shrugged. "I don't know yet. Wherever I can find a place I can afford in town. Which means I have to get a regular, paying job."

"But your writing. Paula, you have got to write."

She grinned. "God, I wish all the readers were like you. I'll write. But I've got to get a little income coming in, so it's a nine-to-five job for me."

"Wait a minute." He stepped closer, close enough to smell

her light perfume, feel the warmth emanating from her body, see the flawless creamy skin. He wanted to kiss the peachy-colored lip gloss off her lips, just to see if it did taste like the fruit, but restrained himself. That she allowed him this close was enough for the moment. "Why not work for me—"

Paula backed up, a funny expression on her face. "Oh, no."

"Just think about this objectively," he said, touching her arm to keep her from going farther away. "I need a receptionist, even you could see that the other night. And you picked it up like a pro. I'll pay you well—"

"You can't afford a receptionist. Isn't that why you want your grandfather's twenty-five million?"

"It's the sanctuary I can't afford," he replied. "That's a huge amount of money. But the vet practice, if it keeps up like this, can support a receptionist. Frankly, I may have to build up the practice a little more, if I have to give up the sanctuary. Like you, I have some financial facts to face." He grinned. "Besides, you could get more people to sign the petition for me. You're prettier than I am."

"No, I should go on that interview." She sounded unsure.

"The economy's good," he said, gambling on reverse psychology. "You should be able to get a job. But as a bottom line, I'll pay you ten bucks an hour for forty hours, and you can bring over your computer and work on your writing in between clients. We have a fair amount of downtime. Or if we don't, you just go ahead and make some. I like the idea of being a patron of the arts."

"You're a patron of the nuts," she said. "Jeff, it's impossible. After what happened, I can't."

"I made a mistake, Paula," he said, running his palm along her skin. Her arms were slender, the bone and muscle delicate yet strong. His lips were so close to hers, he could easily kiss her. "I lost you again."

"I can't trust you," she whispered, turning her face away from his. "How can you ask me to?"

He sighed and stepped away. "I can't. That's how bad I know it was. But I can offer you a job, a real job, no strings attached."

She shook her head. "My father would kill me."

Anger boiled over at the old words used so often in their past. "When are you going to start doing what you want and stop doing what everyone else wants, Paula?"

To his surprise, she didn't disagree.

"You're right," she said, taking the wind out of his righteous sails. She grimaced. "I know I want everything smooth and easy and nice with my family. I want their approval. I owe them and I love them and I don't want them angry with me. I know I bend over backward too much sometimes with my father, because he is my father. But I have to do what I *need* to do, not what everyone else wants me to do. But your job has a whole lot more baggage than just my father's reaction."

He conceded she wasn't wrong. "Go on your interview, but my job's open for you if you want it. No strings. No baggage. No humble pie. This is business."

She just smiled and got in her car.

When she returned from her job interview, however, the look on her face gave Jeff pause. "What's wrong?"

"I hate this," she said, sighing and sitting down on the steps in front of the side door to his office. "I hate job interviews. I'd forgotten how awful they are. People looking your résumé up and down, being continually dubious about your abilities. I started writing because I hated nine-to-five politics and the structure of an office job. I've had books on the biggest chain bestseller lists, and the guy asked me to take a typing test. A typing test!"

Jeff sat down next to her, letting her nearness seep into his being.

He had never realized before just how lucky he had been in his life. His family's wealth had put him beyond things everyone else had to go through. He'd known, of course, that if his grades had been bad in high school, money would have paid the way to any college, including Ivy League schools. His grades had been excellent because he'd liked school. He'd gone directly into practice after graduation and had the money to establish the sanctuary. Now, however, he'd run through just about all of it to keep the sanctuary going. "Better teach me how to type. I may be out there with you."

"You?" she scoffed, laughing. "Jeff, you could buy the place I was at today ten times over."

"Once, maybe, not anymore." He raised his eyebrows. "Don't you think that if I had the money, I wouldn't be in a panic about the variance? I can't fund the sanctuary single-handed anymore. The vet practice pays and would pay more if I devoted more time to it, but it won't pay for all this." He waved a hand. "I may need a job in the real world soon."

"Then why were you offering me one before?" she asked. "Sounds like you need the charity as much as I do."

"I just said the practice pays, just not enough for the sanctuary, too. It'd pay more if I had someone other than me keeping up with it." He was quiet for a moment. "Matter of fact, if you…*someone* took care of the administrative stuff with it, I'd be free to devote my time to getting the sanctuary back on its feet. You offered me an apology for your father, Paula. Why not put my money where your mouth is and really do something about it? Like working for the practice, so I can work for the sanctuary more."

She was silent for a full minute. She was silent for the longest time. "You don't make it easy."

"Nope. And I hope I never will." He smiled at her, waiting.

"This is not the clean break I mean to do," she said. "All right, I'll be your receptionist. Ten dollars an hour. God help me."

"That's the spirit."

Jeff sat back and let the sun shine on his face. The gentle

heat beat down on him. He had just found the first few steps out of the hell he'd been in.

"I MUST BE NUTS, Paula murmured under her breath as Jeff squeezed behind her chair on his way to the file cabinets to return the last patient's record, an overweight dachshund with a propensity to eat everything his doting owner put in front of him.

Jeff's body brushed intimately against her shoulders, the rough jeans only adding to the sensations he sent coursing through her.

He leaned over her, his lips practically next to her ear. "We have anyone else coming in today?"

"Ahh..." She tried to focus on the appointment book, couldn't, then forced herself. "Two. Peterman and Kravitz."

"Sounds like a law firm. Okay." His breath was hot and sweet on her neck. She wished she'd worn a ski mask. Anything to stop her awareness of him.

He straightened, to her relief and disappointment, then squeezed on past. All she had to do was turn her head an inch and she would be treated to a bird's-eye view. Too bad he was wearing clothes.

"Stop it," she muttered, disgusted with herself.

"Beg pardon," Jeff said. "I missed that."

"Nothing."

The door opened and a woman with the worst permed hair Paula had ever seen entered. A matching mound of riotous fur on a leash trotted alongside her.

"That you, Theodore?" Jeff asked, bending down and brushing aside the fur until a pair of eyes were visible. "It *is* you, boy. Well, come on, let's see if we can find the rest of you in there."

The whole back end of the mound wagged in happiness as dog and mistress followed their vet into the examination room.

Paula slumped at the reprieve from Jeff's presence. Yet she

smiled at his affection for his client. He endeared himself to her when she least wanted it. She never should have taken this job; she liked it too much. In the week she'd been Jeff's receptionist, she had found the job convenient for herself and her sons, who could stay all day with her. The patients were a little challenging with lots of variety, and the working hours didn't conflict with her natural writing rhythms. Best of all, she was being paid for it.

On the downside however was Jeff himself. She shouldn't have mixed feelings for him, but she did. More and more she had to force herself to stay cold. But her anger was slowly dissipating ever since she'd said "yes" to being his receptionist. If only the twenty-five million had never come up.

Face it, she thought. She would have found out sometime and the later she did the worse it would have been. She wished the twenty-five-million-dollar bet had never existed. Then, to have Jeff again, she would only have had to work through her father's disapproval. That was nothing compared to the damnable bet. She couldn't get past it.

Theodore Peterman eventually emerged, his owner following dutifully behind him.

Jeff leaned over, resting his elbows on the desk right next to her, his close proximity setting her senses into a tailspin again.

"You're doing a great job," he said. "How's the writing going?"

"Well, actually," she admitted, trying to focus on the subject. Or anything. "What kind of dog is Theodore?"

"Part English sheepdog, part Airedale terrier and part God-knows-what-else. His mother got loose from her pen when she was in heat and mated with a neighbor's mutt. Marge is a retired Air Force colonel with a soft heart. Theo was the ugliest puppy you ever saw outside a Mexican hairless, but when no one would take Theo, Marge kept him." Jeff brushed his finger against her forearm. "Someone's got to love the mistakes in life."

Paula shifted her arm. "He's a sweet dog. What's not to love."

"There you go." Jeff smiled, his gaze filled with amusement. "What will your father say when he finds out you're working for me?"

"Probably he'll say, 'Get out of my house.'"

"You don't sound worried."

Paula shrugged. "I've got to start somewhere. And you know you made the opportunity too good to pass up."

His smiled turned intimate. "I'll make it an even better one if you like…"

"You'd better get the Kravitz records. They'll be here any minute. Then you have to see to Popeye, Orville and the rest."

He leaned against her, his mouth a scant inch from her cheek. "Duddy Kravitz can wait—"

"This is not a good idea," she interjected, trying to pull herself away. Her rebellious body had different ideas, however.

"What's not a good idea?" he asked, not moving.

"Anyone could come in," she said lamely, not moving herself.

"So?"

"So" was right, she thought. He was only leaning next to her at the desk, chatting. Millions of people did it every day. Millions of people weren't Jeff. She had every right to be the last angry woman with him, yet that emotion seemed senseless. If she didn't want him, she should just tell him so.

She said nothing.

Duddy Kravitz, a Doberman with a physique a bodybuilder would envy, saved her from herself. Jeff left her to tend to the big dog and she barely kept herself from slumping in relief.

"I knew I shouldn't have taken this job," she muttered, disgusted with her lack of willpower. He could have kissed her, and she wouldn't have protested.

Her boys came in from their chores and, after a sweet greeting, went off in search of a snack. Paula smiled after them, feeling warm and cozy, then realized how "Donna Reed" the situation was. But it was a skewed "Donna Reed," one that had all kinds of warps within. This was not the clean break that she'd needed to a new life.

The next "patient" was a trio and they came into the office, their fur all puffed up, their short, little legs prancing at a brisk pace. Paula had met their tall, elegant owner once before. Moira Carson, in cool lemon trousers and a navy silk camp shirt looked as elegant as ever. Yet the woman's mouth was drawn down, and she had circles under her eyes that no amount of makeup could totally erase.

"Paula, I didn't know you were here," Moira said, pausing at the desk.

"I'm working for Jeff," she replied, shrugging again.

"Oh. Well, you're seeing each other, I understand—"

"No," Paula said firmly, to convince herself as much as to inform Moira.

Moira's eyebrows shot up. "You're not? But I thought…Julian said… Why not?"

Paula wondered what Moira knew about the bet. If Moira did, then clearly it didn't matter to her. If Moira didn't, Paula would ruin the woman's life should she inform her.

"I have to sit down," Moira suddenly said, while finding the nearest chair. The three Pomeranians clamored to sit on her lap. "No. Sit."

The three sat on the rug, but looked distinctly disappointed.

"You know about the bet," Moira said.

Paula nodded. "You, too, I take it."

"I no longer see that coldhearted, banker's dream named Julian Diamond." Moira thrust out her jaw before saying, "I suppose you heard about the scene we had at the Viennese Café."

"No." Paula grinned slightly. "You had a scene?"

"Right over his head. I'm surprised it's not all over town."

"It probably is, but I don't know many people well anymore," Paula replied.

"I won't be a winning bet for anyone," Moira said.

"Neither will I," Paula vowed, liking the woman more and more. But Paula understood the currents below the surface and sympathized. Moira was in love with Julian. Paula knew her heart was in the same boat. And the damn thing was sinking.

After their conversation, Moira came and went with her dogs as did several other patients. When the last patient trotted out the door, Jeff shut it behind the mixed-breed beagle and its owner.

"Done," he said, sighing. "But it's money in the bank and God knows, I need it."

"I've got more signatures for the petitions," Paula said, tapping the clipboard. "They sign in, then they sign up."

"Great." He picked it up and read it. "Wow. We're already on the second page since you gave me the idea. Moira says it's going to take more than this, however. She told me she has appealed the decision with the county courts."

"She broke up with Julian over that stupid bet," Paula said before she could stop herself.

Jeff looked at her. "I know."

"Now's your big chance to win the bet," she said. "Just get yourself a woman with kids and you're in. Give it a year or two and you can get a divorce. You'll have the money then and save the sanctuary. Heck, for than kind of loot you could set it in Central Park."

"Sarcasm becomes you," he said with a smirk. "You forget. I didn't want just any woman. I wanted you."

Paula swallowed. "I'm not a prize."

"No. I thought it was a good thing, and the bet was an added plus." He waved a hand. "Look, I can't take back what happened, as much as I wish I could. But I don't want to be at

war with my receptionist, especially when she's doing a fabulous job.''

Paula knew she didn't want to be at war, either. But she did
have to be wary.

"Mom, what's for dinner?'' Stevie said, coming into the
waiting room. His voice had the wonderfully whiny quality that
only kids could achieve.

"I don't have a clue,'' Paula admitted, grinning when he
came over and leaned against her, clearly tired and hungry.

"I've got hamburgers in the freezer,'' Jeff said. "You could
stay for a barbecue.''

"Yeah!'' Stevie cheered.

"Oh, no,'' Paula said automatically.

Bobby came in. "What's for dinner, Mom? I'm hungry.''

"Yeah, Mom,'' Jeff added, grinning. "What *is* for dinner at
your house?''

"Not stinky lima beans and lamb chops, I hope,'' Bobby
commented.

Stinky lima beans and lamb chops had been on the menu,
Paula admitted, knowing she'd planned to use her mother's last
frozen, home-cooked meal before vacation. "Well, actually, it
is.''

"Boo,'' Jeff said, summing up even her feelings about the
meal. "Stay for burgers on the grill.''

"Oh, wow,'' Bobby said, brightening. "We never get that.''

"It's settled then.'' Jeff patted Bobby on the back, just for
good measure.

"You're undermining me with my children,'' Paula told
him, pursing her lips.

"Somebody's got to, when it's lamb chops and lima beans.''
He raised his eyebrows. "I don't bite. Well, let me rephrase
that.''

"Never mind. We're here for dinner and that's enough.''

"Yes, it is.''

Halfway through the far-better meal than she would have

presented her sons, Paula admitted that it was enough just to be here. She felt right with Jeff, despite everything. The four of them, however, sitting around a picnic table, the smoky meat flirting with their senses while they ate, was so family-cozy that her heart and brain had trouble distinguishing right from wrong. The sense of togetherness left her feeling as if she were missing something by *not* accepting her lot with the bet. If only…if only…if only…

She'd lived for fifteen years on "if only," wondering about and regretting what she hadn't done before. Now, the decisions she'd made to keep her relationship with her parents unbroken seemed minor against being used as a tool to win a bet. Yet half of her—more than half of her—couldn't believe Jeff could truly be that callous.

"What are you thinking?" Jeff asked from across the table. "You have a dreamy look on your face."

"Do I?" She smiled, rather than give a hint what she was thinking. "I guess it's gas."

"Lovely. Nice to know I give you gas."

"Boy, I hope not," Stevie began. "When Mom gets gas, she really—"

Paula clamped her hand over her younger son's mouth. "*That* is not dinner conversation, young man."

Jeff roared with laughter, clearly having a good idea what the rest of the sentence would be.

Bobby snickered. "Yeah, Mom. You—"

"That's enough from you, if you want to survive the night," Paula said firmly.

God, she thought. Less-than-stellar conversation at the evening meal. It *was* like a family.

Bobby just grinned, looking as unrepentant as Jeff. Paula's heart beat harder as she realized how much better a father Jeff would have been to her son, both her sons, than their own had been. And if she had run away with Jeff all those years ago, she would have lost her parents, but what would she have gained? She had been too afraid of losing family to find out. If only there had been no bet this time around. If only she could trust him to want her for herself.

Here we go again with the "if onlys," she thought.

But they still lingered as she helped him clean up the dishes after dinner. Yet she responded to his closeness, just as she always had. The boys were in the other room watching television so they wouldn't provide a distraction.

"This one's got catsup still on it," he said, handing back a plate for her to rewash.

She blinked, becoming aware that she had been concentrating on his corded forearms rather than the dirty dishes. "Oh. Why don't you have a dishwasher? You of all people could afford one."

"Yeah." He shrugged. "It's just me out here, so it seemed silly at the time for just a couple of dishes every day. Besides, I like manual labor. I told you to leave them, and I would do them later, whiny girl."

"I pull my share of the chores, thank you very much. If I didn't you'd probably stick some bird on my head again." She dunked the plate under the water and rubbed hard with the dishcloth before handing it back. As she did, their hands touched. The warmth of his dry skin seemed to burn into her dampened flesh. Paula made a noise in the back of her throat when her whole body reacted with a wave of desire.

"Did you say something?" he asked. "I missed it."

"Nothing." Her voice cracked. She cleared it. "Nothing, not me."

"Oh. So when are your parents due back?"

"In a few days."

"And do I still have a receptionist then?"

She chuckled, although his smile sent her blood pumping heavily through her veins. "Yes, you still have a receptionist."

"Good." His smile turned sad. "I'll really need one. I'm

going to have to start looking at new properties, to move the birds if I can.''

"Can you afford it?'' she asked.

"No, but I'm going to have to make every contingent plan I can think of. Maybe if I sell this place, I can get something a little smaller and even more rural.''

"Moira might be able to get this settled for you before that,'' Paula said optimistically. "Or the petition might change the council's mind.''

"I ought to be prepared for the worst. Maybe I'll just stake a claim somewhere up in the mountains, like a frontiersman.'' He grinned. "Can you see the headlines? Wealthy Diamond Now a Squatter. My grandfather would pass bricks.''

"Maybe he'll give you the twenty-five million just to keep that out of the newspapers.''

His jaw suddenly and very visibly tightened. "I deserve that, but it still hurts.''

"I didn't mean it as a jibe, just as a joke,'' she said, handing him another dish.

"Okay.''

He said nothing more, just wiped the dish with the towel. Paula said nothing, either. The tension, always under the surface, grew stronger, nearly dominating the atmosphere. At first Paula was just purely angry with him and hating the urge she had to further defend herself. Eventually another awareness pervaded her senses...the strength of his hands when he touched hers while handing off wet things to dry...the leanness of his hip that occasionally bumped hers. She continually caught his profile out of the corner of her eye. Always, she had loved to look at him, just look at him and know he wanted her. He always made her feel desirable, perfect.

Her resistance faded, and she wanted to feel his arms around her one more time. She wanted to have him strip away her clothes and strip away his. She wanted him inside her, being one with her. The fifteen-year separation had only shown her what she had missed. Her anger and her common sense had turned into pure lust. He'd always had the ability to do that to her.

"Paula."

She twisted her upper body to face him fully, her hands still in the sink. His face was flushed yet looked carved in stone. His gaze went straight to her soul, burning her as it did. She could feel the sex emanating from him. He no more knew how to hide it than she did.

He kissed her, pulling her into him. She wound her wet hands around his waist, her fingers toying with the belt loops of his jeans. His tongue caressed hers slowly, rhythmically, as their mouths melded together. Sight and sound gave way to taste and touch. His hands curved around her derriere, his fingers kneading her flesh as he pressed her against his burgeoning erection. Her lower body throbbed heavily. She wanted him, but most of all she wanted love. Unencumbered love. It was an emotion she couldn't trust Jeff to give to her.

Slowly she pulled away. "We can't do this."

"Why not?" he asked, clearly confused.

"Twenty-five million dollars," she replied. "I'll never know if it's for me and you or for the birds."

He didn't laugh. "It might have been at one point, not for the sanctuary, but that you came back at the time when I needed you the most. It felt right. It *was* right. I just couldn't say it right."

She shook her head. "Jeff, you don't really know what it is, and that's why it will never work. Right now you need a receptionist, and I need a job. We both need to just concentrate on that."

Several days later she repeated the same thing to her father, whose fury mounted with every word. Her mother gasped at her, shocked and clearly appalled at where she was working. Paula had waited to tell them until they were settled in from their cruise and had finished chatting about what they had seen and done.

"It's a job, Dad," she said. "I need one and it pays well. I have to accept that I'm not making a living from my writing anymore. And I can't live with you two forever. That's not fair."

"That job better be enough to get yourself a home, because you won't have one here," he threatened.

"Fine. I'm going out looking right now," Paula replied without thought. She realized she'd just countered everything she had been scared about for years. Only she wasn't frightened. Instead, a huge waterfall of relief shot through her. She felt taller and straighter. And sadder. Sad that what she'd always known might happen probably now would. Avoiding it all these years, for the sake of family peace, hadn't done any of them any good. "I hope you will accept me living my life, Dad, not what you want for me."

"Not when you rub it in my face," he replied.

"The only one who rubbed it in your face was you. Dad, get past the Diamonds. For your sake." She called her sons and headed for the back door. As she turned the doorknob, she added over her shoulder. "You might as well hear it from me. Jeff's got petitions all over town to protest the sanctuary losing its longtime variance. I suggested it. Sorry about that."

Her father yelped, but Paula went out the door. The boys caught up with her a few seconds later.

"Boy, Mom, you really ticked off Grandpa," Bobby said.

"He was real red in the face, like he's got a sunburn," Stevie added.

"I know. Grandpa's mad because we're all working for Jeff now. Boys, it's time to move on."

She herded them to the car.

Chapter Ten

"We're looking for a new house!"

Jeff nearly fell out of his desk chair at Stevie's announcement. The boy and his older brother were grinning as they came into the office, while Paula gazed heavenward. Popeye wandered across the room, totally unconcerned.

"Don't you two have work to do?" she asked, shooing them out of the waiting room. "And take that silly bird with you. He ought to be in his barn, anyway, before he decides someone's near death's door and therefore is Snack Territory."

"Popeye wouldn't hurt anyone," Stevie said defending the bird.

"We'll take him out," Bobby said, nudging Popeye and Stevie toward the door. "He scares everyone, anyway."

The three went out, Popeye waddling between the humans and looking for all the world like a little old man. Extraordinary, Jeff thought, acknowledging how adept the boys were with the birds. Popeye in particular. But then, Popeye was an extraordinary bird.

Paula turned to Jeff. "They shouldn't have told you that."

"Why?" he asked, regaining his physical and emotional equilibrium.

She shrugged. "I don't know. I guess I'm feeling like it's personal business."

"Oh." It hurt to know she hadn't wanted to share this major

life change. "Okay, I won't ask why. Where are you moving to? Just for the W-2 form."

"You're paying me under the table, remember?"

"I've got to know where the table *is,* don't I?"

She eyed him. "You're not going to let this go, are you?"

"Hell, no."

"That's what I thought. I'll give you the whole thing, and this is the first and last time we'll talk about it. My dad is kicking me out because I'm working for you and starting a petition on your behalf, even though I had already told him I was moving."

"What!" Jeff stood up, excited, restless and wanting to move, but he didn't know where. Paula had clearly had a fight with her father and stood up to him...to the extent that she was moving out. "You are moving out?"

"That's what I said. There's an apartment in town that's not great...in fact it's pretty bad, but it's cheap." She sighed, looking unhappy. "I'm taking it. Things are too tense at home to stay—"

"You could move here," he broke in.

She gaped at him, then said, "That is unacceptable, even if you weren't getting evicted at any moment."

"All right, cheap apartment," he conceded. "Where's it located?"

"Over the drugstore on Main. It's not the brightest-looking place, but the plumbing and heat are sound." She smiled slightly and sat down at her desk. "So I'm here for a *long* time, if you need a receptionist, because God knows the publishers aren't biting."

"Good." He grinned broadly. "Very good. I don't know where I'll be, but it's good to know you're the receptionist."

"Fine. That's settled." She read off the appointment book. "You've got a Lydia Farnham in fifteen minutes. Her cat needs a checkup and boosters before kenneling."

"Thank God for human vacations," Jeff said. "It gets the

owners in for their pet's vaccine updates. Since we have fifteen minutes, you can finish telling me about you and your dad."

"I've already said it." She bent her head over the appointment book.

"Oh, no. You're not getting away with that." He put his finger under her chin and lifted her head. "You finally tell your father to go to hell, and I am damn well going to hear about it."

"I didn't tell my father to go to hell," she replied. "I told him it was time I moved out."

"Same thing. You never would have done that before." He paused. "Let me put it this way…you didn't do it before when I wanted you to."

"I was seventeen and too scared to defy my parents for anybody. Now I'm an old lady, and I can see peace will never be had unless it's on my father's terms." She smiled sadly. "I wish I could accept that but I can't. I came home to start a new life because I needed to. I guess I have to start other things over, as well."

Jeff's mind reeled with the information. What did it mean, this final breaking with her parents? Where did he fit into it? Something other than employer, he hoped. If only he had never taken up that bet. Paula would be with him emotionally—where he needed her. Dammit, but he'd made a mess of things yet again with her. Still a step had been made, an extraordinary step, and he was in the mix somewhere. *Extraordinary* was becoming his favorite word.

Her moving gave him an idea, especially since he had a reality to face himself. "Since you've found a place right away how about helping me find a new home for the sanctuary."

"Oh, no," she said.

He chuckled. "You always say that. I could get a complex. Look, I'd like a good opinion about properties, and you know what I need. You always have."

She flushed, a pretty reddening of her creamy cheeks. "Now I really say no."

"Stop or I'll think you're flirting with me." He sobered. "Seriously, Paula, would you help me? I may not have much time."

She was quiet for a moment, then smiled. "All right. When do you want to start?"

"Today, after practice hours and working with the birds. I did have Will Garrison in town research a few open spaces or old farms for sale. How much do you think your dad would give me for this place? You know he wants it to develop."

"Not what it's truly worth." Paula snorted. "He'd want to get it cheap just to rub it in. He's really got a 'take no prisoners' streak."

"Thank God his daughter didn't inherit it."

She smiled archly. "What makes you think I haven't?"

"This."

He leaned over and kissed her soundly, loving the way she kissed back without thought. Her mouth was sweet fire, never changing and yet as new as the first time they'd kissed. How she did it, he didn't know and didn't care. He only knew he needed it. He had taken hope from the kiss of the other day. Her body told him something different than her brain did.

The door swung open and they broke apart as the boys came in. They didn't seem to notice the kiss or the adults' tension. Jeff grinned at them and knew he wanted to raise them as his own. He was as much in love with them as he was with Paula. Whoever fathered them didn't matter to him. They were children and they needed him as much as he needed them—for himself. He needed Paula for himself. Her recent kisses showed that she needed him, wanted him, certainly. Maybe the damnable bet hadn't killed everything.

The office got busy after that and stayed busy. It was as if everyone in town was supporting him, at least with business. Each patient signed Paula's petition, if they hadn't already, and

wished him luck. People liked the sanctuary. Jeff was feeling
very good about everything until he was finished working with
the birds and Paula reminded him they were supposed to look
at properties.

"I don't want to," he said, holding the keys to his SUV but
not moving to get in.

"Okay," Paula said. "Boys, we're not going."

The boys groaned. Jeff sighed. "All right, all right. I'm facing reality. Everyone get in."

He drove them all, with great reluctance, to an abandoned
farm about an hour from Diamond Mount. The barn was in
such bad shape he wouldn't let the boys go in with him, but
made them stay outside with Paula. Inside, he brushed against
a beam and immediately heard an ominous groan of protest.
He raced outside and turned in time to see a part of the roof
cave in.

"Oh, my God!" Paula exclaimed, watching with horror.

"I know. I called Him, too," Jeff commented, a shiver of
averted doom coursing down his spine. "Too many acres, too
few trees and too much work."

"Just the barn." Paula pointed to the house which looked
in good condition. "That might be worthy. Got a key?"

"No. I just told Will I wanted to look around and get a feel,
then if I liked it, I would have him come back with me and
we'd go into the house."

"I don't like it," Stevie said. "That barn could fall in on
Popeye or Oscar or Maria. Everybody! I'm not gonna work for
you, Jeff, if you buy this place. Why don'tcha just go yell at
my grandpa? Maybe kick his butt—"

"Stevie," Jeff broke in. "That is enough. You will respect
your grandfather. You will respect all adults and say only nice
things about them. They have lived longer than you, and they
have earned it."

Stevie looked at him, a mulish expression on his face.
"Okay."

It was a measure of Paula's parenting that he didn't remind Jeff he wasn't his father and therefore didn't have to listen.

"But I'm not workin' for you in *that!*" he added, saying the last word and pointing over his shoulder to the rickety barn.

"Deal, because neither am I."

He dropped them off at the house, after a jaunt to the ice cream stand on the old highway, a favorite summer hangout when he and Paula had been younger. This time he drove straight up the driveway to her father's front door.

"What the hell," he muttered. If she could move, he could do a little standing up of his own. "Thanks for coming with me."

"You're welcome," she said, after the boys said their good-byes and scrambled out of the car.

He put his hand on her seat back, all too conscious of the console that separated them. He only wanted to close the space and kiss her senseless, then tell her not to get out of the car. Tell her to stay with him always. He remembered how many times he had wanted to say it when they'd been young and in love.

"I want to kiss you," he said.

"I know. You shouldn't."

"Not 'you won't.' I like that."

She smiled, a sexy, little, knowing smile. "I'll see you to-morrow."

She opened the door and ducked out, not that he would have stopped her. He supposed she had enough to contend with, and he shouldn't add to it. Still, as he made a U-turn and drove by the house, he couldn't resist waving enthusiastically to Bob Helpern, who looked ready to split nails. Jeff hoped to high heaven that Moira would get the variance decision reversed.

At home, in his house filled only with the voices of avian imitators, he knew he was living in a shadow of what could be. He wanted a life with Paula and the boys. The sanctuary, the money to save it, meant nothing next to her and her sons.

He did good work with the birds, but that didn't satisfy his soul. Not like Paula did.

He went out into the night and looked at the stars. A loon called mournfully in the distance for its mate. Silhouettes flew across the half-moon as a flight of starlings or bats moved to another feeding ground. Mosquitoes droned around his ear while one suddenly bit his neck. He slapped at it, then made a decision.

It was getting downright easy to hop the fence that separated the properties. He watched the darkened windows, looking for any sign that the house was awake. Only one window was lit—like a beacon.

He tossed a few pebbles against the screen.

The light went out, then the screen moved, and Paula's head came into view.

"Are you nuts?" she hissed in a loud whisper.

"I thought we already established that," he said, while climbing up to her. "Move over and let me in."

She did, although she said, "I must be nuts for doing this."

"Hey, you're already kicked out of the house so what else can your father do?"

"Good point. Why are you here?"

"Because I love you."

"Oh, God, Jeff." She stepped away from him. "After all that's happened, how can I believe that?"

"I would say, because I've just said it, but I know you'd probably have a problem with that." He knew he had to tread carefully here. Julian had really messed things up with Moira— not that he already hadn't with Paula. Somehow, he had to make it better. But did he still really want to win the bet? The birds, he reminded himself. He had the sanctuary at stake. He just had to ensure Paula understood he loved her *and* they could benefit the sanctuary. "The bet doesn't change how I feel about you. It's just an added bonus—"

"It's not a bonus," she interrupted. "It's what makes you

feel like you do. You should be very angry with me over my father. My God, look at what he's done to you, just since I came back. Yet you still love me. So you say. If all that money wasn't there, would you still feel the same way? I don't think so. I wouldn't.''

"I think you would. I know I would. What can I do to convince you?" he asked, seeking her out in the dark.

"Nothing. There's nothing to say."

Her body felt warm, belying her words. Her robe was silky, his fingers sliding up and down her arm easily as he tried to reassure her with his touch. "I don't blame you. I understand. But I'm going to keep trying, Paula. Because I think you love me. I know you do."

He kissed her, their lips clinging tenderly with emotion, not fire. But the fire surfaced, fast and hot, burning through Jeff, driving his need to prove their feelings in the most intimate of ways.

As the kiss deepened, she pressed herself to him, her breasts flattening against his chest. Her hips met his, and her thighs shifted restlessly. The blood coursed heavily through his veins. He caressed her back, her sides, sliding his hands between them to touched her already-hard nipples. Her breasts were soft, malleable, a phenomenon he didn't remember from before. She moaned into his mouth, her hands clenching at his waist. Her palms coursed down to his buttocks, her fingers digging into his flesh. Jeff's senses spun out of control.

They tumbled to the bed, stripping away their clothes. Hers were easy, and Jeff knew he needed that, because his hands were shaking with desire for her. Her skin was heated, almost scorching him. She slung her leg over his hip, opening herself to his touch. He rubbed his fingers against her woman's flesh. She tensed and rested her head against his shoulder, her teeth nipping his shoulder to keep herself from crying out.

To his bemusement, she raked her nails lightly over his nipples in her eagerness to touch him, and the sensation sent sparks shooting everywhere inside him. She captured his moan with a blistering kiss.

"Paula," he whispered. It sounded like an explosion to his sensitive ears.

He rolled her onto her back and entered her swiftly. Her hot, moist flesh embraced him tightly, making them one. He thrust slowly. Her thighs cradled his hips, taking him in even farther when she wrapped her legs around his waist. She met him with each movement. She was a temptress, making him greedy for all he could have of her. However he could have her.

All too soon, his control broke just as hers did. They swallowed their cries of completion even as her body swallowed his. Jeff collapsed on top of her, pressing her into the mattress of the small bed.

But he knew she loved him. For the moment he was content.

"I LOVE YOU."

Paula wanted to push his words away and just feel his naked body buried in her own. Just give and take physically and leave the emotions out of their lovemaking. Yet even this second time, she couldn't deny that she loved him. Always they had had a passionate relationship. Fifteen years ago it had all been wrapped up in sex. Great, wonderful, incredibly intimate, once-in-a-lifetime sex that she had never experienced again and knew she never would.

But now she could never be sure he meant it, not with twenty-five million dollars right there for the taking. No matter what it saved, no matter how noble the cause, she would never know if Jeff truly loved her for her or for the money. Logic told her that any other man in the situation Jeff was in, any other man with a past track record like Jeff had had with her and her father, would *not* want her fifteen years later. But that incredible sum of money could make a lot of things palatable.

He nuzzled her neck. "I know you don't believe me."

Tears leaked out of Paula's eyes. She hadn't expected any and couldn't quite hold them back. "This is all such a mess."

"I made it," he whispered. "Just give me a chance to prove myself."

"No, you don't have to prove yourself." She hated the thought that he even felt as if he had to. "I've made the mess, too. I shouldn't have come home. I knew I shouldn't have—"

"Hush." He kissed her tears and held her closer. "Don't cry. What will your father say if he comes in and catches us?"

"Just like old times?" she quipped, giving a watery laugh.

Jeff chuckled. "That'll be the day."

She ran her hands down his bare back, loving the expanse of muscles under his warm skin. He was like a furnace, his nakedness always having driven her desire for him beyond the bounds of control.

Footsteps suddenly sounded outside in the hall. They froze. Paula heard a *flick,* then light shone under her doorway.

"Move!" she said through gritted teeth, pushing at Jeff. But he was already sliding off her bed.

He was sliding under it.

"What the—?" she gasped, goggle-eyed that he wasn't flinging himself out the window and down the porch roof.

The door opened. Paula yanked the covers up to her chin. Her father stood in the doorway, wearing only his boxers, his hair wild.

"Dad! What's the matter?" she asked, hoping she looked startled and not guilty. Jeff shifted under her mattress, his head bumping her butt through a foot of stuffing and box spring. She nearly yelped in surprise and fear that he'd give his position away.

"I thought I heard a noise," he said, running his hand through his thinning hair. "I guess I'm just hearing things."

"I guess so."

He turned, then turned back. "Paula, you don't have to move out if you don't want to."

Paula stared at her father, even as she sensed Jeff under the bed, just as still. It was as close to an apology as she'd ever received from her parent. "I...thanks, Dad. I appreciate it."

"Could you find another job, though?" he asked plaintively.

Paula chuckled. Something pushed at her from under the bed; she could easily guess who.

"I've got room at the office for you, if you like."

Paula sobered. She wondered how to say "Are you nuts?" diplomatically. "Thanks, Dad. I've taken enough charity from you already. I really couldn't take more. I hope you understand."

"I guess. I didn't want to work my old man's farm. That felt like charity to me when I was young. Still, couldn't you get another job?"

"I'll think about it."

"Could you back off that petition thing, too?"

"Dad, don't push your luck."

"Just thought I'd try. Maybe your writing will pick up again."

"From your mouth to God's ear."

"Good night."

"'Nite."

The door swung closed. Paula slumped, wondering how she'd made it through her father's sudden appearance—and apology. Never would she have expected that from him.

Something rustled along the floor. Jeff's head appeared over the edge of the mattress. He hoisted himself back onto the bed. In the barest of whispers, he said, "That was a little too close to old times."

"Yes, it was." Paula swallowed, feeling her emotions beginning to go out of control.

Jeff put his arm around her while she pulled herself together. "Here we are, once again, in your bed, in your parents' house, making forbidden love, and then I have to hide under the bed. I actually found the special ties I made with the strings hanging down from your mattress. I used to do that when I was bored while waiting for your parents to finally be asleep.''

She giggled. "We've got to stop meeting like this.''

"I don't think so. I don't think we can.''

"For a romance writer, my love life is a mess," she admitted, sighing.

"Trust me," he said. When she opened her mouth to protest, he added, "I know, I know. But, Paula, what can I do to make things right? Just tell me and I will do it.''

"I don't know." She shivered, feeling like she was hearing a death knell. "I don't know if you can do anything. I think we're just doomed not to be together.''

His arms tightened around her. "Don't think like that. Look, I'd better go before we really do get caught. I'll see you at the house tomorrow.''

She said nothing, but nodded.

"Good." He kissed her goodbye, and she couldn't resist, winding her arms around his neck.

"Tomorrow.''

He said it like a promise, before he disappeared out her bedroom window. But she was no Scarlett O'Hara. She was more like Ally McBeal, a mass of insecurities surrounded by a sea of confusion. Most confusing of all was Jeff.

Paula lay back and rubbed her temples, trying to rub in some common sense. She wanted to believe Jeff so badly, believe they could have it all and the whys would sort themselves out by the twenty-fifth wedding anniversary. Only it wouldn't. She needed badly to trust him, and she couldn't see how, when she was the means to win the bet and save the sanctuary. More important, she had to be careful with Bobby and Stevie. She knew he cared for them, but she still didn't see how she could risk their hearts. Her own didn't matter compared to that.

"I've got to stop fooling around and get a *real* job," she muttered to herself. She chuckled wryly, remembering how often people told her to get a "real" job when she first started writing. Then again, people told her she needed to read "real" books after she started reading romance novels. She amended her vow. "Okay, I've got to stop fooling around and get *another* job."

That was more like it—and no Daddy employment, either.

The next morning she wondered if she'd wished on a star the night before when she answered the telephone to find her agent on the other end.

"Well, this new one got 'em," Sally announced baldly. She named a publisher who had just made her an offer for Paula's latest proposal, the one she had started here in Diamond Mount. The offer was extremely handsome and better still, the publisher was committed to rebuilding her sales. "You're right back in the book business again."

"Oh, God," Paula moaned, her heart beating happily. She thought she would faint with joy. "I can live anywhere again, can't I?"

"No more home-with-the-folks," Sally agreed. "And no more nine-to-five, unless it's with your writing where it damn well should be. It's been a long dry spell, honey, but you are back."

When she arrived at work and saw the lambent promise in Jeff's gaze, she knew she had to tell him right way. "I sold my book!"

He paused, then grinned, then whooped and grabbed her up, spinning her around in a circle. "The one I inspired?"

"What a ham you are," she said, but grinned and hugged him. Never had she felt such pure pleasure in telling another human being about selling a new book. It felt so special, like it was her first book all over again.

"We'll go for a celebration lunch, then we'll look at another sanctuary property, then we'll go to a celebration dinner," he said. "Hey! I'm losing my receptionist. Oh, what the hell."

He kissed her fully on the mouth.

Paula forgot about books and money and being out of the

financial hole she'd been in. She forgot everything except the feel of Jeff's mouth moving over hers, his tongue swirling with her own and his breath warm against her cheek.

"Ohh, you kissed Mommy!"

Stevie's shout took them both by surprise, and they jumped apart. The little boy grinned ear to ear at her and Jeff.

"Your mom sold her book," Jeff said.

"She always sells books," Stevie said blithely.

"No more living with Grandpa," she said. "This time for sure. And no little apartment, either."

"Hot dog." Stevie focused on Jeff. "You like my mom, don't you?"

"I always have," Jeff replied, smiling at him. He smiled at Paula. "And I always will."

"Do you like Jeff, Mommy?"

Oh, boy, Paula thought. "He's all right."

"Thanks a lot," Jeff griped, glaring at her.

She chuckled, then noticed Stevie visibly relax. Clearly the boy was banking on her liking Jeff a whole lot, maybe enough to make him a part of their family. She wanted to hug her son and explain all the problems, all the mess, that had been created by the adults.

"Come on, sport," Jeff said, picking Stevie up and whirling him around. "Let's go find your brother and Popeye and let's get out of your mom's hair. I'm taking everyone on a celebration lunch. Maybe then she'll like me. Maybe she needs a few more sleepless nights and she'll *really* like me."

She shook her head at the man who had driven her crazy for fifteen years. She had done the wrong thing all that time ago, and had run from it ever since. Now she just wanted to raise her boys here in Diamond Mount and write her books. Part of her life was back on track.

But the other part... How much she wanted to have her emotional life back on track. But Jeff needed the money from the bet. No matter how she tried to compromise herself, her values, she would never truly know if he loved her for her. Not in the way she really wanted him to. No complications, no strings, nothing but love, pure and simple.

After fifteen years, she knew she wanted that.

Julian

~ Part Four ~

Yeah, the Bet's Not Won Yet

Chapter Eleven

Julian Diamond sat at his desk in his inner, glass-enclosed office and watched his employees walk by, glance at him, then turn away, shoulders shaking with mirth.

The whole town knew of his imitation of a birthday candle at the Viennese Café. The whole town knew Moira had dumped him, just as she'd dumped that birthday cake all over his best Armani suit. Good thing he liked chocolate.

The cake didn't matter, he thought, sighing heavily and running a hand through his hair. Neither did it matter if the town had a laugh over its banker. Moira mattered.

He knew it when he went to bed at night and realized she'd never be there again. Granted their relationship had been...cautious for a long time, but dammit, he had gotten to like the new Moira and the new closeness. He wished he hadn't been so wary for so long. Now he had lost her.

A pain sat heavily in his chest. Julian wondered if he were having a heart attack, but it didn't feel physical. It hurt to know Moira was no longer his. It hurt deeply.

Julian cursed, wishing he could take back everything he said that night. Somehow he had made a mess of his business proposal. Who could have known she wouldn't respond as she usually did? A little thought, a little mulling over of the advantages, and she should have realized the tremendous potential in marrying him. But that hadn't happened.

"To hell with this," he snapped, getting up from the chair and striding out of his office and out of the bank. He hadn't explained his plan right to her. Somehow, he had made a wrong turn and offended her. All he had to do was apologize and start all over again.

His strides ate up the distance between his office and hers. He waved absently to people as he passed them. When he got to her building, he walked right past Nancy, the receptionist, and into Moira's office.

She looked awful.

Julian gaped at her hair pulled back at her nape, strands haphazardly escaping in an unattractive manner. Dark circles framed her eyes, and her color was too pale.

"You look terrible," he blurted out.

"Go away."

Her secretary came rushing in belatedly. "Mr. Diamond! She doesn't want to see you. Please."

Julian clamped his jaw shut and glared at the secretary, who stepped back in self-defense. "She'll see me, and we will not be disturbed. Do *you* understand?"

"Never mind, Nancy. He can stay. I've got a little time before his brother's appointment," Moira said.

"Jeff's coming here?" Julian asked.

"Business," Moira replied succinctly.

When the receptionist closed the door behind her, Moira pointed to the chair opposite her desk. "Sit down. I can't say I'm glad you've come, but I do have a few things to say to you."

She sounded cool, but he wasn't about to let that stop him from his mission. He sat, but he had things to say first. "Moira, about the other night. I must have sounded like a jackass. I know I didn't explain everything so that you would understand."

"I understand, Julian. You see our relationship as deepening, therefore it's the perfect time to get married, since we'll win twenty-five million dollars from your grandfather. I will receive a handsome endowment, really an embarrassment of riches, in a business marriage, forged to produce a child. And the sex is great, too."

"Well, I didn't mean it to sound so blunt," he said lamely, admitting she did understand the basics. "I care for you, Moira—"

"That's lovely, but I am no longer interested," she said, her gaze cold as ice at minus forty degrees.

"You really don't look well," he said, frowning. "Is it that virus thing again? It comes and goes. I don't like it. This time I think you should go to some specialists in Pittsburgh—"

"I don't need specialists in Pittsburgh, I know exactly what's wrong," she interrupted.

"You're not…dying?" he demanded in a panic. His body actually shook at the thought of truly losing her forever.

"No, I'm not 'dying,'" she snapped. "I have a message for you, and when I am done you will know exactly why I look this way." She paused, stared at him for one long moment, then said, "I'm pregnant, Julian."

His jaw dropped, and then his body, his brain, his blood, his entire body froze in astonishment.

"You are the father," Moira went on, pushing some stray hair from her face. "Since you have little interest in anything beyond your investment-oriented mind, I don't expect, nor do I want, any emotional support from you. However, I do expect you to pay child support and eventually schooling costs. We'll halve that. I have drawn up a contract that spells out payments and visitation rights. Should you want to actually participate in your child's upbringing, I've even spelled out how many diaper changes you're entitled to make in a week."

She slid a wad of papers across her desk.

"Last, but never least, you'll be happy to know, Julian, that love doesn't enter into the paperwork anywhere."

Julian stared at the contract, all drawn up nice and neatly, that said he was having a child. *Him.* He and Moira.

He believed her. He didn't think for a moment that she was lying to him. He didn't doubt for a moment that he was the father. He couldn't explain why he believed her. Just that his heart knew. He had created life. He and she.

The realization broke over his head like a barrelful of confetti being tossed on New Year's Eve. Joy shot through him and shot him right out of the chair.

"I'm having a baby!" he shouted, leaping and throwing his fist up. He couldn't be angry about the contract. She hadn't been herself for weeks, and now he knew why. A *baby.* Somewhere in the mix of emotions was the thought that he had won the bet. But it was such a small little thing, a perk at best, in the big scheme of things involved in having a baby. Visions of hugs and kisses and ball games and amusement parks and first days of school danced through his head. A baby…with Moira. Nothing was more wonderful.

"*I'm* having the baby," Moira said.

"Right, right. How long have you known?" he asked happily, coming around the desk to hug her.

She reared back in her chair, actually rolled her chair away from him. "Don't touch me, you shallow piece of slime."

Julian gaped at her. "What'd I do?"

She laughed hysterically. "You let me hang for a year, keeping me at arm's length unless we were having sex. When you actually got all lovey, it was only to get me to agree to your ridiculous proposal to win the bet, and then, *then,* you have the nerve to jump with joy over a baby that only means that you get twenty-five million dollars! You couldn't have been more obvious about your feelings."

"I'm just happy about the baby *for* the baby!" he shouted at her, trying to get it into her stubborn brain. He calmed himself. She was pregnant. She wasn't rational. "This is getting us nowhere. The baby changes everything. Of course, we have to get married now—''

''Oh, no!'' Moira exclaimed, looking wild-eyed. She gripped her desk as if she needed a lifeline. ''No deal, Julian Diamond. We do not have to get married just because I'm having a baby. I'm perfectly capable of raising this child on my own. He doesn't need a father who only cares for dollars instead of diapers.''

''I am tired of you portraying me as some kind of ogre,'' Julian snapped, glaring at her.

''You're not an ogre, Julian. Just a man who doesn't know love and doesn't want to. I'm not marrying without it.'' Moira's expression changed. ''I loved you, Julian.''

Julian stared at her, stunned by this second revelation that turned his world upside down as much as the first did. More, maybe.

Moira nodded. ''Almost from the beginning I loved you. I could see you wanted distance, but I thought it was temporary. I thought if I were cautious and patient, if I didn't push you for a commitment, you would see that love wouldn't hurt you again. I *thought* I was making progress. Instead, it was just because you wanted money.''

''I...'' What could he say? He'd had no idea she felt that way; she'd hidden it so well from him. ''I care for you, Moira.''

''No, you don't. You just think you have to still say it. I have consulted with your grandfather over the terms of the bet he made with you and Jeff. You can win on a technicality, Julian.'' Her voice caught, as she added, ''Nowhere did the bet require that you be married to the same woman having your child. Right now, you could go out and find another woman, marry her and you would win.'' She rose from the chair. Her voice rose from her. ''You would win, Julian, so just get the hell out and find yourself the first available woman who'll marry you, while I have your baby and you get your stinking rotten money. *Get out!*''

Having screamed the command in his face, Moira suddenly turned pale and proceeded to get sick all over her Oriental rug. Julian yelped and grabbed her around the waist with one hand, holding her steady while she was violently ill.

Her office door burst open and Jeff raced in, followed by Nancy. Both looked as shell-shocked as he felt, although for an entirely different reason. They all watched Moira be ill on her very expensive, imported carpet.

The outer door of the office opened and voices drifted in. Bob Millstein, Roger Gunnarson and Dick Hammermil, all town council members, stood on the threshold of Moira's inner office and stared open-mouthed at the scene before them.

Moira's spasms finally calmed. Julian helped her straighten and return to her big, leather office chair. She was like spaghetti in his arms and actually leaned against him for strength. She sank into the chair and glanced once at her former breakfast, then at her audience.

"Don't worry," she said. "I don't charge for the show."

Jeff said, chuckling, "Gee, I thought that was part of my appointment. Are you okay, Moira?"

"Fine, really. Just something disagreed with me." She looked pointedly at Julian.

"Oh." Jeff said, clearly catching her drift. He smiled at his brother.

"I'd say something really disagreed," Roger Gunnarson commented. The others grinned and nodded.

"I'll get that cleaned up," Nancy offered. "Of course, I want a raise since this isn't in my job description."

Moira shuddered. "You've got it."

Julian looked at his brother. He wanted so much to tell Jeff about the baby, but knew it wouldn't be the best of news to his brother. Somehow, the idea of the bet tied with the baby was repugnant to him. He didn't want anything else to close that gap, and telling Jeff would.

"I guess we'll come back," Dick Hammermil said.

"I will say we came with good news," Bob Millstein added. "We're looking for a new city solicitor. We'd like you to consider it. So consider it while you're in between being sick."

Jeff laughed. "That's interesting. I came to talk about my lawsuit against the town and the council for revoking my variance."

The three councilmen exploded with protests. Jeff protested back until it looked like war was about to erupt.

Julian bellowed, "Gentlemen! Can't you see Moira's sick? Or do you have to look at the rug again?"

"Thank you, Julian," Moira muttered in disgust. "Just what I needed to feel better."

"We're going," Jeff said, waving at the other three. "Let's all go outside and brawl there. We'll give Mike Cartman a good lead article for this week's *Mountain Weekly*."

The other three actually chuckled. Jeff ushered them out. He looked back at Julian and said, "Call me, little brother," before he shut the door behind him.

"I'm three inches taller than he is," Julian commented, with a grimace. "Why am I always the *little* brother?"

He turned to Moira. "We're getting you the best care right now. I don't like this sickness you have."

"It's called morning sickness. It's normal." Moira leaned back in the chair, her face still as pale as milk.

"This…this getting sick when you're upset. That can't be good for the baby," Julian replied in frustration, coming over to her.

Nancy came back with cleaning implements, interrupting further discussion. Julian helped her clean up.

When Nancy left and the rug was spotless once more, Moira said, "I can't believe you did that, Julian. Got down on your hands and knees and cleaned. I almost got sick again just watching you.''

Julian grinned. "Jeff's not the only one who could have been a doctor. I've got a cast-iron stomach...most of the time.''

Moira closed her eyes. "I wish I did.''

"Honey, this can't be good for you," he said. "Let's go to the doctor and—''

"No. I've got an appointment tomorrow, anyway.''

"Good, I'll go with you—''

"No.''

Julian eyed her speculatively. He had the urge to send her to a corner for being like a stubborn little kid. He decided to change the subject. Besides, now that the interruptions were gone, burning questions began to surface again. "How long have you known about the baby?''

"Several months, although I had my first appointment a few weeks ago. I'm over four months pregnant now.''

"Four months!'' Anger flared at her not telling him. "Damn it, Moira, you should have told me—''

"Why?'' she scoffed wearily. "So you would have whisked me away in a marriage, then said, 'Oh, yes, here's half of twenty-five million dollars. Thanks for the great timing, honey?' I'm so glad I didn't tell you. I don't love you anymore, Julian. Thank your lucky stars that you're off the hook with me.''

Julian didn't feel like he had any lucky stars. Instead, his star had fallen down to Earth and wiped out all life on the planet.

It had certainly wiped out his.

"SO YOU TOLD HIM and he liked it.''

Jenny Carson swept back her silvering hair and smiled at Moira. She looked a little too pleased with Moira's description of her office earlier in the day. They sat at Jenny's dining room table for dinner. Anastasia, Sergei and Doodles lay at Moira's feet. She had gone home and couldn't stand being alone—not after her day—so she had packed up her dogs and sought out mother love. Mother love had come through for her with a listening ear.

"He didn't mean it," Moira said, toying with her green beans. "Or he only meant it for the bet."

"Oh, I don't know." Her mother shrugged. "He could have been pleased only for the bet, but he didn't have to protest so much when you presented him with the technicality about the bet. That's what makes me think he was pleased with the news."

"But you don't even like Julian, Mother."

"He's the father of my future grandchild, so I'll give him some leeway. What did old Bart say when you told him about the pregnancy?"

Moira blushed. "He whooped with joy and told me to get in there and tie Julian up."

"Bart always was kinky."

"I don't want to know how you know that, Mother."

Jenny just smiled. "I never tell, and stop playing with your green beans. You're eating for two."

"I don't think even the baby wants any part of these. I know I certainly don't," Moira told her, giving up the thought of eating them. She would only have done it for health's sake anyway since she never had been fond of them. "I reamed Bart a new one, to use an expression I dislike but one which is very appropriate to the situation. He's put both Julian and Jeff in untenable positions."

"They must want to be there," her mother said. "Who wouldn't, for that kind of money?"

"Both of them are desperate for it." Moira flung her fork down and burst into tears. "He'll get married now, Mother! Probably today or tomorrow. Because of the baby, I won't be able to walk away from him. I'll see him and her together all the time. I can't do it. I can't do it!"

She wailed her unhappiness, tears streaking down her face. The dogs got up on their hind legs, their front paws clawing her thighs as they whined in commiseration and vied to comfort her.

Jenny reached over and patted her daughter on the shoulder. "Honey, that's the crazy hormones talking. They'll do that for a few more weeks."

Moira felt a little better after her dinner with her mother, especially after they discussed baby matters. Her mother had pages of advice, some Moira thought good and others Moira thought overwrought. Surely babies with colic didn't cry literally around the clock. Her mother exaggerated that part about her own parenting experience.

As she got out of her car in her own driveway, she was still thinking baby things when, out of the darkness, Julian suddenly loomed in front of her. She shrieked for a second in panic, then realized he wasn't a mugger or worse.

"You scared me," she said. As the dogs jumped down out of the driver's side like little lemmings, she turned on them. "I can't believe you three didn't even bark at him!"

The dogs looked innocently at her, as if to say, "What? Us bark?"

"They know me," Julian said. "Where have you been?"

"At my mother's."

"I was worried, especially after the way you were ill this afternoon."

She wanted to say something sarcastic, but his voice sounded so sincere that she couldn't muster the venom. Instead she glared at him. "Why are you here, Julian?"

He didn't answer at first. Finally he said, "I wanted to see you, to apologize for my behavior."

"Thank you for the apology," she said gravely, then walked by him to her front door. The dogs were at her heels.

Julian followed her. "Could we talk, Moira?"

"I'm really tired tonight," she said, excusing herself as she unlocked her front door. The dogs swooshed past her into the house. They turned and barked at Julian. "Oh, so now you're rottweilers, you stinkers. Quiet!"

The dogs stopped barking, although they milled restlessly in the doorway.

"Moira, we need to talk," Julian said.

She sighed, feeling every moment of the tremendously emotional day weighing down every fiber of her being. Maybe she was exhausted enough that she would be able to get through this calmly if not even woodenly. That ought to keep her stress level down. "Come in."

She led the way into her formal living room, not wanting to use the den, their favorite place in her house. She didn't need cozy memories on top of their "talk."

She didn't offer him anything to drink, although that went against her ingrained manners, but she didn't want to encourage him to be comfortable. Her crying jag at her mother's came back to her tenfold, and she nearly cried again at the thought of him marrying another woman.

He sat on a Queen Anne's chair, while she sat on the love seat with the dogs for company. She made sure they joined her, needing to keep him at arm's length. She ought to feel cold toward him, but her gaze kept admiring his features, and she was far more conscious of his body than she should be.

He said, "Why didn't you tell me about the baby from the beginning? As soon as you knew?"

"I didn't want to pressure you into feeling like you had to marry me for the baby's sake." Moira laughed at the irony of that.

"I had a right to know."

"Yes, you did. Now you know."

"Now is late, Moira. You should have told me as soon as you knew."

She said nothing, just stroked her dogs who snuggled closer

to her belly as if already aware and welcoming the newest member of the family.

He ran a hand through his hair. "I guess I understand why you would hesitate. Considering what our relationship was, I suppose you might have felt on uncertain ground about my reception to the news of a baby."

No kidding, she thought. "I appreciate that."

He was silent for a moment. "I read over that contract you did. It was thorough. Do we really need one?"

"I thought you would be comfortable with that," she said, feeling a little ashamed, however, because she knew she did it as a catharsis more than anything else.

He made a face. "I'm not comfortable with it. When my parents divorced, Jeff and I were Ping-Pong balls in a lawyers' feast of paperwork. I don't want to do that. Can't we just work this out between us? I promise I'll change diapers whenever you want me to."

Moira envisioned the very elegant Julian Diamond elbow-deep in dirty diapers, and burst into laughter. "Could I have a picture of that?"

He grinned. "I'll pose naked if you like. Me and the kid."

His words didn't evoke a sexy image but a tender image…of a sweet little, dark-haired baby, skin to skin on his dark-haired father's naked chest, while Julian rocked him to sleep. Her heart flipped over, and she knew she wanted that image to be as real as sitting here with him.

"I'll skip that." Her voice cracked. She cleared it. "You'd probably regret the baby not wearing a diaper."

Julian chuckled. He was silent for a moment, the time filled with a comfortableness. At last, he said, "This is nice, Moira, talking about the baby. I like it."

He wasn't making it easy for her to keep her perspective. She knew she must or he would break her heart, and maybe break the child's heart, as well, if she weren't careful. He wouldn't mean to, but his priorities kept him cold.

"Are you feeling all right?" he asked. "I still don't like what happened at your office today."

She shrugged. "Being ill is typical. It's not the first time I've suddenly become ill at the office. I usually make it to the powder room first."

He grinned wryly. "Did you see the look on their faces? I thought we were about to have the aftermath of an all-night college kegger."

His amusement was hard to resist. She laughed with him. In her laughter, she found her defenses lowered somehow, more open. How it had happened she didn't know.

"I expect I lost the opportunity for the solicitor's job," she said. "Oh, well."

"I think my brother ruined that with his lawsuit. I know you have attorney-client privilege, but did you really file an appeal for him over the variance?"

"I can answer because I honestly haven't. Since it'll be on the docket in a few days, I can tell you, yes I appealed to the county courts for a repeal of the revocation."

"I hope he gets the variance back," Julian said, sounding like he meant it. "He doesn't deserve what they did."

"No, he doesn't."

"Okay, now let's get to attorney-client privilege, namely mine. Among other things, I came today to make sure you were still my lead attorney in blocking the takeover. The baby changes things."

"Why?" she asked, bristling.

He looked nonplussed. "Well, I mean, I thought pregnant moms need to rest a lot and cut their hours."

"My doctor says I can work all I like. However much I feel comfortable with."

"Oh, then good." He paused before adding hesitantly, "I was afraid that after our fight, you wouldn't want to handle the case."

"That is a different story," she said.

"Oh."

She thought for a long while, weighing the pros and cons of continuing to lead the battle against the hostile takeover. "I hate to let clients go. I'll still do it, if you want me to. Besides, I'm already established with that corporate shark tank we hired in Pittsburgh."

Julian laughed. "I love it when you trash your own profession."

She laughed, then yawned, the reflex taking her by surprise. "I beg your pardon."

"Well, I should go." He stood. "You need your rest, since you're sleeping for two."

That old expression really brought home to Moira the enormity of the life change she was about to experience. Alone. Julian's excitement was a surprise, but it wouldn't translate into his having a high interest in the daily grind of raising a child.

She pushed back the threat of tears and nudged the dogs off her lap so she could stand. Julian took her hand and helped her off the love seat. He held on to her hand afterward, making it awkward to pull free without showing her vulnerability.

"Can I feel the baby?" he asked shyly.

Moira gaped at him, the request so unlike the Julian Diamond she knew. "You want to feel the baby?"

He nodded.

"Julian," Moira said, trying to control a flood of emotions. "There's nothing to feel yet. It's only four months."

"I know. But I want to feel. I need to."

She nodded.

Almost reverently, he laid the flat of his palm against her abdomen. His hand was warm and strong, the span of it nearly stretching from hip to hip on her. He pressed his fingers slightly into her flesh, then smiled.

"I can't feel a thing, and I don't give a damn." He looked extremely pleased. "A baby. Wow."

They walked to her front door together, the pups following

behind, their paws scrabbling over the foyer flooring. Julian still held her hand. Moira found herself gripping his palm tightly.

He opened the door and turned to her. "I'm very happy about the baby, Moira, and it's got nothing to do with the bet. I just wanted you to know that."

She nodded once, not trusting her voice.

He kissed her cheek and left her gazing after him.

The bet brought to mind the technicality she had discovered. He hadn't said he was taking a wife to fulfill the terms and win the money.

Then again, he hadn't said he wouldn't.

Chapter Twelve

The stuffed mouse was huge.

Julian wrestled the thing out of his passenger seat, grunting when the three-foot-high toy didn't budge at first. Finally he got it disentangled from the seat belt and hoisted it into his arms. He flipped the seat over with his free hand and snagged a large bag with the emblem of the most famous toy store in the world.

"Damn!" he muttered, eyeing the rest of the baby gifts crammed in his BMW and wishing he could carry them all up to Moira's front door at once.

He struggled along her walkway with his representative offering, very pleased about his game plan. He knew, after their discussion the other evening, that he had been a fool with her. He'd had no idea she wanted deep feelings from him all along. Yes, he'd been leery, but that was behind him. What he had to do now was show her he wanted no more sterile relationships, not with her nor with their child. Some major emotional investing on his part, and Moira should understand he meant business. He hoped.

He wrangled a finger free from the bag's straw loops and rang the bell. Barking erupted immediately, growing closer than a speeding bullet. Julian grinned. The rug rats were up, and that meant Moira was, too.

The door opened a few moments later. Moira's eyes popped

wide as she took in the huge mouse. Anastasia, Sergei and Doodles surveyed the stuffed animal, then started jumping up, trying to sniff it.

"The saleslady said girl babies get teddy bears and boy babies get mice," he announced, holding the toy out of the dogs' reach. "I wasn't sure, so I went with the mouse, since the Diamonds mostly produce boys. But I can take it back, if you know it's a girl. I'd love a girl, too. Do you know?"

"Wha...?" Her mouth stayed open, as if she were either drunk or stunned.

"Are you all right?" he asked solicitously. Moira wasn't drunk. She rarely drank more than a glass of wine at any time. "Dammit, woman! That's it! Get in the car. I'm taking you to the hospital right now—"

She waved her hands. "I'm fine. Just shocked. What *is* this?"

Julian smiled proudly, very pleased with himself once more. "I went shopping for the baby."

Her expression turned odd, and he was as unsure of himself as he had been proud a second ago. She stepped back into the house and said, "I've got to sit down."

"Oh, God." Julian dumped mouse and bag and grabbed for her, afraid she was about to faint.

"What are you doing?" she asked, stiffening in his arms.

"Aren't you fainting?" he asked.

"Not that I'm aware of."

"But you said you had to sit down."

"Because I'm shocked that you went shopping for the baby."

He let her go. "I've been a jerk at times, I admit that, but you obviously don't know me very well." He paused. "That's my fault, too."

She said nothing.

He noticed the dogs crawling all over the mouse. "Hey! Scoot! That's not for you!"

He grabbed it up. Doodles came with it, little needle teeth gripping the material like it was the dog's last meal. Julian reached under the dog to pry it away. Doodles growled.

"No!" Julian roared in Doodles's ear.

The dog yipped and let go. Julian held the Pom tightly around its furry middle, the canine almost as light as air. Doodles opened and shut his mouth several times, as if to rid his tongue of excess mouse fur, then looked up at Julian once before licking his hand in clear apology. Julian set the dog down on the step. Anastasia and Sergei sniffed their brother before the three of them trotted back to Moira.

She picked up the bag and looked in it. "Oh! Julian, you bought rattles and a baby mobile." She shuffled through the bag as she walked back into the house. "Oh, and more stuffed animals. And a little football!"

"I was a punter for my college," Julian said, following her. "Who knows, maybe our daughter could be, too."

"And a soccer ball. And a baseball." She turned to him. "Julian, you don't like sports."

"Actually, I do. I just never get a chance to watch them anymore. Too busy with work." He realized he was making one of her points about him all too well. "I want to get back to it. Once I get past the takeover problems."

She held up a videotape— *"In and Out?"*

He snatched it away. "That's not for the baby! I just stuck it in there. I thought we could watch it tonight. You and I."

Moira grinned at him, very amused. "At least it's not a Streisand musical."

"Ha, ha, very funny." He set the stuffed mouse on a chair. "I'll be back."

He went to his car and gathered up as many packages as he could. When he got inside her foyer, he unceremoniously dumped them on the floor.

"Julian!" Moira gaped.

"There's more." Two armloads later, he set the last of the

packages down in the foyer, including a portable bath filled with bath toys. He grinned at her astonishment and said, "Whenever you're ready, you can go to The Baby's Cradle and pick out whatever crib you want. I arranged it with the owner. They had a couple of spectacular ones, Moira, all soft white, sort of like a space-age crib, and another was a replica of a Louis XIV piece. I couldn't choose, and I didn't want to guess what you wanted. Just get it, and I'll pay for it."

"Now, I've really got to sit down." She did. On the steps. Tears trickled down her cheeks as she stared at the gifts. "I don't know what to say."

"Don't say anything. Just enjoy." He sniffed. "Got any coffee? I was in a hurry to show you everything, and I haven't had breakfast yet."

"In the kitchen…" Her voice trailed away. She clenched her jaw for a moment and closed her eyes. Suddenly her eyelids flew up and she bolted off the steps. In a blink she was in the powder room. The door was left open, and Julian didn't have to hear to know she was ill again.

He went into the tiny room and braced his arm under her, his other hand across her forehead. When she was finally spent, she rose shakily to her feet.

"I'm sorry," she said, not looking at him.

"It's okay for me. But I'm worried for you," he replied, rubbing her back.

"The doctor says a few more weeks and it'll be over. It should have been over already, but my mother says she was sick nearly every day her entire pregnancy with me. God, I hope I'm not," she added fervently. "I am so sick and tired of being so sick and tired."

Julian smiled. He kissed her hair, feeling protective of her. "I couldn't do this, have a baby."

"No kidding."

They walked out of the bathroom, him helping her. "Why

don't you go back to bed? I'll stick around to make sure you're okay."

"But I want to see the presents you bought," she replied, like a little kid. Her cheeks already had their color back.

Julian smiled. "Then lie down on the sofa, and I'll show them to you."

He helped her to the sofa, even though she walked more strongly with each step, her temporary indisposition passing about as quickly as it had arrived. Moira settled on the sofa. The dogs hopped up one by one and curled at her feet, behind her calves and by her belly as she lay on her side.

Julian unveiled all the gifts he had bought. The little nightgowns and T-shirts, the charming outfits, the baby bottles, the bassinet, the stroller and more toys and more toys.

"Julian, this is all so wonderful," she said, delighting him with her delight. "I can't believe you walked into a store and bought all this. Especially the little gowns and tees."

"Well, I went into the baby section of a department store and just told the lady I was having a baby and I needed everything," he said. "She picked it all out."

Moira chuckled. "Now that's more like you."

"You make me sound like…I don't know, but not good," he complained. "I really wanted to do this, Moira, just for you and the baby."

She smiled tremulously. "You are sweet. I'm sorry about making you sound like an ogre. I only meant that no man is going to ooh and aah over baby nighties, let alone even think to buy them. You especially could lead the pack on that score."

"I don't know," he said. "I liked picking the toys myself and I examined and approved everything the lady brought to me. I must be in touch with my feminine side."

"Despite the video, I don't think you have to worry about that." She laughed. "Someone told me once that some men mimic the pregnancy symptoms. This should be interesting."

"Please." He shuddered. Holding her when she was ill was tough enough, let alone experiencing it himself.

The dogs, almost as one, started scratching furiously at their necks, whimpering while they did.

"Damn!" Moira said, putting her hand over her eyes. "The poor things have fleas, a hazard of summer. I planned to dip them this morning, but it'll have to wait now until I'm up to it."

"I'll dip them," Julian volunteered.

"You!" She scoffed. "Thanks, but that's okay."

"No. Really. Besides, you shouldn't be around anything like that, should you? It's chemicals."

"I suppose not." She frowned. "I didn't think of it. I only saw the dogs scratching and itching and knew it was flea time again."

"That's settled. What do I do?"

Moira gazed at him, clearly assessing his ability to handle the job. At last she said, "It's not difficult. I've got the stuff in the kitchen already mixed. You just wipe it on their bodies with a rag, starting at their head and working back. Get it everywhere, even in their ears and between their toes."

"Yuck," Julian muttered. Although the dogs were finally a little better with him, he doubted they were game enough for him to dip them. Better him than Moira though. "Okay."

"Take Anastasia first," Moira advised. "She's the worst, and if she smells it on the others, she hides under the bed and is hell to drag out. Sergei never realizes he's getting the torture until you actually start putting it on him, but he's not too bad even then. Doodles, the little dingdong, actually likes it."

"Okay." He got up and approached Anastasia, coaxing her prettily in a singsong voice. "Come on, sweetie, let's go have a...fun time out in the kitchen."

"Take the pot out in the backyard and wear gloves. They're on the counter."

"And we'll have fun out in the backyard, too," Julian amended, not missing a singsong beat.

He picked Anastasia up, without incident, and carried her into the kitchen. He spotted the pot on the stove. It was clearly filled with the liquid dip, the gloves on the counter just a short distance away. Anastasia squirmed when she saw the pot and gloves, but to his surprise she settled down, even sniffing the pot gingerly. She actually tried to lick the contents.

Julian held it away, saying, "Honey, I don't think you want to do that."

He juggled dog, pot and gloves in his arms, while using his elbow to turn down the handle on one of Moira's terrace doors so he could go outside to the deck. He was careful not to spill any of the liquid. Who knew what the stuff could do to deck finishes.

Julian set dog and pot on the grass, getting down on his knees himself. He wished he had worn jeans rather than Armani casual trousers and a good golf shirt. But he got to work.

Anastasia fussed at first, when he stroked the dip around her neck to begin. Then she stilled and her nose twitched a few times, faster and faster. The dog relaxed and "grinned," her lips pulled back and her tongue out and panting happily.

"Not bad, eh, Annie?" Julian murmured, while stroking the golden liquid on the now cooperative Pomeranian. The dip had a familiar odor, not unpleasant, for which Julian was grateful. It seemed "Annie" was grateful too. When he saturated her head and muzzle, she began to lick furiously.

"Hey! Stop that!" Only the dog didn't stop. Julian frowned. "This can't be good."

He managed to finish the job, but it was a fight to keep Anastasia from licking off the dip. Granted the stuff smelled decent, he thought, if that dog killed herself, Moira would blame him. He wondered if this was what Moira meant by Anastasia "fussing" over being dipped. The moment Anastasia looked like a drowned rat, he whisked her up and put her in the laundry room, to let her dry without ruining the furniture. That he had actually thought to do this pleased him. He knew it would please Moira that he had been considerate of her house.

Moira napped on the sofa and Julian didn't disturb her as he got Sergei and Doodles. The dogs came willingly into his arms. In fact, they licked at the wet spots of his shirt while he carried them out to the deck. While he wiped down Sergei, Doodles, the dingdong, tried to stick his head directly in the pot to lap up the dip. Julian yelped and pushed the dog away, pulling the pot closer. This time Sergei tried to drink the stuff. They both licked his gloves furiously whenever he wasn't paying attention.

He managed to keep them all from killing themselves with the dip. When the chore was done, he felt very good, knowing he had helped Moira and maybe gotten closer to the rug rats in the process. The three weren't bad, when they weren't trying to take one's hand off.

Grinning, he went into the living room. Moira was still on the sofa, her eyes closed, her chest rising and falling rhythmically. He sat down on the floor next to Napping Beauty and stroked her hand, marveling at Moira's long slim fingers. He hoped the baby had her hands, not his. Especially if it was a girl, he thought, amused with the notion. More and more he knew he had been the biggest fool with Moira. Granted, never once did she give a clue that she cared for him beyond a sexual affection. Granted, he would have run if she had shown it early on, just would have run. But none of that would have stopped the truth.

"What an ass I was," he murmured, shaking his head. He would almost trade all his plans for his bank, let the takeover go through and walk away if he could reverse the clock with Moira.

As if hearing his words, Moira stirred, her eyes blinking open sleepily. She smiled and murmured, "Hi."

"Hi." He smiled back, his heart filling with an emotion that lifted him dizzyingly into the heavens. He took a breath just to settle himself back to Earth a little.

"I dreamed you came with a ton of gifts for the baby," she said, frowning in puzzlement.

Julian chuckled. "A ton is about right. I dipped the dogs, too. I put them into the laundry room, just to keep them from rubbing against everything while they're still wet."

"Oh, good." She let out a deep breath. "I'm hungry, and I actually think it's safe to eat. But I'm going easy on my tummy."

Julian helped her to her feet and walked with her into the kitchen.

"You can go ahead and let the dogs out," she said. "They'll stay in here with us."

"Okay." He opened the laundry room door and the three came rushing out, their fur a little less wet and a little more puffed up. The dogs greeted Moira enthusiastically, then ran straight to Julian, jumping and leaping on his legs, their tails wagging furiously.

"Hey, guys," he said, grinning helplessly at the trio's sudden fondness for him. He patted each one on its little, bony, still-wet, fur-covered head.

"Julian, I thought you told me you dipped the dogs," Moira said, standing by the sink.

"Right," he replied, trying to keep the dogs from licking themselves again. Maybe he shouldn't have put them in the laundry room together. He hoped they hadn't licked each other to death—literally. Time would tell.

"You couldn't have dipped them."

He looked up. "What? Yes, I did. They're still wet. See?"

She lifted a pot from the sink. "But here's the dip."

He frowned. "No, that's not it. The pot was over there. On the stove, with the gloves next to it on the counter."

Moira set the pot down. "Julian! That was my chicken broth!"

He gaped at her. "No."

"Yes! I stewed a chicken earlier for the broth. It settles my stomach so I make a lot and freeze it for working days." She started laughing. "How could you not notice the difference?"

"No," he repeated, walking over to the sink and stared at the large, banged-up pot sitting in it. Its contents had a slightly more golden color than what he had used on the dogs. He bent over and sniffed, then straightened abruptly. "That stuff smells like medicine."

"And what you used smelled like chickens, I'll bet." She laughed harder now. "Oh God…you dipped the dogs in soup stock. You're more of a dingdong than Doodles."

Julian looked over at the rug rats, walking in a circle while licking each other intently. "No wonder they were going crazy for the stuff. And no wonder they love me now."

Moira collapsed against him in laughter. "You are an amazing man, Julian."

Julian grinned and shrugged. He put his arm around Moira. She sagged into him, her whole being filled with affection for him. She also laughed herself silly.

Oh well, he thought. Clearly, a little male stupidity went a long way when it came to amusing women. Moira's relaxed features were filled with wry affection for him.

Amusing Moira was possibly a very, very good thing.

AFTER DINNER Moira found Julian sprawled on the floor in front of the den's television, his head in the fat lap of the giant mouse he'd bought. He watched an inane program, something he never did before. Anastasia, Sergei and Doodles lay across his legs like the sporran of a Scotsman's kilt.

Normally he would only watch public television, if he watched at all, and he would never lie on the floor to do so and never would the dogs be sprawled with him. But despite having to be shampooed clean and redipped properly—with proper supervision by her—the dogs had clearly decided Julian would provide another mistake of major proportion which would net them another treat to end all treats.

"I hear you laughing again," he said, not moving.

She covered her mouth to try and stifle the giggles that escaped anyway. "I think I'm going to call you Julie the Dip from now on."

"Good. Maybe a gangster name will scare the bejammers out of Parsons and they'll withdraw from the takeover of my bank." He lifted his hand and pressed the remote control he held. The movie he'd brought came on. "How about lying on the floor next to me? The mouse is well padded. We could be slobs together."

She couldn't resist. "Okay."

She sank down next to him, crossing her legs yoga-style. As she did, she had a feeling that in a few months she wouldn't be able to sit this way so easily. She probably wouldn't be able to get down on the floor, let alone up again, without a crane. Already her equilibrium didn't seem quite the same as it had just a few weeks ago.

Julian pulled her to him, forcing her to stretch out along his flank. She could feel the lean line of his ribs, the tautness of his waist and hips and the muscles in his thighs. Her blood began to pump more warmly in her veins.

She didn't want to experience any kind of sexual tension with him, but all the toys and clothes and furnishings for the baby had touched her deeply. They had been so unexpected. But the smaller kindness of dipping the dogs had wheedled its way into her heart—as did the laughter. Never in her life would she forget his surprised face when he'd discovered what he'd done. Her anger, her resentment toward him about the bet was slowly fading.

The small of her back kinked little by little, as if in a vise. She shifted around on her side, trying to find a more comfortable position. Her head had no support and she scrunched up on the stuffed mouse's leg.

"Here," he said, stretching his arm out under her neck.

"That's okay," she replied, straightening away from his body.

"I don't bite," he said, snagging her with his reach. "Just as the dogs don't try to bite me anymore."

His hand was perilously close to her derriere, and her breasts pressed against his ribs. Her pelvis all but touched his hipbone. She bent her knees to keep the intimacy at bay. She knew she ought to get up and go sit in a chair, or even ask him to leave, but the words just wouldn't come out of her mouth. She'd been trained to think on her feet, to verbalize at any moment anything that would help a client with his or her rights under the law. Now she was dumbstruck, only wanting to snuggle closer than she already was, to hook her leg over his thighs and nudge her dogs off the junction of his legs to place herself there, naked, flesh to flesh conjoined.

She tried to watch the movie. She really tried. But she couldn't concentrate on anything but Julian next to her. The sweet Julian who bought a three-foot-tall mouse for a boy baby and dipped her dogs in chicken soup. The ramifications of that ridiculous bet faded in her mind. How could she be so angry with Julian after all this?

She hadn't realized her body had unfurled itself and was warmly against him, nor that she had been stroking his side until he touched her fingers lightly, then pressed them into the hard wall of his chest. A rumble of pleasure emanated from under her palm. She chuckled. She couldn't help herself.

"That feels good," he said.

She turned her face up toward his as he spoke. He cupped her chin and kissed her deeply. His tongue mated with hers in slow, blissful strokes. Somewhere inside Moira a smidgen of logic pointed out that kissing a man who would make such a bet that used a baby for money wasn't the wisest move. She didn't care. Her body throbbed with the desire she knew all too well and was recently denied. Her breasts ached for his mouth. Her belly quivered at his nearness.

"You taste so good," he murmured, shifting to his side to draw her even closer to him. The dogs, dislodged, plopped onto the rug unnoticed by either of them. Disgruntled, they hopped up on a wing chair and piled into a snoozing mound again.

Moira couldn't stop the whimper that escaped her as his fingers deftly caressed her breasts. Tender from her pregnancy, she felt every touch as an electric shock. Each left her gasping, while the throbbing deep within her became almost unbearable. She clutched at his shirt, then pulled the buttons free to run her fingers through his chest hair. She'd never told him how much touching his chest turned her on. Many, many times she had nearly screamed with delight just to feel the silky-rough strands tickling her palms. His nipples were well-defined, small nubs that just made her go insane. She always wanted to lick them, worry them with her teeth, let herself really just do whatever she wanted. But always she had had to be in control, to keep her emotions tamped down so she wouldn't be hurt by the inevitable rejection from him.

Well, the inevitable had happened. A far different inevitable than she'd expected. It didn't matter anymore, she realized. She no longer had to hold back her emotions; they were out in the open now, exposed by a chocolate cake over his head. One time, she thought, taking a deep breath, she could indulge herself this one time—and show him what he had really been missing in an emotional-physical relationship.

With a triumphant, very feminine smile, Moira bent forward and kissed Julian's chest. He sucked in his breath, clearly surprised by her sudden aggressiveness. With biting little kisses, she worked her way around his skin until she found a flat nipple. Her tongue rasped across it like a contented cat's.

"Moira," he murmured, intimately brushing against her thighs. His voice held tenderness and wonder.

She became fiercer, even more sure of herself and what she was doing. She teased and tormented with sure mouth and fingers. She played with his senses, heightening her own, as well. In her need to arouse, she became more aroused. Her body cried out for a quick release, but she refused to indulge it.

Their clothes slowly fell away as Julian at last began to tease and torment her back. His mouth was pure heat on her own impossibly swollen nipples. She writhed against him as he ran his tongue around the hard points. She was hot and cold, emboldened and submissive, hurting so sweetly that she thought she would die from it. His lips were firm, nipping on her flesh, even more so as they lowered to her slightly rounded waist.

Julian became reverent, kissing her tenderly once, twice. His hand covered the new shape of her. He looked up and smiled. "Honey, it's amazing."

She smiled back, tears pushing at her eyelids. "I know."

He reached up and kissed her mouth, their lips clinging in a moment of incredible satisfaction that had nothing to do with baser pleasures. Moira's heart melted to share such a kiss. She was glad that she hadn't listened to the little voice of logic. If she had, she never would have had such a moment like this with Julian.

The kiss turned more sensuous. Primitive needs rose to the surface, and Moira became the aggressor again. Suddenly she wanted Julian so badly she didn't need more intimate stroking. She didn't need anything but him inside her. Throwing her leg over his hips, she rose over him, her mouth not releasing his from the kiss. Julian's hands cupped her breasts, his thumbs rubbing hard over her nipples. She cried out into his mouth as tiny shocks of pleasure ran all through her body. Instead of bringing contentment, they only urged her forward.

She took him easily inside herself until she completely surrounded him in her hot, moist flesh. He gasped for breath, and she opened her eyes into cat's slits. His face was flushed with his pleasure, his features like hard stone under the red glow of his skin. And yet it was obvious that he was savoring their union, as if it were unique, an experience he could only have with her. He opened his eyes and stared at her, his gaze searching her features. She knew he would see the same incredible joy at their joining that she saw in his.

"I love you," she said, not willing to skimp one bit on truly making love.

She didn't wait for an answer, for she knew none would be coming. Instead, she began thrusting, nearly releasing her body from his before plunging down the full length of him. His hands guided her hips as he met her each time. Their bodies knew every trick, every movement that heightened and hastened their completion. Moira moved harder and faster, riding him until the first great pull of pleasure burst through her belly. It surged along her veins, that incredible rush of satisfaction. She cried out with it, as it engulfed her totally, bringing her down into the warm darkness.

Julian cried out with her, his body shaking with his own release. His hands nearly crushed her as he held on, but she didn't care. He was with her for the moment, and that was all that mattered.

FOR LONG MINUTES Moira sprawled on top of Julian. She said nothing, just content to hear his heart beating rhythmically. His skin was warm, warming hers. His arms were strong around her shoulders and back, his fingers slowly stroking her shoulder blades.

"Marry me," he said, breaking the silence.

Moira closed her eyes against the impulsive answer. How she wanted to make an impulsive answer. But she wouldn't. He didn't love her. Even knowing that if he didn't win his grandfather's money, Julian would probably lose his bank in a takeover, she still couldn't say the word. The bank meant everything to him. She couldn't blame him for wanting to win, for wanting to see his dream of rebuilding Diamond Bank back to where it used to be. But not at the expense of her child…their child.

"No, Julian," she said finally. He would have to marry elsewhere to fulfill the terms of the bet. He probably would.

Her heart seemed to seep out of her slowly, burning up with pain as it faded away inside her chest. Julian said nothing, just let out a short breath of acquiescence.

Loving Julian was just not enough.

Chapter Thirteen

Julian cursed and pounded on his favorite den chair. No one was there to hear it.

Probably just as well, he admitted, disgusted with himself. He was miserable, too. He had proposed to Moira, a sponta- neous emotion that had erupted out of him at the most intimate of moments...and after intense lovemaking. They had made more love during the night. The next day. And every night since.

It was getting better and better each time, he thought ab- sently, wishing the Historical Society wasn't meeting at her house tonight. Otherwise he would be there in a heartbeat, bear- ing more baby gifts and himself, for her pleasure.

His brain steered him back to the most important issue before him. She had said no. After saying she loved him, after he had asked her to marry him because he *needed* to, she turned him down. In the saddest voice he had ever heard from her, she had turned him down. He had been afraid to ask again, afraid he would hear that voice again. Never had his house sounded so damned empty.

"It's your own damn fault," he said to no one. But he hung hope on their subsequent lovemaking. All wasn't lost while they were still doing that.

On his lap sat a pile of papers, faxes sent over by the Pitts- burgh attorneys regarding possible ways to block the hostile takeover. He knew he ought to be working on them, although none looked good. He really should be in Pittsburgh, working night and day with the lawyers Moira had hired to outfox Parsons. He had lost his bid for expanding, to them; he wouldn't lose his own bank. Diamond Bank, except for a five-year period after his family had sold off the chain, had been the flagship bank of the family banking firm. It had been important to him to restore that flagship to the town and begin to build from there.

Logic told him the quickest and best way to outfox his enemies was to marry *any* woman and fulfill the technical terms of the bet. Old Bart could huff and puff but he'd pay up. In fact, he'd probably admire what his younger grandson had done. Julian couldn't chuckle over the notion.

His heart grew sick at even the thought of anyone but Moira. He couldn't do it—not until he'd done everything to persuade her to marry him. How could she have his baby and *not* marry him? It was ridiculous.

Julian sat straight up, his bank problems completely forgotten once again. It *was* ridiculous, and that's how he had to appeal to Moira. Somewhere under the emotions, she had a fiercely logical mind. So logical he'd often thought she was wasted on wills and estate plannings and small-town property disputes, even though she'd eschewed the corporate work left behind in New York.

A baby needed its mother and its father. Now that was logic.

All of sudden, the entire problem smacked him right in the forehead like a two-by-four. The resounding *bang* nearly burst his brain. This wasn't about logic. This was about love.

He loved her.

"Idiot! Idiot, idiot, idiot!" he shouted, smacking himself in the forehead with his palm just for good measure. Of course he loved her. He always had, probably, but had been too stubborn to recognize it. He had to tell her. Now. He glanced at his watch. "Damn! That stinking meeting is still going on."

He rose from his chair, anyway, too frustrated and too restless to sit idly by while time was wasted. To hell with it, he thought, heading for his car keys and his vehicle.

Cars lined the road outside her house when he arrived there, and he had to park way down the street. But he walked right inside without knocking, knowing she'd leave the door unlocked for the society people to come in. About twenty people sat in chairs set up theater-style in her living room. That upstanding historical member, mayor Robert Helpern, who was becoming as big a pain in the butt for him as for Jeff, glared at him. Julian glared back. He'd deal with Helpern later. The only ones missing from the meeting were Anastasia, Sergei and Doodles. Julian half wished they were here. He needed allies, even newfound, canine ones.

Moira's mother rose, her mouth open in astonishment. But it was Moira who spoke. "Julian! What are you doing here?"

"Making history," he said. "I love you."

"What!" The babble of voices came from everyone but her. Moira just stared at him. She said nothing.

"I love you," he said stubbornly. "I just realized it tonight. I love you."

"Julian, you're making a scene," Jenny Carson said.

"Damn straight I am," he said. "Moira, you *have* to marry me."

"No." The word was so final it almost chilled his heart.

"The baby needs its father."

Their audience "ohhed" but Julian ignored them. Having an audience was an advantage. Maybe Moira would agree to his proposal just to shut him up. Julian grinned. He'd take her any way he could get her, at this point.

"This is the best thing since Lila Mae Turner shot her husband in the babymakers for cheating on her during the Fourth of July Community Picnic," someone commented. Everyone snorted with laughter. "That was in 1931, and we haven't had a community picnic since."

"I think Julian's babymakers have already done the job," someone else said.

"See!" Jenny Carson exclaimed. "You're making a complete ass of yourself, Julian."

"Probably," he admitted, not caring. "Moira, marry me."

"No."

"But I love you!"

"I'm sorry." She was so stiff and mechanical when she answered. She loosened her stance as she looked around the room. "Everyone, the meeting is adjourned for tonight."

"We have to have a vote," Robert Helpern said. "*Robert's Rules.*"

"Stick *Robert's Rules* where the sun doesn't shine," Jenny Carson told him. "If Julian is intent on making an ass of himself, then let's not give him a forum to embarrass my daughter further."

A few others protested the disbanding, but it was from nosiness rather than any sense of meeting protocol. Jenny Carson herded them all out of the house. Julian gazed at Moira, who gazed back.

When her mother returned, she started right in. "Julian Diamond, I know you think you own the town—"

"Mom, that's enough. I want to talk to Julian alone. Okay?"

Her mother pursed her lips. "Are you sure?"

"Absolutely."

As Jenny, clearly reluctant, gathered up her things, Julian said, "Jenny, I do love your daughter. I know you don't believe me, but I do."

Jenny only snorted, clearly dubious, but she said, "I hope so, Julian."

After Jenny left, Julian turned to Moira. "I didn't do this to embarrass you. I did it because I wanted an audience. I wanted to make a commitment to you in front of everyone." He grinned slyly. "This way I couldn't back out of it."

Moira found a chair and sat down. "I wish I could believe you."

"You can."

She shook her head. "No, I can't. Not with twenty-five million dollars on the line."

"It's got nothing to do with the bet!" he said, exasperated with her. "I realized tonight that I've loved you for a long time. I was scared of being used again, and I was afraid of commitment. Gun-shy they call it. Love-shy is probably more accurate. But I was an idiot about it."

"And what made you suddenly realize this?" she asked.

Pulling one of the extra chairs over, he sat down opposite her. He wanted to reach for her hand, but was afraid of being rejected. It occurred to him that he had spent too much time worrying about that before. Whatever her response, *he* had to try.

He took her hand. She didn't attempt to shake him off, leaving his fears unfounded. Taking heart, he held her fingers tightly, lacing his between them. Her skin was warm and silky, the touch giving him hope.

"I realized how I felt tonight because I was hurt," he said. "When you refused to marry me, I felt like I lost my best friend, Moira. The other half of myself. And then it hit me. I love you."

"Julian…" Her voice choked for a moment. "Julian, I wish I could believe you. I do. But I think you think you feel this way because you're losing much more than a best friend. You're in danger of losing your bank. You need that bet. And I think you want the baby tied to you, acknowledged to the world that it's yours. The baby *is* yours. I won't deny it. You'll have all the visitation rights you want, joint custody. I know the contract I drew up was out of anger. Julian, we can work that out. But I won't marry you, not when I know that you're fighting to win the bet. I can't trust you."

"Dammit!" Frustrated, he dropped her hand, stood and began to pace. "Look, look at our relationship. We've been together a year. A whole year! Doesn't that count for anything about my feelings for you? Why the hell would I be around for an entire year if I didn't love you? I realized that tonight, too." He stopped and faced her. "It's got nothing to do with the baby and the bet. How you can even think it, is incredible."

"Then we're at a stalemate," Moira replied, her voice trembling, "Because I do think it. I can't help but think it when your sudden declarations come at a time when you've got so much to lose if I don't marry you. I don't blame you. I understand. I do. But, Julian, I will not use our child to save your bank."

"You're not using the child!" he exclaimed, waving his hands. "Now that's the hormones talking nonsense."

"I wish. Julian, what if we can't stop the Parsons takeover?" she asked. "What if you need an immediate infusion of cash, twenty-five million dollars, to buy up enough stock to hold an overwhelming majority, keeping Parsons out? You know where it's sitting. You know what you can do to get it. What would you do?"

He paused, not wanting to face what his answer might be. He wondered if he would be so desperate to marry someone else if he couldn't persuade her to be his wife.

"See?" she said sadly. "You have to think about it."

"Of course I have to think about it," he said, angry with her obtuseness. "You asked me a question that needs thinking about."

"You don't get it."

"Help me, Moira," he said, desperate as he felt her emotionally slipping away from him. "Help me *to* get it. I want to marry you, I love you, and I have been an idiot. I'm still being an idiot."

She sighed. Her face was pinched and drawn as if she were very weary. "I don't know what to think."

"That's good," he said, gathering hope. "Let's do this.

Don't reject me outright, just start to think about what I've said. How I've been trying to change. Let me show you that I mean what I've said tonight.'' He grinned. ''I'll keep saying I love you in front of everybody. Wherever you want. The town council, the Boy Scouts, the mall, the Campfire Girls. I'll be a declaring fool for you.''

Her expression cleared, and she smiled at him. But she didn't agree.

''Moira,'' he began.

''I'll think about it,'' she said finally.

Julian let out a huge sigh of relief.

THE COUNCIL meeting had more of an audience than usual.

Moira looked at the crowd and felt sick to her stomach. But it wasn't the baby and it wasn't that she was being openly discussed as township solicitor. It was Julian's marriage proposal.

Once, she would have given everything to hear one from him. But now it was too late because it was for the bet's sake. Probably even for the baby's sake. Julian was right; he wasn't an ogre and he would feel responsibility to his child. The proposal hadn't been for *their* sakes and that was what made it unacceptable.

Even now as she looked around the room one more time, she didn't see Julian here to support her. Oh, he could load a luxury car with stuffed mice, but he would never understand what truly mattered.

''Solicitor candidates,'' the council secretary said into a dais microphone, announcing the next item on the agenda.

The council had already discussed the matter in a ''working'' session, so this was a formality nomination and acceptance. Moira's supporters had urged her to be present this evening. While no one had said exactly who had won the job, she had received smiles from most of the council members when they had filed in to take their seats. Only Mayor Helpern was sour-faced.

"I nominate Moira Carson for township solicitor," Bob Millstein said, looking especially pleased. His call was immediately seconded.

"Discussion?" Paula's father asked.

No one spoke…at first.

"I have grave misgivings about this," Robert Helpern said, smiling slightly. "Ms. Carson, while qualified on paper, has several conflicts of interests that would preclude her eligibility for the position."

Moira's stomach churned faster. She could feel every eye in the room on her back, and didn't like where this was going.

"We discussed this," someone said. "And she wouldn't be taking the job until the first of the year, anyway, when Joe officially retires. By then those matters should be resolved."

"What if they're not?" Helpern said, glaring at his fellow council people. "Even if they are, several of those matters are diametrically opposed to this council's decisions. I don't think we want to hire someone who's representing people suing us."

"Maybe we wouldn't be sued if we used our brains upon occasion," Bob Millstein snapped in clear exasperation.

"One more outburst like that and we'll censure you," Helpern threatened. The rest of the council looked ready to protest that, but they remained silent. Helpern continued, "I have reason to believe, as well, that Ms. Carson will need a leave of absence the moment she takes the job."

"Why you old goat," she whispered, angry that he was using her pregnancy as yet another objection. Next, he'd be asking for a scarlet *A* to be sewn on her chest.

"We can do better," the mayor said before finally shutting up.

"No, you can't."

The voice came from the back of the room. Moira turned, although she knew who she would find. Julian strode up the aisle, tie crooked, hair ruffled. He looked exhausted and ready to shoot someone.

Helpern banged down the gavel. "The public session is *after* all our business. You can speak then, Diamond. Not before."

A low rail separated the public seating area from the raised council dais, which doubled as a municipal court on Tuesdays. Julian hopped right over it and walked right up to the dais like he owned the place. Technically he had once, since the Diamond family had built the city hall.

Moira grinned, just liking the way the cavalry had ridden in to her rescue. Her application was in a shambles, and she would never get the job now, not with an open objection against her, but it was wonderful to see Julian taking up her cause. Hell, she thought, it was just wonderful to see Julian.

Helpern banged his gavel. "Order! Order! Where's the chief? We need this man ejected for disrupting the meeting."

"First of all, anyone can require a legitimate leave of absence right after taking a job," Julian said, speaking over Helpern's continued pounding, and taking advantage of the chief being especially slow in removing him from the room. "What you imply and the reason you imply it, Mister Mayor, is outright sex discrimination, something I'm sure the council will not tolerate. Second, Ms. Carson would not put herself up for a candidacy if she felt she would have a conflict of interest when she would actually take over the job. You object because she's opposing injustice *by* the council. This council and the people of Diamond Mount ought to take a good look at what's going on here. We have a long-standing variance suddenly revoked against my brother's sanctuary, a place of open space and learning for our children."

The room gasped, then burst open with conversation.

Julian didn't let that stop him. "I have no wish to criticize council's current legal advice, and I'm sure he advised you properly. Whether he was listened to, is another matter. However, when individual council members interfere with the commerce of the town, you better have a solicitor who *will* do the right thing even if you don't like it. Moira Carson will be best for the town after our current solicitor retires. Okay, Bill, I'm moving along now.''

Julian grinned at the police chief who had finally come up and taken his arm, to lead him away.

"Moira, honey," he said, when he passed by, "don't forget to bail me out."

"I won't," she promised. She stood and said to the council, "I remove my name from consideration. I thank those who supported me for the job."

The room erupted, the inhabitants of Diamond Mount having never seen such doings in normally deadly dull council meetings. They applauded Julian and Moira, who followed him out of the council chambers. Mayor Helpern banged and banged his gavel, shouting for order. He was completely ignored as people called out their personal complaints about council agenda items—and other things they didn't like. Helpern banged so hard that the gavel broke, the head flying into the crowd to whack someone on the shoulder.

"Hey, Moira!" a man shouted over a howl of pain. "Joe Frattera's got a lawsuit over here for you."

"Tell him to come see me in my office tomorrow," she called back. "I believe I'm free to look at his case."

People hooted with laughter. The reporter for the *Call* wrote furiously on a memo pad. He looked happy as a clam in mud.

Outside council chambers, Police Chief Bill Gruden let go of Julian's arm and said, "There ya go, Julian, escorted from the fray."

"And a damned fine job you've done of it," Julian replied.

"When I got around to it," Bill amended.

They both laughed.

"Darn, and I came to bail Julian out before some inmate decided he looked cute," Moira broke in.

"Thank you." Julian put his arm around her and kissed her

on the cheek. "I'm sorry I was late. The BMW wouldn't start, and I ran all the way from the bank. Three blocks in five minutes."

Moira shook her head in amusement. Nothing like leaving it until the last moment. But she wouldn't complain. "You were right on time. In fact, you were marvelous."

Julian grinned. "The brownie points add up, I hope."

She sobered slightly. "Maybe."

"Well, I better get back in there," the chief said. "Someone's got to get that meeting in order and it ain't gonna be old Robbie boy. Pardon my French, but he'd make a whole lot more headway if he stopped pissing people off, although he's been like this since kindergarten. Don't know how Darlene married him."

The chief trooped back inside, although a peek inside showed the fracas had cooled down somewhat.

"Why did you withdraw?" Julian asked, frowning. "You heard that crowd in there. They wanted you for the job."

Moira smiled. "That was nice, wasn't it? But it would have been hell working with a divided council. If someone doesn't want you there, they will spend their whole time actively trying to oust you. Besides, I was more flattered than anything else to be offered the job. I really don't have the time for it."

"More fool them." He chuckled. "I think you got a new client tonight. Did you see that gavel head fly across the room? I thought it was a meteorite."

She laughed with him as they walked out of the building. "Did you see the *Call* reporter? The article will be on page one."

"I bet he's cursing that he didn't have a photographer to catch the action. By the way, can I bum a lift home?"

"Sure, but don't you want to check on your car?"

He shook his head. "The damn thing can rot tonight."

She drove him home, the two of them laughing over the proceedings. She kept glancing over at Julian, just wanting to admire his smiles and amused expression. The whole of Diamond Mount knew about them now. Probably after the Historical Society meeting, the town had to know about the baby. The funny thing was that at one time she had been so fastidious in her relationship that she might have packed up and moved out of town. Now she didn't truly care. People could think what they wanted. She had a feeling that tonight she'd garnered many sympathies.

When Julian asked her in to have a coffee, she didn't refuse, although she opted for a fruit juice and seltzer water. He brought her a huge tumblerful, and a glass the same size for himself.

Moira gazed at it mournfully.

"What's wrong?" he asked.

She grinned. "I drink this much juice, and I'll be up all night, anyway."

He chuckled, catching her meaning. "I'll make it smaller."

"No." She took a healthy swallow. "I doubt I'll sleep much, anyway, after tonight's excitement, so I might as well have something to do. Julian, you were wonderful."

"I was, wasn't I?" He looked far too pleased with himself. "And Helpern always thought my brother gave him the most trouble."

"Stir up a banker and you stir up a sleeping lion."

"Piss off an attorney and you live in court forever."

She laughed. "I'm not angry. Surprisingly, I'm grateful. That job would have been too much. And I would have had to take a leave of absence."

Something in her stomach fluttered, as if confirming her words. She frowned, knowing she'd felt the funky butterflies before, just a wisp upon occasion then gone. All of a sudden she knew exactly what it was.

"The baby!" she exclaimed in delight, holding her tummy.

"What! What!" Julian leaped up, dumping his drink unheeded on the expensive, hand-knotted, Afghan rug. He rushed to her, falling on his knees before her, his big hands hovering while he clearly decided on whether to hold her or catch her. "What's wrong!"

"I felt the baby," she said, looking at him, her eyes filling with happy tears. "I just recognized these little flutterings I've been getting lately are the baby moving. I thought it was gas."

He gaped at her for a moment longer, then sank back on his heels and laughed. "Thanks a lot. My kid is *not* gas."

"I know that. Oh!" The flutters hit again.

"Can I feel?" he asked.

She nodded and took his hand, pressing it firmly against her abdomen. The baby was quiet for a moment, then fluttered, hard this time.

"That little gurgle? That's him?" Julian asked, looking unsure.

"Either that or it is gas."

He grinned when it happened again. "I think we've got a baby in there."

He looked up at her, gazing at her with naked emotion in his beautiful green eyes. "Moira, marry me."

She smiled sadly. "No, Julian. You know I can't."

"The baby needs a stable home and two parents," he argued.

"The baby needs loving parents and parents who love each other. We can provide the first part separately, Julian, and not marry just for his sake. Or for money's sake. We have to marry for our sake, and we wouldn't be doing that."

"Yes, we would."

"No, you know in your heart we wouldn't."

She leaned forward and kissed him. Gently, tenderly. She touched his face, tracing his temples, his cheeks, the line of his jaw. He touched her as gently, as tenderly, learning from her. But he had to have love in his heart, and that, she knew despite his words, might never happen.

She loved him back instead. Loved him with all the emotions she had…touched him with her soul as well as her fingers...accepted him inside herself with all the joy...and wrapped her love around him in the aftermath, wanting nothing more than for him to feel what she felt.

"Marry me," he said at last, as they lay naked and spent on the intricate designs woven into the wool under Moira's back.

Moira shook her head, not trusting her voice to give the right answer. How she wished it was the wrong answer. Until she knew he loved her for her, she couldn't give any other response.

The baby fluttered inside her once more, as if he or she understood.

Jeff & Julian

~ Part Five ~

All Bets Are In

Chapter Fourteen

The dinner wasn't a happy one.

Seated in his carved wing chair, Jeff stretched his feet out on his worn carpet in front of the unlit fireplace. Absently he swirled the fine brandy Julian had brought in the big globe snifter. They had sought each other out for a meal together, both commiserating over the mess of their love lives. Chinese takeout cartons littered the floor at their feet. Popeye rooted among them, looking for leftovers. He wasn't having much success.

"Look out below!"

"Bombs away!"

"Geez, it's the cops."

Screeching followed each pronouncement from the parrots' room, the squawks growing louder and louder until the cacophony of sound hit earsplitting decibels.

Julian glanced up from the fireplace. "What the heck are they doing in there?"

"Seeing who can intimidate the others by being the loudest, along with a medley of thirties movies, I think," Jeff replied, explaining the parrots' chatter. "I've got a women's club appearance coming up, and it's mostly older women, so I added a few things for the mature crowd. If they break into 'Boogie-Woogie Bugle Boy,' don't be surprised."

"Who? The parrots or the women? And why is Popeye staring at me like that? Am I dinner tonight?"

Jeff smiled at his brother's worried expression. "In answer to your questions… The parrots will sing, not the women, and he's staring because he likes you. Probably he's trying to figure out why you're not me."

"I wish I was," Julian muttered.

Jeff sat up, frowning. "No, you don't. Paula was offered a big book contract. She's moving out on her own."

"That's good, isn't it?" Julian asked. "Hasn't she been under her father's influence too long?"

"Wouldn't you think that if she moved out of her father's influence, she would move straight in with me?" Jeff shook his head. "I lived for that day, once upon a time. Like up until last week. Hell, you know it better than anyone how much I wanted us to be together. I still want it. But she won't marry me now, all because of that stupid bet of our grandfather's. Instead, she'll only be working for me for a little while longer, until I find another receptionist, and then she's gone. To write her books. Without me."

"I didn't know you were her collaborator," Julian said.

"From your mouth to God's ears, because I'd kill to collaborate with her every night for the rest of my life. But you know what hurts the most? Her boys. They're here every day. I've become a part-time daddy to them, Julian, and it's meant a lot to me. More than I want to admit. But every day they leave, they go elsewhere, and I'm not part of the rest of their day. I can no more wall off those feelings than I ever could wall off what I feel for Paula."

"I'll have that right from the beginning," Julian said, patting Popeye on the head when the vulture gazed up sorrowfully at him. "Moira won't marry me, either. She's having my baby and she won't marry me."

"She's pregnant!" Jeff gaped at him in shock. "You never said."

"I didn't know until recently," Julian replied, feeling depressed. "But it didn't feel right to say anything to you."

Jeff was silent for a moment. Julian looked over to find his brother's jaw working. Slowly a smile spread over Jeff's features, reaching his eyes. He patted Julian's arm. "Congratulations! A baby. I want to be jealous, but it's too terrific to not like it. Damn! I'll be an uncle."

"Godfather," Julian said, grinning. "*If* Moira lets me at the christening."

"To hell with you," Jeff said. "I know she'll let me."

"Unfortunately I think you're right."

They grew quiet, the only sound left was Popeye's beak scrabbling through the *lo mein* carton.

"Your child," Jeff said in awe. "You know, I felt like Paula's boys are mine."

"You'll marry someday. You already did it once when she left you before," Julian replied. "Then you'll have children of your own and get past that feeling."

"No, that's the point, Julian. We're more fraternal than we look. I can't have children the natural way. That's what broke up my marriage." Jeff stared at his brother, finding his long-kept secret now easy to reveal. "I'm sterile. I never told anyone before, not even you, because I felt…I don't know, just a lot of things back then. It's a helluva thing to announce to people. After a while, it didn't matter anymore, to tell anyone. What was the point?"

"Wait a minute," Julian said. "How can you be sterile? You took up Grandfather's bet."

Jeff chuckled ruefully. "I got goaded into it. We both did, remember? I wondered what I was going to do, and then Paula came home with two sons. At first, it hurt that she had kids that weren't mine. But they clearly had no father who cared, and I would have no natural children of my own. I began to think I'd win on a technicality. Old Bart said we had to be 'in the family way.' He didn't say we had to achieve that state through only one method.''

Julian stared at him. "Damn, you could have been a lawyer."

"No birds in it." Jeff shrugged and added, "I guess I got to feeling like I did have children in an unusual fashion, sort of like the egg laid in the wrong nest and the chick gets raised by the parents who are there, not the biological ones. The bet mattered less and less where the boys were concerned. I imprinted in those boys."

"I'm sorry, Jeff," Julian said, sighing. "Sorry as hell for both of us. We were Diamonds, raised with everything we wanted. Except parents being around. Probably that's where we learned to put up emotional barriers. Look at me. I was so intent on not being used again by a woman that I've thrown away the best relationship I ever could have had. Just tossed it. And can I get it back? No. Moira won't budge from not marrying me. Even her dogs finally like me. And I actually like them."

Jeff laughed, those three little characters having delighted him for years.

"It's ironic," Julian added. "I had no idea Moira was already pregnant when that stupid bet was made. None."

Jeff nodded. "If it weren't for the sanctuary, I wouldn't be in this predicament. Paula would have come home and nature would have taken its natural course. We would be together finally. I truly believe that. I think that's why she came back here when her life in California was over."

"Probably." Julian straightened as the sounds from the other room reached crescendo volume again. "How can you stand the noise?"

Jeff smiled. "It fills up the house, little brother."

"I think I'd rather have those Hanson kids than that." Julian looked at his brother. "Jeff, you could still win the bet. Just marry a woman with children. It doesn't have to be Paula."

"Fancy you helping me," Jeff commented. "You could do the same. Just marry a woman and get her pregnant, not necessarily in that order."

Julian grinned and gazed into his now-empty brandy snifter. "Actually, my little attorney pointed out another loophole to the bet. I don't have to be married to the person with whom I am in the family way."

Jeff burst out laughing, amused by how much their grandfather didn't think about the terms of the bet he'd proposed. Then he stopped laughing. "You don't suppose he was mean enough to leave loopholes on purpose, do you? Think about what marrying a woman with children or deliberately getting someone pregnant just for money would do to those kids."

Julian shivered. "I know I'm pretty mercenary, but I couldn't have done that. If only I didn't have this other bank breathing down my neck. Twenty-five million would buy me a nice hunk of stock, enough to keep my majority voting power."

"Twenty-five million would endow the sanctuary for twenty years at least," Jeff said, sighing with regret. "I looked into buying another property, but I can't afford to do it. What I can afford would need so much work that it wouldn't be affordable. It's looking bleak for me."

"Maybe Moira will get that variance decision reversed. Everyone was pretty angry with the council the other night. And you've got that petition going. I see it everywhere." Julian laughed. "In fact, I've caught hell a few times from people because I haven't signed on their particular petition list. Hell, I can only sign the damn thing once, and I already did. But my point is that public opinion goes a long way toward government decisions."

"I can't depend on it. I'm going to start looking into zoos and other sanctuaries to take the prey birds. The others I can probably support through the vet practice." He shook his head.

"Paula really revived that for me. She revived a lot of things for me."

"Would you marry someone else to win the bet?" Julian asked.

"No." The answer was easy. "The way's clear for you."

"I can't marry anyone else, either," Julian admitted. "It kills me to say it, thinking about that money. But I can't."

"So what do we do now?"

"Good question. I guess we move in and become old farts together."

The notion of what to do hung in the back of Jeff's mind the next day as he took a tour of a house on the outskirts of Diamond Mount.

Paula put her arms wide and whirled about the center of the deserted living room. "What do you think?"

Truthfully, he couldn't tell her. He'd walked through the place with a feeling of impending doom. She was making a new life for herself and her sons, while his was falling apart.

"It's nice," he said finally.

She dropped her arms and looked at him. Her beautiful eyes were so wounded he couldn't stand it.

"Paula, honey, it's me, not you," he said. "I'm happy for you, honest I am. But it hurts to know that I can't be a part of this."

"I shouldn't have asked you to see the place," she said. "I didn't realize how uncomfortable it might make you. I was just happy to find a cute little house and I wanted to share it with you."

"I'm glad you did. In fact, I want to make sure you're getting a good deal for the place. I just wish my enthusiasm level was all it should be." He glanced around, then back. "Marry me instead."

"I can't."

He wished she hadn't been so quick with her answer. "Paula, what can I do to change your mind?"

She ran her toe across the floor like a shy little girl. "I don't think there's anything you can do. Jeff, you need that money."

"I hate it when you're on my side," he commented, feeling the distance between them growing to the size of the Grand Canyon.

"I'm always on your side," she said. "Even when it seemed like I wasn't."

The boys rushed in from the outside. Stevie shouted, "Come on, Jeff! You should see the big tree in the backyard. I'm gonna climb it."

"Oh, no, you're not, young man," Paula said sternly, drawing his attention.

"Well, I am," Bobby said.

"Oh, no, you're not, either."

Jeff chuckled. "Well, let's go see if I can climb it, because a tree needs climbing sometimes."

Paula glared at him. "Don't you dare take those boys up that tree."

"Yes, Mom," Jeff said.

The boys raced ahead to the large maple, spreading its low limbs across the width of the yard. Jeff duly admired it, then climbed it as promised. He looked out at the small, white, vinyl-clad Cape Cod with its dormers. The house screamed rose-covered cottage and traditional family life. How much had he envisioned this with her? And why would he never be allowed to have it?

The mystery questions of life, he thought, and wondered what he could do to still get the positive answers to them.

JULIAN PONDERED THE IDEA of Jeff and himself becoming two old men together, like one of those oddity stories for the tabloid shows.

He shivered, not liking what he envisioned at all.

"Do I have the air-conditioning turned down too low?"

Moira asked solicitously from across the conference table at her offices. "I always seem too warm recently."

"No, it's just me." He glanced at the papers and reports spread over the cherry wood top. "Is there anything in here that the Pittsburgh people found useful?"

"Not really," Moira said, sighing. "Parsons is very intent on the takeover. Our friend Mayor Helpern really stirred their interest."

"I bet he's promised them all kinds of perks," Julian said. "Free infrastructure…a break on taxes…rezoning for expansion. You name it, and he's probably given it away. I know I would."

"Mmm. I wonder if the council knows about this," Moira mused.

Julian grinned. He loved being with her like this, watching her mind at work, seeing that beautiful face in a mask of concentration. She never was sexier to him than when she was talking business—but especially his business. "You're wasted out here in the hinterlands. You should still be in New York, playing hardball with the big guys."

She eyed him speculatively. "So should you, Julian. So why are you here?"

"Because I hated New York," he admitted. "This is my home."

"Sometimes, when I'm at my worst moments with the Brooks Brothers suits and the coffee beans imported from Africa, I look around and know those *Absolutely Fabulous* women, Patsy and Eddy, who are on top of every trend and fashion statement to come down the road, would never set foot in Diamond Mount. But I have, and I love it. That's when I know I'm okay." Moira laughed.

He laughed with her, knowing he felt more "in place" here than in New York, for all his need of Levenger furnishings in the study and range-fed chickens in the oven. He had a yuppy exterior and a small-town heart.

"I wonder how the merchants on Main would feel about the mayor giving special privileges to outside commerce," she said, getting back to their meeting subject. "You know he blocked a property tax break for them a few years ago when the economy was in a recession, and they've never been happy about it. If we could show favoritism, that might stop whatever package he offered to Parsons. Then maybe Parsons wouldn't find this area so attractive for expansion. That would stop the takeover cold."

"It's possible." Julian remained dubious. "Rezoning might help my brother's cause better, however, if the mayor did offer some variance to Parsons, especially after the zoning board took Jeff's away."

"Maybe." Now Moira was dubious. "They are two different cases, and whether they relate looks to be a stretch. Now if they rezoned to kick Jeff out and move Parsons Bank in, willy-nilly, *then* I might have something."

Julian reached out and riffled through the papers. "We don't have a white knight to rescue me?"

"I've always loved that term," Moira said smiling. "Not yet. They're still working on it. Unfortunately, the banks they've approached want a deal similar to Parsons. I'm afraid I wouldn't be able to get you out of it so you could eventually expand your bank like you want to."

All roads led to twenty-five million, he thought in disgust, hating the idea. That he had liked it before shamed him now.

He looked over at Moira. She had her eyes closed, her head cocked to one side and a dreamy smile playing around her full, kissable lips. One hand was below the tabletop, obviously resting on her belly. The baby was moving.

Julian's heart broke, split like a tree limb did with a sharpened ax. He would only ever look on at her and his child, neither of them truly his. He had brought it upon himself, knowing he could have married Moira six months ago, even earlier. Knowing he should have. Instead, he'd allowed himself to get caught up in that damnable bet.

Moira looked up and smiled at him, a secret knowing smile that only broke his heart even more. "He's kicking again. I think he wants to get his two cents in about Parsons." Rocking her head back and forth, she chanted in a singsong voice, "Yeah, yeah, we hate them. Yeah, yeah, that's mean. Yeah, yeah, we hate them anyway. Oh!" She chuckled. "I got a really strong flutter that time. Or else I'm about to lose my lunch."

"I hope not," he said fervently. Although he had been a master of stoicism in those moments when she had lost her lunch or breakfast or dinner or all three, he had no wish to be stoic again.

"Would you like to feel?" she offered.

He thrust out his jaw and nodded, not trusting his voice. He came around the table and put his hand on her abdomen. She pressed it down hard into her flesh, her fingers warm and sweet against his wrist. Once again, he felt a brush of something along her tummy from inside her body. That single moment of life growing, life he helped create. The sensation left him in awe.

"It's getting more noticeable," Moira said. "My mother says boy babies are more active in the womb than girl babies."

"Do you think it's a boy?" he asked, feeling the flutter of movement again.

She shrugged. "Could be. My obstetrician says she can tell me if it's a boy or a girl. I don't know if I want to know."

"If you decide you want to know…can I go with you when you find out?" he asked hesitantly.

She smiled at him. "Sure. After all, you bought the mouse. You ought to know if you have to take it back or not."

He chuckled. "God, I have mouse privileges."

"You have all the privileges you want," Moira said. "This

is your baby, too. I know I drew up a contract, and I'm sorry—''

"No. Don't apologize. I was a jerk. I have been all along. How did you put up with me?"

Her expression went all funny, and he couldn't tell at all what she was thinking. "I put up with you for a moment like this one."

"Marry me," he said impulsively, his hand still on her belly, over their child. "Please."

"I wish I could, Julian," Moira replied, her voice trembling. "I truly wish I could."

"What can I do to change your mind?" he asked, lowering himself so he was little less than eye level with her chair.

"Nothing. How can I ever believe you love me, love our child just for us?" she asked. "Not when that bet motivated you to begin thinking seriously about marriage and children."

"Let me ask you this," he said. "What if it *were* just the pregnancy, Moira? What if no bet ever existed, that we were going along in our relationship as usual, and you got pregnant?" He paused. "I guess that's what you thought was happening."

She chuckled, amused through her sadness. "That's the truth."

"Okay, then what did you intend to happen when you didn't know about the bet?" he asked. "When you eventually would have come to me and said 'I'm pregnant, Julian, and you're the father.' If I had said then that I would marry you, would you have?"

She looked him straight in the eye. "No. I was terrified to be in a loveless marriage with you. I still am."

"But I love you!" he nearly shouted in frustration as he leaped to his feet, finally taking his hand from her body. "Dammit, I do love you."

"You bring out the big guns during negotiations," Moira observed, getting back some of her spunk. "Julian, the unexpected pregnancy is one thing to work through. At least I could get a feeling that you truly loved the child. I would hope I would. But the money...that's obscene, somehow, to marry and have a child for that."

He wanted to say that the money would be a bonus, but it sounded hollow even as a thought. *Obscene.* That word did seem more correct than it would have before.

"There's nothing I can do?" he asked.

"I don't know," she said, looking up at him. "For the baby's sake, I don't know."

PAULA GATHERED UP the last of the petition lists on her desk and gazed at them, goggle-eyed.

"The whole town signed, I think."

"Really?" Bobby moved closer, looking over her shoulder. He should have been in the parrots' room, cleaning out their food and water bowls, then refilling them. Before she and the boys had come to work, Paula had stopped at several places where the shopkeepers had agreed to collect names for their petition. In every place, she had been handed over thick wads of papers. She and her sons had been excited to look them over as soon as they arrived at the vet's office.

"I want to sign!" Stevie exclaimed, leaning way over the desk and swishing a petition page around to face him. "I want to sign the 'tition."

"You can't even print yet," Bobby scoffed.

"Can, too!" He turned to his mother and asked hesitantly, "Can I, Mom?"

"I think it's time he learned," Jeff said, coming in from the falcon barn, to get ready for his practice's hours. "Wow! Look at all that."

"It's amazing," Paula said, shaking her head. She grinned a little. "I don't think my father's going to like this."

Jeff smiled slyly. "Somehow I don't see him jumping for

joy. I wonder if all these names could do anything with the judge.''

"Probably not, since a judge is bound by law, not popular opinion,'' Paula said, knowing that much about even small-town political life. "But the zoning board would sit up and take notice. Or the council itself. I'd present it to either of them. Both would even be better.''

"It's still a long shot,'' Jeff said. "I called a friend in the Federal Conservation Service, who's arranged for zoos and sanctuaries to take the birds if this doesn't work. He was very disappointed that the breeding and eventual release program for this state would be stopped.''

"Let's hope the council acts on the petition then,'' Paula said, looking proudly at her own name, the first one scrawled boldly on the first page of the petition.

"Can I sign, Jeff?'' Stevie asked. "I live here, don't I? Mom says the whole town signed, but I didn't.''

"You sure do live here, pal.'' Jeff stepped over and handed the child a pen. To Paula, he said, "It's not like it's a recall petition where everything has to be perfect.''

"I'd like to start one for my father,'' she muttered. "Did you hear what he did to Moira?''

"Hey, the man's entitled to his opinion.'' Jeff's grin widened. "He did me a big favor, though. If she had become the town solicitor, she wouldn't have been my attorney much longer for the appeal. We may have to go farther than the county court for that.''

"And are we?'' she asked.

"Depends on her pocketbook, because mine's shot.''

"I want to sign!'' Stevie demanded, interrupting them. "Ple-e-e-ase.''

Jeff ruffled the boy's hair. "Here, let's use the back of this page. It's been my experience, when I get thank-you letters from kids, that they like to have a *lot* of space to write their letters.''

"I'll sign after Stevie," Bobby volunteered. "I want to keep Popeye and Elvis here."

Jeff helped Stevie hold the pen right, then closed his large fist gently over the boy's small one. Carefully, Stevie made the letters of his name with Jeff's help. Bobby looked on, patiently waiting his turn. Paula suddenly couldn't see through a blur of tears. They fell down her cheeks and ran under her jawline. She didn't bother to wipe them.

"Mom, you're crying," Bobby said, dismayed when he glanced over from watching his brother and Jeff and saw her.

"Paula, honey," Jeff exclaimed, taking his hand from Stevie's and wiping gently at her tears. "What's wrong?"

"Nothing. Everything." She sniffed loudly. "Oh, I don't know why I'm crying. PM you-know-what, I guess."

"You never did that before."

"I'm old now. I cry. Okay?" She sniffed again and, brushing his hand away, swiped at her tears.

"Mom, are you crying because Grandpa will be mad at us for signin' the 'tition?" Stevie asked.

"No, I'm not crying about that," she said. "I'm crying because you spelled your name for the first time."

"Yeah, it looked that bad," Bobby teased.

"Did not!" Stevie yelped, defending himself.

"Knock it off, you two," Paula said, gaining her equilibrium. "It looked pretty."

But she knew it wasn't Stevie spelling his name that made her cry. It was Jeff's gentle enclosure of her son's fist, as teacher, as mentor. As a father would do. How could she not cry at such tenderness, knowing her refusal to marry him kept him and the boys apart? Yet how could she marry him, knowing the bet might have motivated his interest in her children? Maybe his sterility had, too. Had he latched on to her sons because he felt genuine affection for them or because they were a means to an emotional and financial end?

She realized she could handle the doubts about the emotional end, but the bet…she couldn't go along with that, no matter how much he truly wanted her children for themselves in other ways.

"Paula," Jeff said in a low voice as the boys went off to their chores. "Why were you crying?"

"Because I needed to, I think," she told him, dabbing at her face with a tissue she'd grabbed from the box on the desk.

"I did it, didn't I?"

"Yes and no. It's old ground that we've been over so many times my head hurts, Jeff. Forget it."

"No. Marry me, and I'll make it better."

Tears leaked out once more. "I can't."

He gazed at her. "I won't ask again."

Her breath caught in her throat. She said nothing, but it pained her to realize he was deadly serious.

The door opened and their first patient bounded in, dragging its owner behind—practically lifting the small older lady off the floor was more like it.

Byron the boxer's hind end wagged furiously as he leaped up and knocked Jeff over in order to give him a resounding kiss across the face. Paula burst out laughing, while Mrs. Hemmilman tugged futilely on the leash and bleated for the dog to behave. Byron, after bathing Jeff thoroughly and totally ignoring the human on the other end of his leash, licked his behind a few times as if to ensure it was still attached, then immediately turned his attention to Paula. Eyes lighting up, he leaped for her, tongue hanging out like a monstrous pink promise.

Paula screamed.

Byron yelped and sat down, startled by the unusual reaction to his happiness. His ears went back and his eyes were filled with hurt.

"He's got the worms again, Dr. Diamond," Mrs. Hemmilman said.

"Then I definitely don't want him to kiss me," Paula said.

Squawking erupted in the parrot room. Frightened, Byron

dived under the desk, his claws scrabbling at Paula's legs. Paula yelped and pushed her chair back, giving the dog free rein. Mrs. Hemmilman almost went under the desk by default.

Jeff wiped his face with his shirttail, then took the leash from the old lady. He dragged a quivering Byron out from under the desk.

"She makes me do the same thing when I want to kiss her," Jeff commented to the dog as he pulled it, splay-legged, into his office.

"How did I get to be the heavy in all this?" Paula asked the world.

But she couldn't marry for money, not with her sons involved. The petition had better work.

Only the petition didn't. When she presented it at the next council meeting—to her father's disapproval—no one on the council took it up or even looked at it. They simply thanked her.

Jeff, facing a long, drawn-out court battle, was out of options. Except for a great deal of money for one "I do" from her.

Paula knew she couldn't sell herself or her children, and that's what she would be doing, no matter how worthy the cause. Of all the things that had held her back from Jeff—family feuds, being too young and all the other barriers that kept them apart—she knew this last obstacle was the worst. If she had to sell only herself to save him, she would do it in a heartbeat and never look back.

But not her kids.

MOIRA HELPED DOODLES get untangled from the trio of leashes, before locking the front door. She turned around and found Sergei tangled in the leashes instead.

She groaned as she bent to undo the second dog from the mess he'd made. The elastic waistband of her slacks bit into her stomach, even though she had stopped wearing her tops tucked in weeks ago.

"I really do have to get maternity clothes," she murmured, while petting all three Pomeranians on the head. "Okay, let's go."

They didn't get very far, just down the walkway, but the disruption didn't come from the dogs this time. Julian's car pulled up in front of her house. Moira straightened with another groan for lost waistlines, as he got out from the driver's side. He was carrying a huge, stuffed teddy bear. A teddy polar bear, for the thing was of soft, pure white.

"I thought about it," he said, reaching her. "And I decided to hedge our bets. Maybe we'll have fraternal twins. It runs in the family."

"Oh, Lord," Moira uttered with the emphasis on the deity. "I totally forgot about that."

Julian grinned. "Hey, the more the merrier."

Moira shivered, thinking of all the diapers and feedings and crying times two. Then she thought about the cooing and the cuteness doubled. It might be worth it, she admitted to herself.

"But it's probably two boys if it's twins," she pointed out. "You were."

"Fraternal could be either way," Julian replied. "In fact, Jeff and I were the less common kind because we were the same sex. Fraternals tend to come in the male-female package and often looking exactly alike. Twins can't be identical if they're a different sex, because even if they did look alike, they wouldn't be truly identical."

"Thank you, Doctor Spock," she said, while the dogs jumped up and tried to sniff the bear.

"Hey!" Julian lifted the bear away. "You guys will get it all hairy."

Moira grinned.

"Where are you taking the crew?" he asked, eyeing her.

"For a walk. They need the exercise and so do I."

"I'll go with you," he offered.

He walked the rest of the way to her door, unlocked it with his key and set the bear down in the foyer. Moira wondered why she hadn't asked for the key back when this whole mess started. Why hadn't she broken ties with him sexually, let alone emotionally? She was still holding out hope, that's what she was doing.

"Walkies!" Julian called out in a falsetto voice, while taking up the leashes from her. The Poms instantly began their pretty, fluttery quickstep on their short, short legs. Julian looked back at Moira, waggling his eyebrows. "Damn! It actually works."

They walked through her neighborhood, Julian holding her hand like they were an old married couple out for a stroll in the park. Only they weren't an old married couple, and Moira forced herself to keep that in mind.

"I talked to the Pittsburgh firm today," Julian said. "Right before I came over here— Doodles, quit sniffing that tree before Sergei uses your head for a watering spot."

Moira chuckled wryly when Doodles didn't listen and Sergei took Julian's advice.

"I'm not bathing him," Julian announced. "I'll probably use a Merlot '86 instead of shampoo."

"Actually some shampoos are close to a white wine color," Moira said.

"See? The dog will lick himself and get drunk. Then the others will lick him and they'll be drunk, too. You'll be calling me Julie the Souse. No, thanks. We'll just hose him down when we get home."

"Better hose down Sergei," Moira said. "Doodles just reciprocated. They're not bright, but they're cute."

Julian reached down and scooped up Anastasia and gave her a little hug. "Now this one's bright and cute."

"She *is* liking you," Moira commented, when the dog "smiled" happily up at him.

"See? I'm a wonderful guy, Moira. The perfect father for

my baby.'' He smiled. ''Who else could be better? And I'm housebroken on top of that.''

Moira knew all the lightness went out of her. She could feel it in the way her smile faded and her throat went tight. She could sense her gaze growing dull, and she heard as if from a far distance. Her heart turned to a numbing ache, and her body became almost lifeless. She knew he would see her sadness and ask what was wrong.

''What did the Pittsburgh attorneys say?'' she asked, to stop the subject before it started.

Julian clenched his jaw. Finally he started walking again, tugging the leashes to get the two males to move from the object of their affections. Anastasia, he carried in the crook of his arm. The dog made no move to get down.

''They can't find a white knight,'' Julian replied at last. ''And they don't hold out much hope of a friendly bank coming in to take over Diamond Bank. Most refused outright, saying they expanded too much already and were leery the downturn in global banking conditions would impact their individual future. Of those who were interested, they wanted terms pretty much like Parsons's offer.''

''Why didn't they call me?'' she asked, feeling out of the loop.

''Because I had called them first.'' Julian pursed his lips for a moment. ''I got a notice from the securities exchange that Parsons had formally put in a bid.''

''Why didn't you call me?'' she demanded, her stomach churning.

He shrugged. ''I thought I'd come over and tell you in person. Which is what I'm doing.''

They walked silently. Moira ran options through her head, trying to find another solution to stop the takeover of Diamond Bank. Their options had been few from the beginning. Now they were nil.

She could marry him. That infusion of cash would probably

put him over the edge for his stock holdings. But she would never feel good—for the rest of her life she would feel she sold her child out for money. She couldn't do it. "I'm sorry, Julian."

He grinned. "I'm not dead yet. I'll find a way to keep what I want."

But he was dead. And she knew it.

THE SIGN WAS ENORMOUS. It was on the outskirts of the town, a billboard more suitable for a state highway than a small place like Diamond Mount. Of course, at one time, before expressways and turnpikes snaked across entire states, a major route to Pittsburgh had run through the town's Main Street. The sign, with its high visibility, had pushed everything from cute terriers with a penchant for disrobing very tanned toddlers to cowboys riding across mountain meadows at breakneck speed while puffing away on cigarettes. Nowadays, it pushed a state fair that had been held ten months before.

PAULA PUT A BOX DOWN in her brand-new living room, grateful that the owners were willing to lease the house to her until her advance check came through. Tension at her parents' house had risen considerably after the petition. Her father was getting flack from every corner of the town, between those who had wanted Moira as town solicitor and those who were upset about the treatment of Jeff's sanctuary. She sighed, knowing her dad created his own problems. Some people just did that.

Finally, though, she had achieved what she had come home to do, and that was make a new life for herself and her boys. She was back on her feet financially—even though she hadn't signed her new book contract yet. Well, she amended, she was on her way. The wheels of publishing could sometimes run right off the tracks, but she doubted it. Her new publisher was solid and well-known as ethical. She would see her paperwork eventually—and her on-signing advance wouldn't be far behind.

Despite reaching her goal, she felt empty, as if a big part was missing from her new life.

When she went outside, a car going down the street slowed. The driver, the owner of one of Jeff's patients, waved, stopped the car completely and rolled down the passenger window. "Hey, Paula! Have you seen the sign on Main?"

"What sign on Main?"

"That big billboard that's been there forever." The man laughed. "It's about you."

"What!"

Stevie tugged on her shirttail. "Mommy, what's the man laughing about?"

"I don't know," Paula said, shrugging.

"You better go see it right now!"

The car sped away. Paula shrugged again, although the thought that she was somehow on a sign bothered her. Finally she told herself the man must be mistaken. Fifteen minutes later someone else stopped and told her nearly the same thing.

"He says he wants to marry you."

"Oh, God," Paula said, horrified that Jeff had done something incredibly dumb. "Get in the car, kids."

"Where we going?" Bobby asked, dumping his box of things on the step.

"We're seeing a man about a sign."

Moira Carson slowed her car along the first part of Main Street, her stomach churning like it was whipping up the grandfather of all ulcers. She remembered the phone call to her office and a person laughing and babbling something about Julian and a sign.

Moira shook her head, then noticed a little crowd of people standing on the walkway, looking off to the side. She pulled her car over and parked, getting out in time to find Paula and her children pulling up.

"Hi!" Moira waved to Paula through Paula's open car window. Glancing over toward the sign in question, she began, "Julian's evidently done something with a..."

She gaped, her voice trailing away. All of her turned to mush inside, her bones too weak to hold her up. Unconsciously, she leaned on the side of her car, as she read:

THE DIAMOND BROTHERS DO HEREBY GIVE UP ALL RIGHTS TO THE BET MADE WITH BART DIAMOND. THEY DON'T WANT THE MONEY. HONEST. THEY WOULDN'T TOUCH IT WITH A TEN-FOOT POLE. NOT EVEN A TEN-THOUSAND-FOOTER WILL DO. MOIRA AND PAULA, THIS IS NO JOKE. WE KNOW NOW THAT EVERY MAN'S GREATEST FORTUNE IS HIS FAMILY, MORE THAN ANY AMOUNT OF MONEY COULD EVER BUY. PLEASE MARRY US AND BE OUR FAMILY. WE LOVE YOU MORE THAN BIRDS AND BANKS, AND WE ALWAYS WILL. WE'LL BE POOR TOGETHER, BUT RICH IN LOVE.

"Oh, my," Paula breathed, coming next to Moira and looking at the sign and the signatures of Jeff and Julian.

"Oh, my," Moira echoed. She began to smile, her heart lightening from a burden that had overshadowed everything. She looked at Paula, who looked at her. They collapsed in each other's arms, laughing.

"Oh, wonderful. We bare our souls, and they think we're Laurel and Hardy."

"Jeff!" Stevie and Bobby's shout wasn't needed to alert either woman to the presence of the sign's culprits. Jeff hugged the boys, who flung themselves into his arms. He looked expectantly at Paula.

"I told you I wouldn't ask again," he said. "I lied. No more bets for love, Paula. I want the world to know I want to marry you just for you. I wanted it fifteen years ago and I want it even more now.''

Paula grinned and slid into his embrace. She held him tight, even as she said, ''You can't mean to give up the birds and their home.''

''They'll survive, but I'm nothing without you,'' he whispered back. ''I've always known that. You and the boys.''

''Will you marry me and live in my new little house?'' she asked. ''We can make the garage into a veterinary's office.''

''Living in a garage. I can't wait.'' He meant it.

Julian stared at Moira, who felt the baby move vigorously. With approval, it seemed.

''That's one hell of a contract up there,'' she said, pointing to the sign.

''I took lessons from the best. You.''

''That's a lot of money you're walking away from.''

''I don't want it. Not if I can't have you.''

She reached up and touched his cheek. ''You don't deserve to lose the bank.''

''Banks mean nothing without love.'' He grinned a little. ''I can't believe I'm saying it, but it is true. Having my bank never would mean anything without you to love and be loved by. Jeff and I both realized that the money would never be worth the loss of you and Paula to us. And the boys to Jeff. We couldn't think of any other way to convince you both that we meant everything we said, so we said it in a way that we could never deny. I want you, Moira. I'd regret it forever if I didn't have you in my life.''

''What about the baby?''

''He can come along if he likes, but I'm still going to be there with you after the kid is long graduated from Yale.''

''Brown,'' she countered, naming her own alma mater.

''Put it in the marriage contract,'' he murmured, as she wrapped her arms around his waist.

''Guaranteed.'' She sighed. ''Julian, will you marry me?''

He grinned. "If you sound any more enthusiastic, I might have to take a stress test."

"You'll need one after the wedding night," she promised, her heart soaring.

"I won't be able to stop saying I love you," he whispered in her ear, "because I won't be able to stop feeling it."

"Thank God," she said.

The crowd, doubled in size and growing, burst into applause.

And the Winner Is...

Epilogue

"I do."

The brides spoke in unison, then laughed. Their friendship had deepened quickly with their happiness until they were almost like sisters.

"I do, too," Jeff Diamond said, anticipating the question. He'd waited far too long for Paula Helpern-Miller, to not immediately put the Diamond on the last of her names now that he had her at the altar.

Bobby and Stevie clapped and cheered, pumping fists in their enthusiasm for their stepfather. The congregation chuckled while the minister raised his eyebrows in disapproval.

"Jeffrey, please," the man admonished. "God has an order for all things, including marriages. Besides, you're forgetting your brother."

"Could we hurry up with the wedding?" Julian asked, watching Moira like she was a pressure cooker about to blow. Perspiration beaded his forehead. "Moira could have the baby at any moment. I told you we should have had the wedding earlier. Or later."

"Relax, I'm all right," she said serenely. "I wanted today because it's the anniversary of the day we met."

Julian grinned like an idiot at the mention of his wife's new-found penchant for sentimentality. A moment later he lost all dignity when his "best men" started yapping and snarling at each other from ankle level. Julian squatted down and made goo-goo noises that settled down the little dogs.

His bride, her form gently rounded under her soft pink wedding suit, made a rude snort of amusement. "Oh, yes. You are right up there in the dignity class with Jim Carrey—"

The minister interrupted, saying loudly, "Do you, Jeffrey Rutherford Diamond, take this woman, Paula Miranda Helpern-Miller, as your lawful wedded wife, in sickness and in health, in good times and bad, in happiness and sadness, as long as you both shall live?"

"I do," Jeff repeated, making it official.

"Julian Cadell Diamond, do you take this woman, Moira Eleanor Carson, to be your lawful wedded wife..."

When the minister finished with the identical questions asked of Jeff, Julian lifted his chin and said, "I do, and I am eternally grateful she will still have me."

The congregation chuckled again. All except one.

Hours later that one unamused person sat in a corner of his own house and harrumphed his way through the reception that was being held there. Bart Diamond admitted that he'd gotten the job done, gotten both boys married and in the family way, and yet he was madder than a wet hen about all the results. His grandsons had refused his money. Both of them! Just outright said "Thanks, but no thanks." They couldn't be Diamonds, Bart thought. No Diamond turned away from money.

And yet, as he watched Jeff chase his new sons around the dance floor, all three laughing delightedly, the old man had to admit that he'd never seen his grandson happier. Or his other grandson. Julian fussed over his new bride, clearly taking pride in their baby about to arrive. He even played with those three little dogs of Moira's. Bart harrumphed again at the propriety of having animals at weddings. Clearly, both sons would be far more dedicated fathers than their own had been. He had only sent best wishes from Palm Springs. Bart wondered where *he* had gone wrong with his own son that the man ignored *his* twins, fine men both of them, and now family men—his personal dream to see in his declining years.

"But I'm still stuck with no tax write-off on that twenty-five million," he grumbled and reached for a piece of wedding cake. That part of his beautiful plan was ruined. Damned impulsive kids.

Paula's mother waved goodbye as she and Paula's father slipped out the door of Bart's mansion on the mountain. Paula sighed and said to Jeff, "I can't believe they came."

"I think it's a truce," Jeff said.

"My father told me he's retiring, going to Florida before the end of the year." Paula tilted her head thoughtfully. "I think that will be very good for both of them, although neither ever liked Florida. But they need a change."

Jeff put his arm around her waist and kissed her temple. "We'll go and visit anytime you like. Keep that line of communication open."

"You ought to. He's made a big concession with a lot of things by coming to the wedding. I'm glad he did."

"I have a surprise wedding gift for you," Jeff whispered against her ear, sending shivers of heat throughout her body.

"You want to do wicked things to me tonight." It was a statement, not a question.

"Not that. Well, yes that," he amended, chuckling at her outraged expression. "It's probably just as well your father's retiring to Florida. He wasn't happy when Moira got me a stay against the variance decision from the county court. Remember the friend I called at the Federal Conservation Department? He pulled some strings and arranged for me to sell the land to the federal government, who will declare it eminent domain and part of the conservation lands. Evidently Pennsylvania doesn't have enough national parkland, so the sanctuary will go on, and it will be designated as a government-protected area."

"Oh, that's great!" Paula flung her arms around his shoulders and hugged him. "But that variance—"

Jeff grinned. "I don't need my grandfather's money. I never did. I only need you."

"We get to keep the birds." Paula hugged him tightly. "There's got to be a book in this."

He laughed. "I volunteer for love-scene research."

The boys nearly raced past him, but he caught them up and hugged them to him, then kissed Paula tenderly. "I have my fortune in all of you. Today I am the luckiest man in the world."

In yet another part of the house, three council members cornered Julian and Moira Diamond. The trio wore worried expressions.

"Parsons is closing your old bank, Julian!" Dick Hammermil exclaimed. "We received the notice from them this morning. Bob, here, found it on the fax tray when he stopped by the council chambers."

Bob Millstein nodded. The man looked miserable.

"Not my bank anymore, remember?" Julian replied blithely. He had negotiated a decent settlement with Parsons since he had to give up the fight of the takeover. A *very* decent settlement, enough to consider partnering with another bank.

"But, Julian, we now have *no* bank in our town center, only their branch which is ten miles away!" Roger Gunnarson exclaimed.

"A good business move on their part to eliminate the competition," Julian said.

Moira added, "Quite sensible, too, from an economic standpoint, since they would have had operating costs for two banks fairly close together."

"Ten miles isn't close!" Roger snapped. "We made a terrible mistake. How can we fix it? What will it take for you to maybe reestablish Diamond Bank? Infrastructure? Tax break? Loan help?"

Julian shrugged. "Gentlemen, please. No business now. I'll be on my honeymoon in just a few hours."

"But Moira can't do anything!" Dick Hammermil said, then clamped his hand over his mouth. The man looked horrified at his indiscretion. "Sorry, Moira. I'm terribly sorry."

Moira stared off into space. Finally she said, "Actually, I can do something. Julian, my darling, my water just broke."

Julian leaped from the chair. "Now?"

"Now." The first deep pull of labor swept through Moira's body. She gasped at its strength. "I think your daughter doesn't want to miss our honeymoon."

"Call the doctor!" Julian snapped at the three men. "I'll get the car. Jenny, you'd better take the dogs home with you—"

"I'm going to the hospital with *you*," Jenny announced and turned over dog duties to Bart, while Jeff ran for the car and Paula helped Moira up. Half the reception went to the hospital with the newlyweds-about-to-be-parents.

Jennifer Julianna Diamond came into the world, screaming at the top of her little lungs. She stopped and looked in wonder when she was put in her father's arms.

Julian gazed back in awe of the little being he held. Suddenly he knew what Jeff felt for Paula's sons, now his sons. The love ran deep and sure though his veins, never to change, no matter what life brought.

"I have a family," he whispered to Moira. "I will never need anything more than my wife and children to make me the richest man in the world."

Moira smiled at him. Her face was red, her hair disheveled, her body limp. Never had she looked more beautiful to him.

Back at the house, Bart eyed his three charges who eyed him back. "Well, you got a little sister to torture you. Hell, I'm talking to dogs now. If I'm that gaga, I might as well pay the IRS and be damned."

After all, he had created a couple of Diamond Daddies. He could live with the rest.

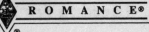

COMING NEXT MONTH

#781 DADDY UNKNOWN by Judy Christenberry
4 Tots for 4 Texans
Tuck was thrilled to see Alexandra Logan back in Cactus, Texas—until she told him she had a little problem. She was four months pregnant—and, thanks to a slight amnesia problem, she didn't know who was the man responsible!

#782 LIZZIE'S LAST-CHANCE FIANCÉ by Julie Kistler
The Wedding Party
Bridesmaid Lizzie Muldoon had resolved to attend the society wedding stag, but somehow ended up with a *fake* fiancé! Groomsman Joe Bellamy was the lucky guy for Lizzie. And she couldn't convince anyone he was not her future husband—including herself....

#783 INSTANT DADDY by Emily Dalton
A whirlwind romance with a stranger resulted in the best part of Cassie Montgomery's life—her son, Tyler. She never expected to see her mystery man's picture in a magazine—advertising for a wife! Breathless, Cassie replied. Would Adam Baranoff remember her—and welcome her gift of instant fatherhood?

#784 AND BABIES MAKE TEN by Lisa Bingham
New Arrivals
A trip to the sperm bank and suddenly Casey Fairchild found herself leaving the fast track behind and taking a job in a tiny Midwest town. But life was anything but dull when her boss turned out to be a sexy stud—and the father of quintuplets!

Look us up on-line at: http://www.romance.net